PRAISE FOR THE KINGMAKER

"Finely tuned political intrigue meets intense sexual chemistry when Washington, D.C., power broker Derek Ambrose catches presidential candidate Jason Melville, one of his clients, having too good a time with London Sharpe, a high-priced escort. Derek is willing to pay a bundle to convince London to stay out of Jason's life, but soon Derek is obsessing over her himself. She's happy to take the money and run, since a scandal could ruin her own carefully constructed double life. No one in London's social circle knows where her money comes from, and in order to stay in business she needs to keep it that way. So when a reporter learns that London spent an afternoon in Jason's hotel suite, everybody has a lot to lose, and there is only one way to save the day. Laurence's tightly woven story is a superb mix of sexual and political tension that's certain to please fans of both." -- Publisher's Weekly

"...an alpha hero with a heart of gold." --The Book Siren

"...a tale that could be right out of our headlines." -- Cyn's Reviews

"The Kingmaker does not disappoint." -- Mile High KINK Bookclub

"...a cross between Scandal and House of Cards." -- Amazon Review

"Selena Laurence's talent shines in this new series. Just wow!" -- Goodreads Review

"Best political romance in a long while!" --Amazon Review

THE KINGMAKER

★★ A POWERPLAY NOVEL ★★

USA TODAY BESTSELLING AUTHOR
Selena Laurence

everafter ROMANCE

Copyright 2016 © Selena Laurence
All Rights Reserved
ISBN 9781635760200

Copy Editing by Proof Before You Publish
Cover & formatting by Sweet and Spicy Designs

All rights reserved. Without limiting the rights under copyright reserved above, no part of this publication may be reproduced, sorted in or introduced into a retrieval system, or transmitted, in any form, or by any means (electronic, mechanical, photocopying, recording, or otherwise) without the prior written permission of the copyright owner of this book. This contemporary romance is a work of fiction. Names, characters, places, brands, media, and incidents, are either the product of the author's imagination or are used fictitiously. The author acknowledges the trademarked status and trademark owners of various products referenced in this work of fiction, which have been used without permission. The publication/use of these trademarks is not authorized, associated with, or sponsored by the trademark owners. This book is licensed for your personal use only. This book may not be resold or given away to other people. If you would like to share this book with another person, please purchase an additional copy for each person you share it with.

For permission to use any portion of this material, please contact the author at: author@selenalaurence.com

Also by Selena Laurence

The Powerplay Series
Prince of the Press (A Powerplay Novella)
The Kingmaker (A Powerplay Novel)
POTUS (A Powerplay Novel)

The Lush Rockstar Series
A Lush Betrayal (Lush 1)
Loving a Lush (Lush 2)
Lowdown and Lush (Lush 3)
A Lush Reunion (Lush 4)

The Rhapsody Rockstar Series
A Lush Rhapsody (A Rhapsody Novel)
Racing to Rhapsody (A Rhapsody Novel)

The Foreign Exchange Series
Speaking Greek (Book One)

The Hiding From Love Series
Falling for Trouble
Concealed by a Kiss
Secrets in a Kiss
Playing With Fire

Dedication

This one is for Jamie. You did it. You're a rock star.

CHAPTER I

He stared at a pair of legs—long and shapely, with dark olive skin that glowed in the low light of the room. They ended in a pair of very strappy stiletto-heeled shoes, and toenails the color of a fine burgundy. Unfortunately, those spectacular legs were currently pressed against a wall while his client—his very married client—mauled the owner of said legs in a swanky hotel suite in southwest D.C.

"You have got to be kidding me," Derek groaned as he stood in the doorway viewing the clusterfuck that had just exploded all of his plans.

"Unh," Jason Melville grunted as he stopped ravishing the woman's neck and raised his eyes to gaze over his shoulder at his very pissed campaign consultant. "Derek," he gritted out. "This isn't what it looks like."

Derek slammed the door and strode across the room to glower at Jason and the woman splayed against the wall.

"What exactly *is* it then, Jason? Because it looks to me like you're about to screw a woman who is not your wife hours before we're supposed to announce your candidacy for President of the fucking United States. Did it ever occur to you that she could blow your entire campaign to hell before it even starts?"

Derek's gaze drifted from Jason's rapidly reddening face to the brunette he had pinned, hands above her head, against the expensive wallpaper. As Jason released her and she straightened her clothes with a huff, Derek could see that the rest of her was as exquisite as her legs. Classic bone structure covered with smooth as silk, flawless skin. Exotic eyes the color of dark chocolate, tipped up at the outside corners, the lashes long and luxurious. And below all of that, a pair of tits that would tempt any president—well, maybe not the current one, since she seemed to swing toward men.

"I'm a *professional* escort," she hissed. "And I'll have you know that I'm very discreet. I would never discuss a client's business with anyone, whether he's the president or a janitor."

Jesus. A hooker? Could it get any worse?

"Look, sweetheart, I'm sure you're the picture of discretion, but the presidency is not something to risk over a tumble with an *escort*." He squeezed out the last word like he could hardly tolerate saying it, and her cheeks turned pink in response, her mouth tightening and eyes narrowing.

Jason exhaled a big breath and stepped further from the brunette.

The woman pursed her plump lips and nudged Jason out of the way before brushing by Derek, heading for the bathroom, her perfectly firm and round ass swaying in the pencil skirt that hugged her like a second skin.

Derek whipped around to glower at his candidate who blatantly adjusted himself in his $1000 Armani dress slacks.

"What the fuck were you thinking?" Derek snarled. "Do you realize what you've done?"

"I'm under a hell of a lot of pressure," Jason muttered. "And I'm tired of being the only one in D.C. who doesn't get to indulge a vice once in a while. I need a goddamn way to relieve the stress."

Derek walked to the thermostat on the wall and turned on the AC to rid the room of the scent of the hooker's perfume, which was perversely turning him on even in the midst of his anger.

"Well, if this is how you handle your stress, I'm not sure you're cut out to be president. While indulging a vice, as you put it, may be commonplace in D.C., it also nearly always ends in scandal that ruins careers. Particularly for a young, good-looking candidate with little kids at home. Do I need to mention Gary Hart and John Edwards to you?"

Jason grabbed his jacket off of the bed. Derek heard the water turn on in the bathroom and wondered exactly how much money he'd have to cough up to make this woman go away, and how long it would be until she came around again wanting more.

"London is known for her discretion," Jason said as he unrolled his shirtsleeves. "No one will ever find out."

Derek raised an eyebrow.

"Fine. I'll stop, okay? Is that what you want to hear? I won't see her again, and I'll be a good boy and jack off in the shower instead. God knows Angela's not going to help me out." Frustration rolled off the Senator in waves, almost palpable in the re-circulated air of the room.

Derek thought of Jason's Patrician blonde wife and their two preschool-aged children. His stomach churned. Why the fuck did these guys get married if they weren't going to make the commitment? It wasn't essential to have a wife in order to be successful in politics these days. He shook off the thoughts and focused on the problem at hand.

"How much?" he asked.

"How much what?" Jason responded, searching for something on the floor next to the bed.

"How much do you normally pay her?"

Jason muttered, "Got it!" in triumph and stood to put on a pair of diamond cufflinks. "London? She's a grand an hour." He checked his watch. "And she's been here about twenty-two minutes."

Jesus. A grand? The last time he'd gotten laid, Derek had spent fifty bucks on two cocktails, and then taken the pretty young reporter home for a couple of hours before sliding her into a taxi and saying goodnight. Final total? Maybe a hundred dollars. A grand seemed excessive.

"So how much do you think it's going to take to keep her quiet?" he asked.

Jason ran a hand through his perfectly disheveled dark hair tipped at the temples with the first smatterings of gray—hair dye to lend him more gravitas—and cocked his head at Derek.

"She won't talk. Really."

"Bullshit," Derek answered just as the woman in question emerged from the bathroom looking every inch the respectable wealthy D.C. wife, a perfectly fitted plum-colored business jacket molded to her hourglass figure, her thick hair in an upsweep, and those sexy as hell strappy shoes still attached to her perfect legs.

"I won't talk," London repeated, casting him a dismissive look.

Derek turned to her, fury simmering only slightly below the cool as steel façade he'd worked to develop and maintain for fifteen years.

"Look, I'm sure you're a lovely *escort*, very trustworthy and all, but you have no idea what kind of investment I've made in Jason here. One wrong word, one wrong look, or a secret shared between you and one of your 'friends', and his career, as well as mine, are shot to hell."

"I don't tell secrets to friends or anyone else, and I've never looked *wrong* at someone in my life." She paused. "So what are you going to do now? Kill me?" Her left eyebrow lifted and he could see the spark of derision in her face.

He rolled his eyes at her. "We're not on House of Cards, sweetheart," he answered drolly. "How much will it take to have you leave the country for a few weeks?"

London smirked. "Really? You want to pay me to take a vacation even though I have absolutely no intention of saying anything to anyone ever?"

"It'd make me feel better," Derek answered.

"Fine. I've always wanted to do the Bahamas. So, what? Ten? Twenty?" She looked at Jason before striding over and adjusting his tie. Jason's face lit up and he licked his lips as he looked down at her like a piece of prime grade steak.

Derek's rage bubbled up threatening to explode. "Senator!" he snapped. "Eyes on me."

London snorted delicately and stepped away from Derek's candidate.

"Jesus," Jason's face flushed. "Just pay her and get it over with," he snapped before he stepped out of the room swiping the screen of his phone as he went.

Alone in the bedroom, Derek and London stared at each other for a moment, and he swore her uber-confident, devil-may-care exterior cracked briefly.

She moved to the nightstand and gathered her purse before walking to him and holding out her hand. "I don't care if you give me extra, but I do insist on the grand I earned."

Derek looked down at her. She was on the tall side for a woman, probably five eight or nine. But he was six two, so she seemed delicate as he stared at her achingly perfect face. She could have been a top model or an actress, and if her snark was any indication probably plenty of professions that required verbal smarts as well. Why was she doing this? Servicing arrogant, careless men who only wanted to have their egos stroked more. Why would such a spectacular woman sell herself so short?

He knew he should pay her and send her on her way, but he was caught in some sort of twilight zone, drawn in by her smart mouth, her resistant attitude, and that damn spicy perfume that floated around her like a tropical flower.

"Why?" he asked, voice soft. "Why do you do it?"

Her eyes turned hard. "I have complete control over my life, Mr. Ambrose. Don't you dare pity me."

"You know my name." Some part of him buried deep sparked with anticipation.

"Everyone knows your name," she answered.

He clenched his fist and then shook his hand at his side, trying to release the urge to run his fingertips across her satiny cheek.

"You're not everyone."

"No, I'm not. I'm nobody, and that's how I wish to stay. Now, will that be cash or--?"

Derek sighed, then removed his phone from his pocket and swiped the screen. "It's Derek," he said, never taking his eyes off of London. "I'll need twenty thousand in cash brought to the Senator's suite. My personal account please. And make it snappy."

**

Thirty minutes later London rode in the back of a taxi on the way to her Dupont Circle brownstone. It was still early by Washington standards and she knew she could call in to Margrite, her boss at the agency, and make herself available for another client, but the morning's dealings had left her with a bad taste in her mouth. And not only because Jason Melville was a boring prick. No, it was Derek Ambrose that had ruined her normally level disposition. The censure that had permeated his face when he looked at her. The way he'd dropped the cash in her hand as if he might catch something if he touched her.

It had been a long time since London had felt the need to justify herself or her profession to anyone. Her work as an escort had begun eight years ago after she'd spent two years as a runaway teen, fighting to make her own way in a world and a city that simply weren't designed for a minimum-wage earner without a high school diploma. She would never claim the job was easy, but she'd learned to do what she had to in order to earn a very nice living, and still maintain some semblance of a normal life.

"Normal" meant she surrounded herself with friends who didn't ask questions and accepted her for who she said she was. She left work at the hotel door, and lived the quiet, upscale days of a woman with money in her off-hours. She had a house in a highly respectable neighborhood, she casually dated respectable men on occasion, and had highly respectable friends like Joanna, who was currently standing on London's front stoop waiting for her.

London exited the cab and thanked God she'd had the chance to freshen up so that she didn't look like she was doing the walk of shame at 11:30 in the morning.

"Hi!" Joanna called out cheerfully, smoothing her silk Alexander McQueen skirt as she wiggled on high-heeled Prada pumps.

"What brings you out before noon?" London joked as she put the key in her front door and ushered Joanna inside.

Jo flipped a strand of perfectly coiffed auburn hair over her shoulder and batted YSL-coated lashes, her big brown eyes sparkling with the mischief that they typically were. "I was at the salon around the corner and wondered if you might be willing to exchange lunch for decorating advice."

Normally London would be happy with an afternoon watching Joanna spend her husband's money on knick-knacks, but the encounter with Derek Ambrose had left her disoriented and dissatisfied somehow. Yes, she'd learned to accept the life choices she'd made since she left home at seventeen, but something about the way he'd looked at her had made regret blossom inside. Now she knew she had to kill it off—fast—before it took root, choking off her ability to reach that space in her mind where she was able to be London the hooker, rather than London the society girl.

"Could we do it next week? I've spent all morning running errands and I'm so worn out. I almost wonder if I'm coming down with something."

Joanna set her Kate Spade bag down on the foyer table and put her hand to London's forehead. "You do look a little peaked. Why don't you lie down and I'll get you some water. Do you have a headache?"

"No. Just tired and cranky."

"Maybe it's PMS?"

"Maybe," London answered non-committally as she walked to the front living room and collapsed on the sofa.

Joanna returned with a glass of ice water and London welcomed the distraction for a moment as she drank half of it down.

"You'll never believe who I met last night," Joanna gushed after she sat in an armchair near the sofa.

"I'm sure I won't, so spit it out." Joanna stuck out her tongue before continuing. "Senator Melville and his wife."

London's heart skipped a quick beat then settled back to its normal rhythm.

"What's so special about him?" she muttered into her water glass.

"The rumors are that he's running for president, and Brian's going to support him if he does. With the kind of resources Brian's firm can throw behind Melville, we're thinking the thank you might include a minor cabinet appointment or a diplomatic posting."

London always feigned ignorance of all things political, and it drove Joanna's husband, Brian, insane. He worked for one of the largest law firms in D.C. and spent much of his time on the Hill lobbying for various clients. His goal was to be Secretary of State someday.

"So when do you find out if he's announcing?"

Joanna looked at the Cartier bracelet on her wrist that had a small clock in the center. "Actually, he's supposed to hold a press conference in just a few minutes. Mind if I turn on your TV?"

London gestured at the flat screen on the wall over the mantle. "Be my guest."

Joanna took the remote from the coffee table and turned the television to WNN. "Oh look! Here it is."

Jason Melville's handsome face filled the screen and London saw the flashes of cameras and heard the shouted questions that reporters tossed from the audience. Melville's words were smooth and polished, just like his appearance. He was flanked by his wife, Angela Vandermeer Melville, his two preschoolers, and his parents, the owners of Melville Industries.

But it was the man standing at the back corner of the stage that captured London's attention. He stood taller than the Senator, and was even better looking. His hair was tousled, but not in an artificial way like Melville's. The dark blonde locks were cropped close on the sides, but longer on top, and had enough wave that London suspected they were impossible to tame.

His broad shoulders and narrow waist were emphasized by the perfect cut of his suit, but his tie was askew, as if he'd been yanking on it, and his body hummed with a kind of restless energy visible even on camera. As Melville gestured around the stage, talking about supporters and advisors, the camera zoomed in, and London got a split second close-up of those eyes. The icy blue eyes that had stared her down not two hours ago in a bedroom of the Renaissance Hotel. Coupled with the hard-as-steel jaw, those eyes were intimidating. But then everything about Derek Ambrose was intimidating. And sexy. Really damn sexy.

"Oh look," Joanna breathed as she watched the screen raptly. "There's Derek Ambrose, he must be Melville's campaign consultant. Isn't he the most gorgeous thing you've ever laid eyes on?" London scoffed. "If you like them big and mean, I guess?"

"How do you know he's mean? Ooh, have you met him?" She turned to face London, her face lit up with excitement.

"Just look at him. Look at his expression. That is not the face of a nice guy." London nodded her head as if it would give her statement more weight.

Joanna pondered the screen for a moment. "I suppose you're right. Melville seems a lot more approachable. And he might even be better-looking anyway."

London wished she could agree.

"Oh. Here we go," Joanna said, turning up the volume.

"So it is with great pleasure," Melville spoke into the microphones set before him, "that I officially announce my candidacy for President of the United States."

The various hangers-on and hired guns on stage clapped loudly and Joanna squealed with excitement.

"He's doing it, he's going to run." She turned to London. "You have no idea how this is going to change Brian's career. He can go from being a minion at the law firm to being a power broker on the Hill. You have to promise me you'll vote for Melville."

London tried not to sigh. "I don't vote. You know this."

Joanna made a face in exasperation. "London, seriously, you can't keep living in D.C. and be so incredibly blasé about our nation's governance."

"Like you care who wins? The only thing that matters to you is whether Brian gets to be Ambassador to some small exotic island where you can lie by a pool all day and be fanned by native boys."

Joanna laughed and London softened the words with a grin.

"That is patently untrue," Joanna said, turning serious—at least for her. "I care a great deal about who runs this country, and I think Senator Melville would make an excellent president. He's young and creative, he's sponsored some of the most important legislation protecting women and children that we've seen in decades, and he seems very devoted to his wife and family. Doesn't that sound like the kind of man you want as president?"

It took everything London had not to fall on the floor laughing. Melville was young all right. That's about all London was willing to give him at the moment.

London cleared her throat. "Well, I hope he wins—for Brian's sake at least."

"So you'll think about voting for him? Maybe you could even get involved in the campaign a bit. You are registered so you can vote in the primaries, right? Please tell me you didn't go and do something dumb like put yourself down as an independent."

London took another sip of water before answering. "I'm registered. And for the right party even."

"Oh thank God. I didn't want to have to unfriend you after all the effort I've put in." Joanna winked and stood. "I really should go, Brian is going to want to talk about the campaign tonight, and I need to have the furniture for the solarium picked out by the time he comes home so that he'll be too distracted to notice the prices."

London smiled. "You're a devious one, Joanna Russell."

"That I am."

After Joanna left, London turned her attention back to the television screen, watching the last of the press conference play out. As the camera panned around the stage while Melville answered the final questions from reporters, it stalled on Derek, his face stony, his expression unreadable, and then just before it moved on, he cracked. His eyes flashed fire and his mouth twitched, those full lips pursing briefly. As London watched, rapt, she could have sworn he was looking right at her. And burning her alive while he did it.

**

Derek Ambrose was the nation's leading campaign consultant. Blessed with the looks and persona that could easily have made him a candidate himself, he'd chosen life on the inside of the political world, but that didn't stop him from being a star in his party, known by the public, often the public face of campaigns, and a darling of the media. When Derek spoke, America listened, and when he posed, they watched. He actually preferred pulling the strings from behind the scenes, but he'd long ago become accustomed to the attention, and used it to his benefit when necessary. Because in Washington you needed every advantage you could get, and Derek wasn't shy about finding his own advantages.

Several hours after Melville's announcement, Derek dropped his jacket and briefcase on the sofa as he entered the large lounge of a studio apartment in the heart of downtown D.C. It contained all the classic elements of a man cave—sectional sofas, pool table, fully stocked bar, big screen TV—and it served as the headquarters for the Powerplay Club.

The Powerplay club was one of the best-kept secrets in Washington. Formed by Derek and his college classmate Kamal Masri, the son of a wealthy Egyptian businessman and currently the Egyptian Ambassador to the U.S., the club's members had been chosen carefully and consciously. Each of the six had a position in a different area of Washington's elite, and each brought unique knowledge and insight to the club. The club's objective was to garner power and influence for its members, and Derek had known that together they stood a far better chance of reaching the top of the D.C. dog pile than they did alone.

The club operated with very few rules. Each member had his special connections and skills, the others would call on them as needed. Derek was a mastermind who could strategize better than anyone in the District. Kamal had connections—legal ones and not so legal ones—who could get intelligence on virtually anything or anyone. Teague Roberts handled all their legal issues from criminal to contracts. Other members had their own skills and resources, and they all benefited from the association.

One of the club's biggest pushes had been to find a presidential candidate they could support, nurture, and place in office. The inside track to the President of the United States was a goal that all of the Powerplay members shared, and one that would give them unprecedented influence. While Derek had personally known every U.S. President for the last decade, he'd never been the campaign manager for any of them. He'd grown tired of waiting to be invited and decided to recruit his own candidate.

By joint agreement the club had settled on Jason Melville, second term Senator from Pennsylvania, and up and coming party favorite. The Powerplay members had been impressed with his leadership on the Senate Foreign Affairs committee, his spotless personal life, and his willingness to listen to their objectives while still standing strong in his positions. It didn't hurt that Melville was dedicated to working for some of the issues closest to Derek's heart—women, children, and workers' rights. Melville was widely known as being one of the hardest-working members of the Senate. He was serious about the issues, and about his part in effecting real change in Washington.

But given what Derek had seen of the Senator earlier in the day, perhaps his workaholic tendencies needed some tempering—in a way other than sex with a hooker. Now Derek was faced with telling his closest friends and confidants that their chosen one was tarnished so badly the whole effort might have been a waste of time.

Kamal, and Jeff, a U.S. Army Colonel and the group's security specialist, had beat Derek to the club condo, and were arguing at the pool table as he approached.

"I did not tap it twice," Jeff rumbled. "It was a clean shot, you just can't stand to lose."

Kamal shook his head of dark hair. He needed a haircut, Derek thought. What the hell kind of Ambassador let his hair curl up over the collar of his shirt?

"You clearly tapped it twice. But since you're afraid I'll win unless you cheat, then we'll call it good and move on."

Derek reached the table, watching as Jeff shook his head and pursed his lips. Kamal had a spark in his eyes that was a clear indication he was in a trouble-making mood. Something that rarely bode well for anyone.

"Is this how you handle delicate international negotiations?" Derek queried. "Tell them they get the win because they're pussies?"

Kamal laughed heartily. "Yes, telling the diplomatic staff of opposing nations that they're *pussies*—as you so eloquently put it—is a highly effective strategy. I think in fact that's how World War II started, wasn't it?"

"You're a dick," Jeff answered with no real heat from where he now lounged against the bar, a tumbler of scotch in hand.

"Ah, but I've been told it's one of my more popular features."

Jeff rolled his eyes and Derek stared at Kamal with disdain.

"It's true," a voice boomed from the front door of the apartment. "I was with him at the Stageline Club last week and the blonde on his lap was very complimentary of his dickliness."

"That's not a word, Teague," Derek answered, turning to watch the dapper, imposing figure approach.

"How are you?" Teague asked as he reached the pool table and gave Derek a hard slap on the back.

"I've been better," Derek grumbled.

"This ought to be your moment of triumph," Teague said. Derek could see the high-powered litigator in him laying in wait just under the surface, ready to do battle with anyone or anything that might have fucked up Derek's day. Teague hadn't made it to full partner at one of the most powerful law firms in the nation by being quiet and compromising. Unfortunately, they were all hamstrung when it came to Jason Melville. They'd chosen him, and now they had to live with the consequences.

"Did you catch the press conference today?"

All three of the other men around the pool table nodded.

"Well, the part you didn't see was when I caught our candidate about to fuck a hooker two hours before that."

"Son of a bitch," Teague muttered.

"Bloody fool," Kamal added, tossing his pool cue on the table in disgust.

Jeff merely snorted. Everyone there knew what he thought of politicians.

"I did clean up as best I could. The woman is apparently known for her discretion, but I wonder how many presidential contenders she's had as clients. I doubt she's dealt with this level of shit before now."

"Who is she?" Teague asked.

Derek reached into his briefcase on the sofa and picked up his tablet swiping at the screen quickly to pull up the report his top-notch investigations team had put together over the last few hours of the day. In Derek's line of work, having highly capable and highly discreet P.I.s at your beck and call was essential.

"London Sharpe. She's been with Double D Escorts for the last eight years, and before that it appears she was an exotic dancer at the Beltway Club."

"So high-end all the way," Kamal added.

"Yes. She's a damn grand an hour."

"Whooo," Teague shook his hand out and whistled.

"And before the Beltway Club?" Jeff asked.

"There are a couple of years missing in her late teens. She's the daughter of a Middle Eastern linguistics professor at Georgetown. Father unknown."

"What's the mother's name?" Kamal demanded, extra alert now.

Derek scrolled through the report he'd been emailed by his in-house investigation team. "Farrah Amid. Iranian dissident who claimed political asylum when the daughter was about two."

Kamal nodded. "Persian. A lot of highly educated women in Iran. I can't imagine her mother is too pleased with the daughter's choice of profession."

"So was she a runaway teen?" Jeff interjected.

"What makes you think that?" Derek asked, something about the idea of the beautiful fiery woman being young and alone twisting his stomach.

"There are years missing right around the time she's what, seventeen? Eighteen?"

Derek looked at the screen. "Yeah, last adolescent record is first semester of her senior year in high school. She would have been…seventeen."

Jeff nodded. "And she turns back up when?"

"At twenty."

Teague looked at Jeff and some understanding seemed to pass between the two men. Jeff's childhood had been spent in the rural south, while Teague's was in a New York City housing project. But both men had clawed their way to the top of their respective fields, and they'd both seen a lot of the darker side of life before they got there.

"My guess is that's as long as she could make it before she had to turn to stripping and prostitution to survive," Teague said quietly.

Derek's gut clenched. There was a vast difference between a confident, beautiful woman choosing to become an escort and a scared, hungry teen turning to prostitution in order to eat. He didn't like either scenario personally, but only the latter made him physically nauseous.

"Luckily she landed in the classier places," Kamal added. "Could have been worse."

"She said something to me this morning," Derek said. "She said, 'I have complete control over my life. Don't pity me.' It sounded so much more like it was a choice than the picture you're painting."

Teague shrugged. "Sometimes it helps to convince yourself of that."

All four men were silent for a moment. Derek knew better than to ask Teague for details about his life prior to the day Teague arrived in D.C. to attend law school at Georgetown, but he'd gleaned enough over the years to realize that Teague had lived through things most people only saw on television shows like *Breaking Bad*. If anyone knew what it felt like to be young, alone, and desperate, it was Teague.

"Now if only we knew whether she'll be satisfied with the payoff I gave her…" he muttered.

"She will," Kamal said with confidence. "Even after she gives the agency their cut she earns a great deal, and she was raised in a culture that highly reveres integrity. Her word is probably as good as gold. You just made her day at work more profitable than usual is all." He paused. "How much did you give her anyway?"

"Twenty grand." Derek sighed. He made a very good living, but twenty grand wasn't chump change, and he'd really been looking forward to having that new Jaguar F-Type parked in his Georgetown garage next month.

"Ouch," Jeff said, grimacing.

"So we think she'll keep quiet?" Kamal summarized.

Teague and Jeff nodded.

"And if she doesn't?" Kamal asked.

"Then we're fucked," Derek answered. "And eighteen months of plans are as well."

No one looked happy at that. The Powerplay club had worked hard to choose Melville. They'd scouted candidates, discussed options, and vetted the Senator very carefully. It was a colossal disappointment to find out he had bad habits they hadn't discovered prior to his announcement.

"How did this slip by us?" Jeff asked. "There was nothing in his background or profile that indicated he was seeing a hooker."

"Escort," Derek interjected half-heartedly.

"Whatever," Jeff replied.

Teague snorted.

Derek continued, "I don't know how it slipped by, I've talked to our investigators and believe me we'll be shopping around for some new talent, but in the meantime I do not like someone else holding the cards here."

"Let me look into options to get us in a better position," Teague said. "Maybe we can find some sort of leverage to insure she keeps quiet."

"I'll ask my contact at the D.C. police department what he can tell us about the escort service too," Jeff added, running a hand over his buzz cut hair. Even though he'd been assigned to the Pentagon for several years, he kept his hair as short as a field officer did.

"Good," Kamal said. "And let's get Scott to keep an eye on our candidate while he's at work on the Hill." Powerplay member Scott Campbell was Chief of Staff for the President Pro Temp of the Senate.

"And I've got him when he's on the campaign trail." Derek scowled.

"Now," Kamal pressed. "What's next on the agenda?"

CHAPTER II

London didn't work that night. Generally she had one client a day, four to five days a week. She took on a new client every couple of months, but most of the time she was dealing with regular customers. She was the most popular escort at her agency, and didn't need to do anything to get new clients referred to her whenever old ones dropped off.

But she decided to stop by the office. She wanted to check up on the next day's schedule and get out of the house, plus she really owed it to her employers to inform them of the day's happenings, since they'd been anything but ordinary. The entire event with Melville and Derek Ambrose had left her restless and unfocused. She'd tried cooking, her usual go-to for stress relief, but that had only resulted in a house full of bread that she really shouldn't eat all in one day, so she wrapped up a couple of loaves and caught a cab to a high-end storefront in the tony shopping district on Wisconsin Avenue. The small luxury lingerie store served as a front for the much more lucrative business of escort service.

The door chimed as she entered the store. Gorgeous French silk in pastels, jewel tones, and neutrals hung from padded hangers and filled glass cases along the walls. Bras, panties, corsets, garter belts, the store was the wealthy D.C. woman's ace-in-the-hole when it came to seduction.

A well-dressed and well-coiffed woman in her early fifties stepped out from the back room, her face breaking into a smile when she saw London. The inky hair that was pulled back into a sophisticated twist had strands of silver through it, but her green eyes were bright and her face was nearly unlined. She also had a style, and the very slightest accent, that told of her French origins.

"Darling," she trilled. "What brings you by?"

"Margrite." London walked closer and kissed her on both cheeks. "I didn't think you'd still be here. Where is Gerard?" she asked, referring to Margrite's partner in the escort agency.

Margrite waved a hand in the air carelessly. "One of his boys didn't want to play as rough as the Deputy Ambassador of Latvia did, so Gerard had to go negotiate a compromise."

London shivered in distaste. "The boys really do have it harder, don't they?" she asked. "No pun intended," she quickly added.

Margrite grimaced sympathetically.

"And is that delicious smell coming from your bag something for me?" Margrite raised her perfectly waxed eyebrows.

"Yes, take me to your lair and I'll give it to you."

Margrite laughed, pulling London by the hand toward the back of the store where they entered a small office space carpeted in deep pile aquamarine, the walls painted a soft cream, and the entire space finished off with Louis XV furnishings.

"First show me what you've baked, then tell me what's bothering you so much that you had to bake all afternoon."

London removed the two loaves of Middle Eastern sweet bread from her satchel and set them on Margrite's credenza. As she busied herself getting out the plates and knives that she knew Margrite kept in a cabinet under the espresso maker, she stayed silent, weighing the best way to explain her morning to her boss.

"Now, to what do I owe this visit?" Margrite asked, delicately bringing a piece of sweet bread to her ruby red lips.

"I had a little problem earlier today. Senator Melville..."

"Oh, do tell," Margrite deadpanned. Decades dealing with D.C.'s politicians had left her somewhat cynical when it came to the nation's leaders.

"We were interrupted by his campaign manager, Derek Ambrose. I'm not sure if you saw, but the Senator announced his candidacy for President a few hours after our date. Finding us in the Renaissance Hotel together was not high on his campaign manager's list of very good things today."

Margrite took a sip of tea from the cup sitting on her desk. "What did he do?"

"Yelled, insisted that I was a risk to the campaign, and paid me off."

Margrite raised an eyebrow. "Paid you off? To keep quiet I assume?"

"And to leave town."

"And are you?" Margrite looked skeptical.

"No! I took the money because he was hysterical and wouldn't stop shoving it at me. You know I don't need to leave town. I'm not going to tell anyone about Melville for heaven's sake. And here it all is, by the way," she added, placing a stack of cash on the desk.

"Don't be ridiculous. Tips are yours, you know that. This was simply a larger than normal tip. It also sounds as though you earned it having to deal with the horrid man."

London couldn't help but smirk at the thought of what Derek Ambrose would say if he heard the owner of an escort service referring to him as 'the horrid man'.

"He was annoying as much as anything. You know me, I don't like drama, and he was full of it."

"He always seems so stoic on TV," Margrite observed. "He's charming to the press, but reserved. He tries to keep the focus on the candidate."

London thought back to the serious way Derek had looked at her when he asked why she did what she did. Stoic. That was one way to describe him. A force of nature was another.

"Oh dear."

"I'm sorry, what?" London snapped out of her reverie.

"You liked him, didn't you?" Margrite's blue eyes were sharp beneath her dark brows.

"No!" London protested a little too loudly. "Didn't you hear the story? He was convinced that I kiss and tell. How could I like someone like that?"

Margrite had a smug smile on her face. "I've seen him on TV, darling. What's not to like?"

London rolled her eyes. "You know I don't go there. I don't have time to 'like' anyone as you put it."

Margrite leaned across the desk and took London's hand in hers. "You could make time. You know I've never thought this was the way for you long term. I had hoped to earn some money and give you a safe place for a couple of years at most. I always thought someone would have snapped you up by now."

London gave her friend's hand a squeeze before she pulled away. "And that's very generous of you, but I'm not interested in having someone rescue me. I do quite well on my own, and I live the way I want to. I don't have to rely on anyone, I don't have to bend to anyone else's ideas about who I should be or how I should behave."

Margrite's eyes turned soft. "Oh my love, someday you're going to tell me what it was that mother of yours did to you. But until then, I wish you'd at least consider the possibility that you might want to be someone's mistress or wife someday. There are plenty of lovely, wealthy men out there who would adore having you on their arms during the day, and in their beds at night. I'm serious when I say that a permanent paramour has many advantages over the hourly ones."

London shook her head and chuckled. "You can have them," she said. "The last thing I need is some man trying to tell me what to do."

"Even one who looks like Derek Ambrose?"

"Even him." Yes, she thought, banishing the memory of those icy blue eyes. Even him.

**

Derek's fists pounded a heavy bag over and over again. Thwack, thwack, thwack, thwack, in rhythm—one, two, one, two. His bare chest was covered in sweat and his shoulders ached from the brutal pace he'd kept up since he arrived at Spar.

"You'd better be careful old man, you're going to strain something," his brother Marcus's voice snapped him out of the haze of frustration he'd been in for the last hour.

He grabbed the bag as it rebounded from his last punch. Steadying it he turned to face his twenty-five-year-old kid brother, a near double for Derek, but with darker eyes and hair.

"I'm just getting warmed up," he told Marcus. "Get your gear on and I'll kick your ass."

"Body punches only from now on," Marcus instructed. "This face is my livelihood."

Derek grimaced. The kid had a point, he'd recently started as a political correspondent for WNN news, and Derek knew that while Marcus was talented as hell, his good looks didn't hurt his career.

"Fine, body punches only, pretty boy, now get moving."

Marcus smirked and loped off to the locker room to change out of the five thousand-dollar suit Derek had bought him. Derek knew he spoiled the kid, but he was so fucking proud of him he couldn't help it. Marcus had graduated top of his class from one of the best journalism programs in the country, worked for two years as a reporter in a large market, and then snagged the political correspondent job at WNN, the biggest news network in the world.

Derek had paid for everything his brother did since the kid was sixteen and Derek got his first good consulting gig. In the intervening years he'd put Marcus through college, grad school, and now gotten him a swank apartment and a BMW to celebrate the new job in D.C. He shook his head as he went back to punching the bag. He probably did spoil Marcus, but it gave him joy to do it, so what the hell.

Some people might think that he ought to be spoiling a woman the same way. But he'd never met one that tempted him to do so. He thought back to earlier in the day and the escort he'd caught Melville with. Now *there* was the kind of woman who deserved to be spoiled by her man. He wondered if she had one—a man that is. Did prostitutes have boyfriends? He shuddered at the idea. Not if the men had any sense they didn't. Oh he knew the cliché, the pimps were their boyfriends, but London Sharpe wasn't some hooker with a pimp. She was far too high-end for that. She probably knew about as much about streetwalking as he did, which was to say, not much.

The fact was, if he'd ever met a woman like London, Derek might have been tempted to spoil her. He'd want to spoil her with protection, companionship. He'd want to have her back—and a few other parts as well. He hit the bag one more time and stopped to wipe his brow. Yes, a woman like her had no business working as an escort. She tried to act tough, but he'd seen it in her eyes. She was far too refined for that kind of life. She needed a man—her own man—to care for her, support her, do whatever she needed done. She was the kind of woman who inspired ancient tribes to go to war over her, and modern day CEOs to stop their manwhoring ways.

Manwhore. The word brought back the vision of Melville with his hands and lips all over the inspiring Ms. Sharpe. Derek growled and hit the heavy bag so hard it nearly popped off its chain.

"What's crawled up your ass?" Marcus asked as he reappeared, headgear and gloves in hand.

Derek scowled at him, but all Marcus did was laugh. "You don't seriously think that'll still work on me, do you?"

"Shut up and get in the ring, junior." Derek gestured at one of the sparring rings nearby.

"Did you reserve it?" Marcus asked as they walked.

"No, but Renee did." Derek saw his brother's eyes light up when he mentioned his secretary's name. "And get that starry-eyed look off your face. I've told you more than once that my staff is off-limits to you."

Marcus shook his head. "And I told you, I'm not going to make a move on your secretary, even if you are out of line trying to dictate who I can and can't date."

Derek seriously doubted Marcus was telling the truth. He knew how his brother operated with women. He was all about the chase and the conquest, then he was on to the next. And that was why Derek wanted to keep him away from the cute blonde who sat in his office lobby. Renee had enough pain in her life right now, she didn't need a player adding to it. She reminded Derek so much of their younger cousin who had been killed in a rafting accident two years before. He couldn't bear to let his womanizing wolf of a brother have at her, even though he knew they were both adults.

As they got settled in the ring and started a slow dance around one another he changed the subject to something less inflammatory than Marcus's love life.

"So tell me what you heard at the office about Melville's announcement?"

While Marcus was a reporter and very serious about his career, he was first and foremost always Derek's brother, and though Derek didn't think he was ready to have his baby brother on the inside of the Powerplay club, he also knew he could count on Marcus to have his back with the press. Marcus would always give his loyalty to Derek before he gave it to a job or a source.

"You know, when I got hired we discussed how this was going to play out—you being related to me—and management decided that as long as they didn't put me on a story directly related to you it'd be fine. But I can see it's making everyone else nervous." He shrugged.

"So you're telling me they're so tight-lipped around you that you're useless to me?" Derek winked and grinned.

Marcus jabbed a hard right at Derek's midsection, catching him off-guard. He spun away, receiving only a glancing blow, but pissed that he hadn't been more aware. Between the press conference he'd held earlier and the wrench that Melville's extra-curricular activities had thrown into the mix, Derek knew he wasn't in top form, but he couldn't afford that. He had to be on the ball at all times.

Marcus danced on the balls of his feet for a moment before raising his fists up in fighting stance again. "No, just saying that I don't hear everything. But today I heard that the consensus is you've got 'the one'. He's the President's heir in the party, and with you managing the campaign he virtually can't lose."

Derek knocked Marcus upside the head with his big padded glove-encased fist. Not enough to hurt him, just a tap. Marcus shoved Derek's arm away.

"Damn straight he can't," Derek snarked.

"Asshole." Marcus shook his head.

"And how about you? You figured out how to get the nightly anchor spot yet?" Derek dodged a blow to his left shoulder and planted a firm shot right in the middle of Marcus's chest. The younger man coughed and rubbed the spot, wincing.

"Jesus, give me a week, will ya? I barely know where the bathroom is in that place."

Derek checked the surrounding area. The gym was crowded, but most people there were working out on the bags or in a training session with the gym owner.

"I had a little problem before the press conference today," Derek said, quietly.

"Yeah?" Marcus asked.

Derek proceeded to describe the events in the hotel room prior to Melville's announcement.

Marcus stopped moving, dropped his hands to his sides and stared. "You're kidding, right?"

Derek motioned for Marcus to keep sparring. "I only wish."

"Jesus. What the hell was he thinking? I mean it's one thing to have an affair, but a hooker?" He looked appalled.

Derek felt heat rise in his face, and his chest tightened. "What?"

Marcus's eyes darted around the way Derek's had a few moments earlier. "You said she was a whore, right?" he hissed.

Derek shoved Marcus. Hard. His kid brother stumbled and cursed under his breath. "What the fuck?"

Derek took a deep breath, his reaction surprising himself as much as it had Marcus. He rubbed the back of one glove across his forehead before he put his fists up again, indicating the spar should resume. Marcus was slow to follow, still shaking his head in disgust.

"I didn't teach you to talk like that," Derek gritted out. "She's a human being, and while I can't agree with her *career* choices, that doesn't make her unworthy of our respect."

Marcus mouthed something silently that looked like, "Wow."

"Am I right?" Derek asked, giving his favorite man in the world a hard look.

"Yeah, yeah, of course. I'm sorry, of course you're right." He was silent for a moment as they continued to dance and jab at one another, taking things slow and easy as if the conversation were enough of a firestorm.

"Have you ever..." Marcus's voice faded away, but Derek knew damn well what he was asking.

"No. Of course not, but I know plenty of men who have."

Marcus shook his head. "Yeah, I can't see ever being that hard up."

"If you'd seen this woman you'd be singing a different tune," Derek muttered.

Marcus sliced a halfhearted uppercut at Derek's chin, but Derek dodged and came back with a jab to Marcus's side.

"So she was hot—the woman?"

Derek gave Marcus another tap on the side of the head. "She was very hot."

Marcus stopped his dancing around the ring, gesturing to the water bottles at the edge of the area. Both men walked to the ropes and reached out to grab their bottles.

"Sounds like you might like to be one of her clients," Marcus joked.

Derek could feel himself bristle, but he knew he couldn't blame Marcus for the question.

"No, I'd never be a client," Derek answered. "But if she were in a different line of work..."

"I want to see this woman," Marcus grinned.

"I'm thinking there's no way that's going to happen," Derek answered as they moved back to the center of the ring and began sizing each other up.

"Famous last words." Marcus grinned as he landed an uppercut on Derek's jaw and did a victory dance around the ring.

**

Derek rolled over and slammed his hand down on the cell phone that was chiming relentlessly. He fumbled with it, finally peeling open his eyes and running a finger across the screen to turn the alarm off.

He groaned and reached for the remote to power up the flat screen television mounted on the wall across from his king-sized wrought iron bed. WNN filled the room and Derek sat up and adjusted his pillows. In his line of work it was essential to be on top of every piece of news out there. Years ago he'd learned never to leave the house until he'd checked the media.

"And in Washington this morning it might be the shortest-lived presidential campaign on record."

Derek's chest felt like it was suddenly coated in ice. He clutched the remote, clicking the volume higher as he climbed out of bed and walked toward the TV.

"Jason Melville, Senator from Pennsylvania, announced his candidacy for president yesterday in a brief press conference." The screen cut to a clip of Melville's press conference while the announcer continued talking and Derek swallowed the bile rising in his throat.

"But this morning WNN has obtained information from a confidential source that may end Melville's campaign before it even begins. Sources say that Senator Melville spent time alone in a hotel suite with a high-end D.C. call girl. Information verified by hotel records and security cameras show a woman identified as a popular D.C. prostitute visiting Melville's hotel suite at the Renaissance yesterday afternoon, only hours before he announced his candidacy."

"Fuck!" Derek yelled in the early dawn gray of his bedroom. "No fucking way!"

"Sources tell us that the as yet unnamed woman, shown here in the elevator of the Renaissance, was sequestered in Melville's suite for about ninety minutes. No word yet from the Melville campaign, but no one can deny that this must come as a huge blow to well-known political strategist Derek Ambrose who has been guiding Melville's presidential plans."

Derek ran a hand harshly through his hair and threw the remote at the wall, shattering it and disconnecting the television.

He picked up his phone and clicked on speed dial number seven.

"Derek," Jason said as he answered.

"She won't tell anyone?" Derek growled. "She's discreet? She'll never say a word? Well, goddammit she said something. It didn't even take twenty-four bloody hours, Jason. Not even twenty-four."

Jason sighed. "I don't understand it, I really have no idea how this happened, but right now I've got bigger problems. Angela's not awake yet, but my father-in-law, Vandermeer is, and he's seen the news. He's going to tear me to pieces, Derek."

Derek gritted his teeth and wondered how he could have ever been stupid enough to think this jackass was the key to getting him inside the White House. "And you deserve it. Stay put. Don't talk to anyone. I'll call your staff and tell them what to do, so don't even answer calls from them."

"Okay, but what am I supposed to do about Angela?"

"Try apologizing, Jason. And keep it up for the next decade or so. Don't bother me unless she cuts your dick off. I'll be in touch."

He ended the call and flicked to speed dial number one immediately.

"I just saw," Kamal answered without preamble.

"He has no idea how it happened." Derek paced the bedroom, rubbing his hand on his bare chest where a burning pain was working its way to the surface. "I think I'm having a fucking heart attack."

"Remember that game we played against Dartmouth senior year?" Kamal asked, referring to their time on the Cornell soccer team.

Derek's scowl deepened. Now was not the time for a walk down memory lane. "Yeah?"

"You thought you were having a heart attack then too, and you went out and scored two goals and got us the conference championship. You're not dying."

"Says you," Derek muttered.

"So what's the next step?"

"I've got a visit to make to a certain high priced call girl."

"You sure that's a good idea? What if you're seen?"

"I'll be careful. Call Jeff and ask him to get me a tail that can keep anyone else off my ass?"

"Done," Kamal responded. "We'll get them over there in the next thirty. Want me to get someone to talk to Melville's staffers so they don't do something stupid like call a press conference?"

"Please. I'll call you as soon as I've seen her."

Kamal huffed out a bitter chuckle. "If she hasn't already taken your twenty grand and whatever else she got paid for blabbing and skipped the country."

"If she has I'll hunt her down," Derek said darkly. "I don't care if I have to go to Siberia in the dead of fucking winter, I'll find her. And she'll be damn sorry when I do."

CHAPTER III

The pounding was incessant. London rolled over in her bed and groaned. "Stop it already," she mumbled. It started again—banging so loud it sounded like it might crack the wood in her custom made front door.

"All right, all right!" she yelled. Who in their right mind would be pounding on her door like that at—she checked the clock on the nightstand—seven thirty in the morning?

She climbed out of bed and grabbed the sapphire blue silk robe that was draped over the footboard of the bed. After she'd donned it she walked to her dressing table and stooped to check her hair in the mirror. It was a mess, but hell, anyone who'd wake her up this way deserved what they got.

"I'm coming!" she shouted, as she walked downstairs and across the cool marble tiles of the foyer. In retrospect, slippers would have been a good idea.

She reached the door and put her eye to the peephole, jerking back as soon as she recognized the very angry-looking Derek Ambrose on the other side. She peeped through again, and saw his cold blue eyes looking right back at her.

"Open. Up," he demanded in a voice that wasn't loud, but still sent shivers down her spine.

She unlocked and swung open the door but before she could say a word Derek shoved past her, entering the house, then pivoting swiftly. He caught the door with one hand right next to her head, and slammed it shut, rattling the pictures on the walls.

"What in the world..." London managed to choke out, somewhat breathless from the rage rolling off of him.

"How much and who?" he snarled, stepping closer to her.

"What are you talking about?" she asked, stiffening her spine so he wouldn't see how afraid she actually was.

"Who paid you to rat out Melville and how much did they give you?"

She stared at him, her mind a blank as she tried to process what he'd just said.

"What? Rat out...what?"

He glared down at her, his eyes flashing like chips of frozen seawater. "I have to hand it to you, you work fast. I'm not even sure how you found someone willing to play ball that quickly. But maybe you've had this planned for a while, huh? You've been seeing Jason for a couple of months. Maybe he slipped and told you he'd be running for the White House, so you decided you could make some extra money. Is that how it happened?"

"I have no idea what you're talking about," she answered, her voice as steady and cold as she could make it.

Derek muttered some sort of curse and grabbed her arm, looking around him for a split second before dragging her through the foyer and into the front parlor.

"Who do you think you are?" she gasped. "You can't come into my house and start throwing me around like some sort of rag doll. I want you to leave immediately!"

"Honey, after what you did to me you'll be lucky if I treat you as well as a rag doll." Derek reached out and flicked on the TV, punching the channel button until he found WNN.

London stood, rapt, as Melville's face flashed across the screen.

Presidential candidate purported to be with prostitute in Washington hotel hours before announcing his candidacy, the scrolling headline read.

"Oh my God," London murmured as she watched in utter horror. The headline went on to describe the reactions of various pundits and the lack of comment from the White House. "How is this possible?"

Derek stared at her, his face no longer the picture of fury. He paused, cocked an eyebrow, and observed her silently. She glanced at him then her eyes went back to the TV.

"Tell me they don't have my name. Please tell me they don't have my name."

"They don't," he answered. "But they have footage of you in the elevator at the hotel yesterday. It doesn't show your face straight on, but that doesn't mean someone won't pick you out."

"Oh God." London collapsed on the sofa, while Derek finally released her arm. She held a hand to her forehead. "Oh my God. How did this happen?"

"My question exactly. But I'm starting to get the feeling I won't find any answers here."

She gazed up at him, her distress replaced with rage. "I can not believe you think *I'd* do this. I'm an escort, so automatically I'm untrustworthy? I'll have you know that the measly twenty grand you gave me yesterday is chump change in my world. You see this house? *I* paid for it. In cash. I have a vacation condo in Vail for God's sake. I don't sell out clients for a few thousand dollars. Or even for tens of thousands. I'm a businesswoman."

Derek looked at her and she watched as myriad emotions crossed his face—surprise, admiration, and something else that made her throat go dry and her palms sweat. She felt her face heat and her pulse rate picked up.

He continued to look at her, his head cocked to the side, his eyes pinned to hers. "You didn't do it," he said quietly.

"No," she answered, her voice just as soft.

He broke the gaze and took a step closer, then seemed to reconsider. "Well with a condo in Vail you've surely got a coffee maker as well," he proclaimed suddenly, turning on his heel and striding toward her kitchen.

Ten minutes later she faced him across her kitchen island, a cup of coffee in hand. "You've got your coffee, now how are you going to fix this?"

He laughed, a deep, raspy chuckle that sent vibrations down to her very center. His smile made tiny crinkles break out around his pale eyes, softening them and warming his whole face. Combined with the light scruff that sprinkled his jaw and the mess of blonde hair drifting across his brow, the smile sent him from attractive to breathtaking and she sighed, struggling to mask her reactions and regain control over her traitorous hormones.

"What exactly is so funny?" she grumbled, taking a sip of coffee to cover her involuntary response to him.

He winked at her. Bastard. "Ah, you're funny. Really." He took a sip of his coffee. She wished she'd poisoned it before she gave it to him.

"I mean it, Mr. Ambrose. How are you going to fix this? I can't believe I don't have friends calling me already asking why they didn't know I was a prostitute."

"I hate being called Mr. anything by the way, and I thought you were an escort," he chided.

"That's not how they'll see it, and you know it." He ran a hand through his hair, his expression sobering. "I'm thinking."

She narrowed her eyes at him in anger. "Your idiot client got me into this. You didn't have him on a tight enough leash. This could ruin me."

He slammed his coffee cup down on the countertop. "And you think it's going to do what for me? Make me a great catch for the next presidential candidate? Who the hell will hire the guy who's forever associated with the shortest presidential campaign in the history of U.S. politics?"

She sighed. "It seems to me we're both victims of whoever leaked this information. Do you have any other ideas as to who it could be?"

He prowled around the kitchen like a big jungle cat, obviously deep in thought. Even with her substantial experience with men of all shapes and sizes, she was held captive, watching his muscles bunch under his dress shirt, the way his broad shoulders dwarfed her cozy kitchen, the way his long legs covered the length of the room in two steps.

Finally he stopped. "I have no idea who it is, but ask me again in twenty-four hours. They won't get away with it."

"And what do we do until then?" she asked, tossing her hair back over her shoulder, determined to shake off the attraction that grew the longer he stayed in her house.

He planted his hands on the kitchen island, and leaned forward. His gaze raked over her, obviously taking in the cleavage that peeked out of the neckline of her silk robe.

He breathed deeply, almost as if he was inhaling her. Her tongue darted out between her lips and she knew trouble was coming, could feel it circling the room, making her breasts heavy and her heart race.

"We're going to date," he said, the ends of his mouth tipping up in a devilish grin.

**

Damn she was gorgeous. No wonder men paid a grand an hour to be with her. He was about ready to empty his stock portfolio if she'd only open the sash on that jewel-toned robe she wore.

He'd been sporting a semi since he stormed in the door and took one look at her lush breasts and smoking hot ass all wrapped in shiny silk, her hair a tumbled mass of waves around her exotic eyes. Even in his rage he'd wanted to grab her, pin her against the wall, fuck her senseless, and hear her scream his name.

That had to explain why he'd concocted the hare-brained scheme that he was currently explaining while she stood, arms crossed, eyes narrowed, and foot tapping.

"No." Her voice was flat, her face a blank wall.

"I *could* let you and Melville take the fall. I'd claim ignorance, you can't prove otherwise. The two of you would be done forever. He'd never get elected to anything again, and you'd be the notorious D.C. escort—not sure it did much for Heidi Fleiss but who knows." He shrugged, and she glared. He was being an asshole, but the point needed to be made. They had very few options here. The sooner she realized that the better.

He paced to the other end of the kitchen, trying not to breathe too deeply when he passed her. She still had that exotic spicy scent wafting around her. It made him hungry in the worst possible way.

"I've put over eighteen months into grooming Melville, I have a lot riding on this, and I'm not ready to go down without a fight. You should be grateful, because it's going to help you as well."

She snorted, and even that was sexy.

"How is dating *you* going to help me? I've seen pictures of some of the women you take to functions—" she rolled her eyes—"it's not really the kind of company I want to be in."

Jesus. What was wrong with the women he dated? They were always attractive, polished, well-bred. He chose them carefully to insure they didn't overshadow him in the press, but also didn't embarrass him.

"What the hell's wrong with my dates?" he asked, truly irked she'd criticized his taste in women.

"Don't get me started," she answered, turning to the sink to rinse out their coffee cups.

He ran a hand through his hair in frustration. *Stay focused* his inner disciplinarian told him.

"Look, let's stick to the issue at hand. We're going to hold a press conference. I'm going to say that you're my girlfriend and that's why you were visiting *me* in Melville's suite. We can't hide the fact that you've worked as an escort, but we can spin it that since you've been seeing me you quit. You're reformed, the love of a good man and all that. It'll go a long way toward damage control for your reputation. We could turn you into a media darling with this. We can talk about stronger laws to protect victims of human trafficking, have you do a couple of sympathetic interviews describing why and how you ended up in that life."

He could feel her wavering, but her jaw was still set, steel under silk. She wasn't a pushover. He could see that she didn't like to do anything others told her to, and he had to stifle a grin imagining what a failure she must be with some of her more *domineering* clients.

"You really think I want to spill my life story to the press like that?"

"No, but I also think you're going to be getting a hell of a lot of attention in the next few weeks no matter what you do. Wouldn't you rather it be sympathetic attention?"

He could almost see the wheels turning inside her head. He wasn't even spinning it at this point, it was the fact of the matter. She'd been outed and there was no going back.

"I'll think about it," she finally answered.

He nodded, knowing that he shouldn't push her harder. If there was one thing Derek Ambrose knew it was how to conduct negotiations, and a fiery, sexy as hell escort was no different than a righteous, portly politician in the end. Some situations called for an iron fist, but others a kid glove.

"Tell me who knows what about your job," he said, propping a hip against her kitchen counter.

She gestured for him to follow her back into the parlor. He watched in fascination as her ass swayed under the soft fabric of her robe as she walked, and his dick twitched for the tenth time in the last twenty minutes.

After they were seated at opposite ends of her brocade and mahogany sofa, she sighed. "No one knows—knew—anything," she answered softly.

He stared at her in astonishment. "No one? You've been an escort for eight years and you've never told anyone?"

"Well, the clients obviously know, and the agency, but other than them? No one."

"Family?" he asked.

"I don't have any family," she corrected quickly, her tone indicating it wasn't a topic open for discussion.

He watched her for a moment, remembering the suspicions the Powerplay members had about her late teens. He tried to slough it off, but it brought back that sinking feeling of nausea.

"What if you run into a *client*," the word was shockingly distasteful on his tongue, "out somewhere? How do you keep people from recognizing you?"

"I've kept a very low profile on both sides of my life. Once I started the more lucrative side of escort work I stopped going to public events with clients, and I've avoided the types of gatherings where my clients might be attendees on the private side of my life. It's driven my best friend to distraction. I refuse to attend political gatherings or large fundraisers with her."

He shook his head, amazed at the whole thing. Eight years she'd kept this secret. Eight long years. She obviously wasn't proud of what she did for a living. She obviously didn't want it to define her. So why did she do it? For money? He couldn't believe that was her only motivation. Her townhouse, while not ostentatious, was lovely, stylish and classy like her. She had a vacation property in Vail, her clothes alone could have paid the rent for several months. She could have quit the escort business and found something else long ago.

"And your friends—how do they think you support yourself? What kind of people are they?"

She raised an eyebrow at him. "Not that you have any right to be digging around in my personal life any more than you obviously already have, but my friends think I have inherited money. I lead the quiet life of a single woman of means. I lunch, I volunteer, I travel. The only difference with me is that I also fuck wealthy men for cash. It all worked very well until this morning."

Derek's blood pressure rose with the cavalier way she described her business. He knew he had no right to judge, but he couldn't help the visceral response he had at the memory of her with Melville. Her beautiful soft body up against the wall as that asshole manhandled her. He shivered, trying to dispel the picture from his mind.

"Well, for the time being that difference will cease. We'll announce that we're dating, and that you realized as soon as you met me that you couldn't continue working at the job you had been. You'll tell your friends that you were keeping me under wraps because you wanted to see where it was going—that's perfectly reasonable considering my track record as a boyfriend is pretty non-existent."

"So is mine as a girlfriend," she muttered.

He stood and strode to the window, not wanting her to see his face while he spoke.

"We'll need to keep up the pretense until the whole thing dies down. Be seen out in public a few times—eating dinner, going to a function or two. I'll pay you for the lost income of course."

He knew he'd have to kiss the Jag goodbye for the rest of the year if he was going to pay her that much money, but if it meant getting his candidate into the White House he'd do it in a heartbeat. The added benefit that it would keep her out of those men's beds was nearly as enticing an incentive. It wasn't logical, but nothing about this whole thing was.

He rounded on her. "So what do you say? We'll be the darlings of the political season." He gave her a crooked smile and a wink that he knew worked wonders on women. He'd been using it since he was twelve.

Her face was like stone. Immobile, expressionless, cold. Figured. Just when he needed a *yes* more than he ever had before, he'd met the one woman who could resist the crooked smile-wink combo. Shit.

"This is not a good idea," she said standing from the sofa.

"Why?"

"We don't even like each other. How will we convince people we're dating? And as we've both admitted, we're not really relationship people, our friends will see right through this horrible charade. Or maybe you don't have friends?"

He rolled his eyes at her snark and the glint that snuck into her gaze.

"I have friends, you'll meet them…while you're *dating* me. Because unless you've got another idea, this is what we're going to have to do."

"I've been so good at staying hidden all these years, I can't believe this has happened."

"Surely you knew you couldn't lead a double life like that forever?" he asked gently.

She sighed in frustration, her perfect brows furrowing. "I've had a lot of fools for clients, but I think Senator Melville wins the prize. You really believe he'd make a good president?"

He coughed, trying to cover the chuckle at her description of the men who paid for her company. Any man who had the chance to be with her and then let her go was indeed a fool.

"I do, even after this. He's a brilliant statesman and politician but he's also human, and obviously we've discovered his fatal flaw." And hell, Derek couldn't even hold it against the man. This woman could become anyone's fatal flaw. She was like a magnet that pulled you in, her sexuality a swirling vortex that could consume you.

"And you actually think this will work? Save the campaign and convince people that I've reformed?" Doubt dripped from her very words.

"Yes, this can work. It's called hiding in plain sight," he answered, striding closer to her. "We've really only got a couple of choices here. We send you abroad for a few weeks while Melville denies it right and left. The press will be relentless looking for you, and as soon as it dies down and we bring you back they'll be all over you again the minute you set foot in the airport. Meanwhile, my candidate will be crippled by the rumors. He'll have to defend himself at every turn, and eventually the press will dig up something or someone who corroborates the rumors. Then it's all over, Melville has to drop out, my reputation is tarnished forever, and you're a notorious hooker for life."

He could see the pain flash across her face. Her lips tightened, and her eyes dropped to the floor as a flush crawled up her cheeks. He hated that he had to be so crass, but this was Washington and politics. There was nothing gentle about it, nothing kind or sensitive. As much as he loved it—the competition, the fangs-bared, balls-to-the-wall heat of the battle—he also sometimes resented it—the demands on his time, the constant maneuvering and jockeying for position, the fake front that he wore like a protective lacquer each day. And right now he wished that there were some way to achieve what he needed without disrupting this woman's delicately balanced life.

"And the other option?" she asked. "The hiding in plain sight one?"

"We give them an alternate story. You were at the hotel to see me, you and I are in love, you're a changed woman. It's a distraction at best, but if we can buy some time, and muddy the waters well enough the story will never get legs. It'll resurface—probably more than once, but it'll continue to go nowhere because we will have planted too much doubt."

One of her perfectly arched brows lifted and her plush lips pursed for a brief moment. "I see why you're Derek Ambrose," she said.

He couldn't help but smile, his chest swelling just a touch at the fact that she realized he was damn good at what he did. He wasn't a terribly vain man, but somehow looking good in front of this particular woman felt good. Maybe too good.

She watched him for a moment, neither of them moving, but his own breath coming in faster huffs as he watched her chest rise and fall. Then her tongue darted out to lick her full, dark lips, and something inside of him snapped. *Want* spread through him like floodwaters filling an empty river basin. The desire seeped into every corner, every spare inch of his being. And it burned. An ember just waiting to take a big gulp of oxygen and burst into flames.

A voice inside his head told him he was fucked. Totally and utterly fucked. And this idea was doomed too, just as he was doomed. But that want, that sizzling ember of desire wouldn't allow him to care. It wouldn't allow for anything but the fixation on the oxygen it needed to fully live.

Her. It wanted her.

She sighed as she turned away, and he saw her hands shaking. Thank God. Maybe it wasn't just him.

"Okay," her voice was quiet, "I'll do it. But I'm not taking money from you. So please don't mention that again."

He stepped closer, raising his hands as if he were going to place them on her shoulders, then he dropped them and leaned forward, his lips nearly brushing her hair.

"But no clients, right? You can't continue working if we're going to sell this obviously." Deep down he knew this was about more than someone catching her working. He didn't want to think about any man being near her if she was his girlfriend—even a pretend girlfriend.

She turned, gasping when she realized that he was in her space, inches from her body, nearly touching, yet not. Her eyes traveled up to meet his, and her lips dropped open slightly, sending a shock of electricity straight to his groin.

"No clients." Her voice was almost a whisper. "Just you."

If it were possible he leaned closer, infinitesimally closer, his lungs straining to function when he hadn't filled them in minutes—or maybe it was hours. A car alarm sounded outside and he jerked back, stunned at how easily he'd lost track of where he was and what he was doing simply because he could smell her, see her, breathe her. "I'll call the press conference for three p.m. so we can make the evening news cycle. I'll send a car for you. Wear something like that dress you had on at the hotel. The purple one. It was perfect."

She pulled back watching him suspiciously. "You noticed what I was wearing in the middle of that disaster?"

"I noticed everything about you," he returned. Then he stepped away and left her standing alone in her living room.

CHAPTER IV

London leaned back in the overstuffed leather seats of the Town Car and sighed. She really had lost her mind. Send a sexy as hell man to sweet talk her and she'd crumbled like a day-old cookie. The damage was done, her life was blown out of the water, and instead of giving up and accepting that she'd lost her friends and the respectable life that she'd built outside of prostitution, she was going to leap from the frying pan into the fire and try to salvage something from this debacle.

It was a disaster waiting to happen. All the media attention was like begging to have her darkest secret exposed, and then she'd be a pariah beyond salvation, beyond even Derek Ambrose's considerable spin skills. If America found out about her family, she'd become public enemy number one. Her friends would never get beyond that. Not in the nation's capitol.

So why the hell was she doing this? The answer was fairly simple—she loved her life. Not her life as an escort, but her life as London Sharpe. Her townhouse, her friends, her charities. Yes, she'd had to tread carefully all these years, making sure to stay away from things where prominent D.C. men might be involved, and in all fairness, she had run into a few clients in places like restaurants and concert halls. But they didn't want to acknowledge her any more than she did them, so it had all worked out.

For eight years she'd been who she wanted to be, not who someone else told her to be. She'd found people who were loyal and kind, and most of all, honest. The irony that she'd been dishonest with them all along wasn't lost on her. But being a prostitute and keeping that from the people she cared about was the price she paid to have control—control over what she did, who she let in. She'd long ago lost control over her history, but she was determined to have control over her present and future.

And now she was ceding control to Derek Ambrose. She was going to let him spin her life, tell the world that she hadn't been who they thought she was, and then she was going to become someone she actually wasn't—his girlfriend. If anyone had told her two weeks ago that she'd be about to stand up in front of the national press and do this, she'd have laughed them out the door. But here she was, and as many reservations as she had, she was going to follow through. Mostly because she couldn't bear to say goodbye to the London she'd built from scratch over all these years. And if she were being brutally honest, she also had a very hard time saying no to Derek Ambrose.

After Derek left, she'd spent the rest of her morning fielding phone calls and messages from her friends. Was it true? Was she actually a prostitute? How could she have been doing that all those years and they'd never known?

The toughest conversation had been with Joanna of course. Jo had been London's closest friend since they were in their early twenties and were in the same Women's Service League class together. Joanna was the closest to knowing the real London of anyone on the planet, although that didn't include information about

London's profession or family. Their conversation had not been an easy one.

"Why didn't you tell me?" Joanna had cried as she'd barreled her way into London's house.

London had blinked at her. How to explain the myriad choices she'd made over the years?

"Because I couldn't bear to hear what you have to say."

Jo bristled yet again. "And you presume to know what I'm going to say?"

London shook her head, letting her hair fall over her face as she dipped her chin. "You've just found out that I'm a hooker, Jo. You're a paragon of D.C. society, your husband is an up and coming diplomatic star. What else *can* you say?"

Jo's brow furrowed and she reached out to touch London's hand. "Before all of those things I'm your best friend. And you never told me about this entire other part of your life. Why?"

"It's not exactly the kind of thing you shout from the rooftops," London answered bitterly.

"Tell me about it now. Tell me how it happened, how it all works. Tell me *why*." Joanna's eyes filled with tears, and London wondered if this was what she'd been avoiding after all. Not the censure, or the abandonment she'd told herself she'd get from Jo, but this—hurt, confusion, betrayal. Joanna loved London, and London wasn't sure whether she could bear to see Jo's pain on her behalf.

London took a deep, shivering breath. "I left home when I was seventeen. I had a falling out with my mother—"

"Your mother's alive?" Joanna's eyes narrowed.

"Yes." London swallowed, her throat dry and tight. "She lied to me, about some very important things in my family, and when I found out I ran away. I managed for a while with fast food jobs and sleeping on other people's sofas, but as time went on it got harder and harder. When I was twenty-one the boyfriend I'd been living with went on tour with his band. I didn't want to go along, so I lost my place to live once again. I was so tired, Jo. So tired of trying to make it on my own. I'd cleaned houses, worked at burger joints, manned a newsstand in Union Station, any low paying job that a woman without a high school diploma could get I'd had. I was sick of it, but I didn't have any other options."

Joanna nodded sympathetically, her mouth a tense line in her face.

"Then one day I was handing out flyers for a window washing company when a man stopped and talked to me. He said he owned a high-end dance club and that I had a great look he thought would be popular. I wasn't naïve, Jo, I knew he was talking about a strip club, but at that moment, as beaten down as I was by it all, I just didn't care. So I went to check it out that night, and it wasn't so bad. The place was clean, the girls who worked there seemed nice enough, and they told me that they made in a single night what it took me over a week to earn at all my other jobs."

"No one could ever blame you for that," Joanna said, patting London's hand like an approving mother.

London nodded. Wondering if Jo was going to be so understanding about the next part of the tale.

"I worked there about six months, and at first it was like a godsend. I made enough to get myself a studio apartment—it was a dump, but I didn't have to be dependent on roommates. I was able to eat dinner out once a week, and even get some decent clothes, but then I got this pain in my mouth—it was my wisdom teeth, one had gotten impacted. You might be surprised to hear that strippers don't get dental insurance." London grimaced wryly and Joanna raised an eyebrow in response.

"It took me six months to pay off the cost of that surgery, and I knew that I might finally be able to keep a roof over my head, but only if nothing ever went wrong. I was still one bad day away from being homeless.

"That was when I started listening to the girls in the dressing room. They talked about this other business some of them worked for, an escort service."

She stopped to look at Joanna, and her heart lurched when she saw the tears in her friend's eyes.

"Jo, don't feel sorry for me. It gave me everything I have—this house, the place in Vail, my clothes, good healthcare. I earn a thousand dollars an hour having sex with men who wear suits to work. There are worse ways to earn a living."

"And better ones too." Jo's voice hadn't been recriminating, only sad, and she reached out and put a palm against London's cheek, looking at her earnestly. "Did you never think about going back to school, even getting some sort of vocational training? Beautician, bookkeeper, something?"

London shook her head. "It sounds so easy when you're looking in from the outside. We all say it, 'why don't those women go back to school?' There are loans, scholarships, all kinds of programs. But here's the thing— you spend every day being this perfect fantasy, creating this flawless shell of a woman, one who doesn't get hurt feelings, or a headache, one who hides it if men touch her in a way that disgusts her. Being an escort is really like being a giant doll, and it takes more mental energy than you might think. And after you're done for the day, you have to try to remember who you were before you went inside that hotel room. You have to find the energy to peel that façade back and be you again. A lot of days you barely manage it. A lot of days all you want to do is go home and go to sleep before you have to get up the next day and do it again."

She reached over to the tea she'd been drinking and took a sip.

"Don't get me wrong, being an escort wasn't horrible. I chose it, I'm not a victim, but it's also not an easy job. It requires you to put a certain part of you away, locked up in a box that you don't dare open. That's the part that might go to college, Jo. I thought I'd put that part away a long time ago."

Joanna watched her thoughtfully for a moment. "It makes so much sense now."

London quirked an eyebrow in question.

"How detached you often are. Those days when I feel like you're not really with me. I always thought it was because you'd been traumatized by your parents dying, but now I see it was the leftovers from your job. You couldn't always come back to the rest of us after…that. Am I right?" she asked tentatively.

"I suppose so." London thought for a moment. "Some days…" She paused, her hand clenching around the delicate handle of the teacup. "Some days are harder than others. Some…clients…are harder than others. And it takes a bit to be in sync with the rest of the world again."

Jo paused, seeming to tumble it all around inside her mind. "I talked all about Melville, said what a great family man he was, and you'd been having sex with him just hours before that?"

Then London had to go further, lie yet again to the friend who was ready to forgive her, trying to understand the twisted path she'd taken to get to where she was.

"No," London was quick to correct. "Melville is not a client."

"So what is all this about then?"

"I wasn't there to see Melville."

Joanna paused. "And?"

London chewed on her bottom lip then put it out there, cringing as she waited for the ensuing tsunami of disbelief. "I was there to see Derek Ambrose. I've been—" she had to clear her throat, "—I've been dating him."

"No way!" Jo shrieked. "No way have you been dating Derek Ambrose! He's rich, he's hot. I've heard he never dates anyone more than twice. My cousin's best friend went out with him once and said that he was the sexiest man she'd ever slept with but he never called her again. Holy shit."

London stayed quiet, resisting the urge to laugh at how quickly Joanna shifted from sophisticated D.C. political wife to gossiping teenage girl. Then she waited for the second wave to hit. Joanna just needed to catch a breath after all.

"So you've been keeping *this* a secret from me too? For how long? Weeks? Months? And yesterday you said Derek Ambrose was, and I quote, 'big and mean'. What was that all about? Were you at that hotel to break up with him?"

Okay, wave two was going on longer than expected. London interjected. "No, I didn't go to break up with him. We did have a little spat, so I said that because I was mad at him right then." Better to stick as close to the truth as possible. "We'd just had an argument. It's already over. We're together, Jo. And I'm sorry I didn't tell you."

Joanna sighed. "Why? Why couldn't you tell me?" The hurt in her voice sliced through London.

"I'm sorry. It was something he and I decided together. He gets attention from the press, they put him in the gossip columns when he dates someone. We were afraid of just what's happened. The press would want to know who I was and discover that I've been a prostitute. Neither one of us has ever been in a serious relationship. We wanted a chance to get to know each other before we had to face all of the things we're facing now."

"But *me?*" Joanna asked softly. "I would never have told anyone."

"You're right. I'm so sorry, Jo. I messed up. I know that now. I've never really tried anything like this—a serious relationship with a grown up man." She laughed self-deprecatingly, her brain trying to sift through the lies mixed with so much truth.

Jo had then been quiet for a moment before she asked the crucial question. "Does this mean you're not working anymore?"

"Yes, that's exactly what it means. Once I met Derek and we wanted to pursue a real relationship, it was clear I couldn't go on working. Now I have to figure out what to do with myself. Luckily I have resources that will last me awhile until I decide."

Joanna had grinned in triumph then. "You have to tell me everything. How did you meet him? What did he say to get you to go out with him? Is he as delicious as I'm imagining?"

London breathed a sigh of relief for her best friend's sweet generous nature. Joanna was spunky, but also didn't have a mean bone in her body and London was the beneficiary of that innate goodness.

"First of all, I'm not certain that you should be imagining the man I'm dating—delicious or otherwise—" London shouldn't care, but something about Joanna noticing Derek's assets rubbed her the wrong way.

Joanna snorted.

"We met at a charity function. He was never a client—I swear. He didn't give me much choice about going out with him, and yes—" London raised her eyes to the ceiling above her wishing like hell this wasn't the truest thing she'd say all day,"—he *is* as delicious as you're imagining."

London had cut the interrogation short at that point, telling Joanna that she had to get ready for the press conference. Joanna had been supportive of the move as it might give Melville's campaign a fighting chance, and thus her husband's chances at a diplomatic post as well.

Now, London was spending the drive to the hotel regretting the brand new set of lies she'd told her friends. She had long ago resigned herself to the lies about her job, but this new layer of deception was something she detested. She had a close circle of friends, more family really, since she had no other. She cared deeply about them—Joanna, her neighbor Rafe and his husband Kevin. Carlotta, the wife of an Argentine diplomat that she'd met at a party several years earlier. These people mattered to London, and it made her physically ill to shut them out of her life more than she already had. But if she was going to keep them, the lies were necessary, and so she bit her tongue, plastered a smile on her face, and prepared to present the new and improved London to the world.

The Town Car pulled up to the curb of the Renaissance Hotel and London shook herself out of the maudlin thoughts. What was done was done, and the best she could hope for was that Derek's gamble would pay off. She took a deep breath and readied herself. As she stepped out flashes blinded her, voices shouted, and hands grabbed. She cringed back against the side of the car while the chauffeur worked to shove the reporters out of her way. Just when she thought she'd be consumed by their hysteria a big, strong hand locked onto her elbow and the sea of journalists parted like something in the Old Testament.

She looked at a broad chest and then up into Derek's eyes. He grimaced at her before pulling her closer and tucking her into his side as he maneuvered them both through the throng and into the large glass doors at the front of the hotel. The noise from the reporters faded as they entered the lobby and London shook her head trying to clear it.

"Are you okay?" Derek asked as he kept his arm around her, walking her through the lobby.

"Yes. A little overwhelmed is all."

"Sorry about that." He gestured for her to enter a large meeting room while he held the door open for her. "We wanted to have a big turnout so we had to leak enough information to spark their interest."

She walked into the room, obviously set up for a press conference, a podium at the head, rows of folding chairs taking up the rest of the space.

In the front row, five men were lounging, each of them with an air of Washington's elite wafting off of them.

"Come meet my friends," Derek told her with his trademark wink before he leaned in to her ear and whispered, "I paid them to pretend we were friends so you'd be impressed." London struggled not to laugh. *Devil.* He was the devil in disguise, she knew it.

"They're like a pack of piranhas out there," Derek said as they approached the group of men. All five stood when they saw London.

"You wanted results," a lean man with light brown hair and amazing green eyes said, smiling.

"That I did," Derek answered, pulling London to a halt in front of the group and putting his arm around her shoulders.

"Gentlemen," he said, "I'd like to introduce you to my *girlfriend*. Honey, these are the guys." Derek's tongue in cheek remarks helped alleviate some of London's panic, and she shoved at him and frowned. His hold on her only tightened. "Play nice," he whispered in her ear, earning a smirk from a mocha-skinned hottie in a designer suit standing closest to them.

"Now," Derek said, gesturing to the designer suit guy, "this is Teague Roberts, partner at Guildhurst, Crandall, and Roberts. Mr. Cheerful there is Colonel Jefferson Thibedeux, Director of Domestic Operations for the Pentagon Next to him is Scott Campbell, Chief of Staff to Senator Hugh Carries." All three men said their hellos and shook her hand politely.

"The one who needs a haircut," Derek continued, "is Kamal Masri, Ambassador to the U.S. from Egypt, and the best damn left outside mid the Cornell soccer team's ever had." Kamal gave her a charming smile and shook her hand. Her heart clutched briefly, his dark features and warm eyes bringing back memories of other people and other times in her life.

"And last, and probably least, is Gage Warner, the president of the Workers' United League of North America. That's right," Derek deadpanned, "he gets Canada and Mexico too."

The dark-haired, gray-eyed man flipped a finger at Derek before reaching out and lifting London's fingers to his lips. "It's truly a pleasure to meet the woman who's finally tamed our boy," he teased. London couldn't help but smile back at him, and Derek stiffened at her side, his voice brusque when he next spoke.

"All right, enough with the introductions, let's run through this performance to make sure we've smoothed out the rough edges."

**

Forty minutes later the conference room was packed with reporters, cameras and microphones. Derek stood at the podium with Senator Melville on one side of him and London on the other.

"Good afternoon everyone," he rumbled into the microphone. "If you could quiet down we'll get started." The room went silent almost instantly and London looked to Derek, marveling at how well he controlled the crowd of hungry newspeople.

"Thank you for coming," Derek began. "You've heard the reports this morning regarding Senator Melville and a mysterious woman who visited his hotel suite yesterday a few hours before he announced his candidacy."

Derek paused, looking around the room with a stern expression.

"You all know that my heart generally beats only for you." The reporters chuckled and a couple wolf-whistled. "But I have to admit I've been unfaithful." More laughs from the audience. "The mystery woman visiting the Senator's hotel suite was there to see *me*, and she is *not*—let me be very clear about that—not involved with

Senator Melville." He gave the room his meanest glare, and London noticed some of the audience balked.

"This lovely woman on my right is London Sharpe. My *girlfriend*. We hadn't taken our relationship public yet because she has indeed, *in the past*, worked as an escort. I did not want her very private history to become public gossip and impact the important work we're doing with this campaign. I did approach Senator Melville when Ms. Sharpe and I started our relationship, and I received his blessing. The Senator is a strong advocate for women in all walks of life, including those who need our protection from human trafficking and sexual exploitation."

There were murmurs throughout the audience. Derek silenced them with another of his icy stares. "Since we started dating, Ms. Sharpe and I have been enjoying getting to know each other without any pressure from the more public parts of my life, but obviously we have to come clean at this point."

Shouts and chaos erupted, but Derek put a halt to it with a hand held up and a look of impatience. "Hold on, we'll get there." Then he winked, and London swore every female reporter in the room sighed in unison.

"Ms. Sharpe is not a public figure, so I'm not going to let you at her, but I will give you a brief bio so you'll at least get your facts straight. London was born in Iran and immigrated to the U.S. as a child. She *is* an American citizen for those of you who seem preoccupied with such things." He nodded at the reporter from Channel F-News who smirked in response.

"London is a volunteer and advocate for several organizations devoted to women's and children's issues. She and I met at an event benefitting the Greater D.C. Children's Farm."

London bit her lip, remembering how she'd sat on the phone for forty-five minutes with Derek's secretary going over their calendars from the last six months to find an event they might both have attended and could claim as their "meet-cute" spot. A flash going off reminded her to relax her expression, and she experimented with a small smile, trying not to let her discomfort with all of this show.

"And that's all you're getting from me this morning," Derek concluded. "I'm going to turn this over to the Senator now, and he's going to discuss his proposal for a new funding structure for the Pentagon's weapons purchases. Let's put this one to rest, ladies and gentlemen. Thank you."

The room exploded, reporters shouting things at both Derek and London. He took her elbow and guided her out a door behind them as Senator Melville stepped to the podium and said, "You guys got me into some really hot water at home." That stopped the shouts and the entire room broke into laughter.

When they reached the lobby, Derek's friends were waiting.

"How'd it go?" Scott asked.

"Fine. Melville can handle it from here. Jeff, can I get the security escort back to London's place to make sure no one follows us?"

"Yep, they're waiting by the Town Car in the underground."

"I think it's a wrap, gentlemen. Thanks for your help." Derek shook everyone's hands and the group dispersed.

London watched the men walk away and a sudden rush of exhaustion hit her, as though the adrenaline coursing through her since she'd been wakened by Derek that morning suddenly poured out all at once. She was left feeling vaguely dissatisfied and questioning her own sanity.

As much as she tried not to engage with D.C. politics, London was hardly ignorant of the game and its power brokers. Derek's friends were every bit as significant and powerful as him. London dealt with men like them in her job every day, but when they entered a hotel room with her she was actually the one with the power. London had learned early in her career exactly how much control she actually held over men in the bedroom. She was blessed with the looks and a body that men desired, and she used it to her full advantage. By the time they'd been alone with her for ten minutes they'd do virtually anything she asked in order to have her, and she preferred it that way.

But this wasn't the bedroom, it was the pressroom, and now she was in the opposite position. Outside of the bedroom with men like these she had no power, and it made her twitchy, reminding her of days long ago when she had no control over her history, no control over how she became who she was. And like in those days when she was London Amid instead of London Sharpe, she suddenly felt trapped, used, and disposable.

The fact was, if Derek and his friends decided to jettison her, they could so very easily. They could also find out her deepest secret—the one that her mother had told her when she was seventeen, the one that she had never come to terms with since.

"Let's get you home," Derek said placing his hand on the small of her back and directing her toward the elevators to the parking garage.

She deliberately stepped away from his hand, irrationally irritated that any of this had happened, that she'd lost all the control in the blink of an eye.

He glanced at her but didn't remark at her rejection.

The enormity of what she'd just done seemed to settle on her all at once. In the last twelve hours she'd allowed a man—a man she hardly knew—to completely dismantle the life she'd so carefully constructed over the last eight years. She'd just gone on national television and tied herself to a stranger for God knows how long. In only a few hours he'd completely taken over her life. London Sharpe didn't let anyone take over her fate. The speed at which things had transpired over the last day made London dizzy. If she could only get a few moments to breathe, think about what was going on, regain her senses.

They entered the elevator and he turned to her. "Are you all right?"

"Fine," she clipped out.

He scowled. "I might not be an expert on relationships, but even I know when a woman's 'fine' means anything but," he chided.

She took a step away from him. "It's been a long day, Mr. Ambrose. I'm tired and my feet hurt. I just want to go home now."

He leaned closer to her and put a finger under her chin, forcing her gaze up to his. "Mr. Ambrose, hmm. You're going to have to call me Derek if you expect anyone to believe what we've just told them." He paused, his voice low and gentle. "You did well today. I know it's not easy, and I'm sorry this happened. I'm sorry Melville got you into this mess."

She sighed, turning her eyes back to the lights in the elevator as he released her jaw from his touch. "It's fine. I'll be fine."

"Yes, you will. Because I'll make sure of it," he added quietly.

She wondered how he could make such a promise. Even Derek Ambrose couldn't replace the life she'd so carefully constructed, and she was terrified that life was about to explode into a million pieces.

CHAPTER V

Derek leaned back in his large office chair, resting an elbow on the supple leather armrest as he pressed his forehead into his palm. His head throbbed, and his mind wandered more than it focused. He'd been staring at a speech he was drafting for Melville for forty-five minutes and hadn't been able to complete one coherent sentence in all that time.

He closed his eyes and all he could see were ruby lips, amber eyes and a rack that would make an angel weep. London Sharpe, his so-called girlfriend who he'd neither seen, nor spoken with in three days. They were scheduled to attend a fundraising event for Melville this evening, and the anticipation was eating him up inside. Try hard as he might, he was going to have to admit—to himself anyway—that he was intensely attracted to the woman.

"Dammit," he muttered as he swiveled around to face the window. His office had a clear line of sight to the dome of the Capitol Building, and it served as a reminder of what he had always wanted most in this life—the power to influence a nation. He didn't feel he needed elected office to do that, it wasn't Derek's style. He knew that many times the politicians themselves were gnarled masses of ego and neediness topped off with a healthy dose of delusions of immortality.

He didn't need to make speeches, get fan mail, and be interviewed to feel like he was loved. He didn't need those things to know he wielded influence either. And he sure as hell didn't have any half-cocked ideas that he would be remembered by generations in the future. No, Derek just wanted to be the man who pulled the strings so that he could help the world reach its potential.

For as long as he could remember, Derek had held a rather unique perspective on life and the world around him. At the age of five he'd come home from playing at the neighbor's house and asked his mother, "Why do Erik's parents keep grounding him when he doesn't clean his room? If they would give him ice cream for cleaning he'd do it right away. He'd do anything for ice cream." If Derek had one exceptional talent it was the ability to see how to wield influence.

He'd majored in Political Science in college and begun working on campaigns as early as his sophomore year. His talent and unflagging work ethic propelled him to leadership roles on national level campaigns by his twenty-fifth birthday. By thirty he'd formed his own political consulting firm, masterminded some of the biggest and costliest senatorial campaigns in history, and made a boatload of money in the process.

As a trusted advisor to several of the candidates he put in office he'd been able to influence their policy platforms, steering them toward issues close to his own heart. His father worked the line at an auto factory in Detroit, pushing his body to its limits every day. As the U.S. auto industry had suffered a long and painful death, Derek's family had struggled to maintain the solid working class lifestyle they'd had when he was a child. Luckily, once his big paychecks started to come in he was able to help his parents and now had them settled into a lovely retirement house in Boca Raton.

But he'd never forgotten the razor's edge that hard-working Americans often walked in the new millennium. His push to gain entry to the White House stemmed from both the urge to wield influence, and to direct the policies of the country where he saw such important need. His special ability was that he saw how to do that in ways others didn't.

Now he was sitting at his desk, on the cusp of everything he'd been working towards for the last ten years, and all he could think about was that face, those legs, and the luscious pair of tits that fell midway between the two.

There was no way he could actually get involved with London. She was an escort for Christ's sake. He had no interest in a woman who made a living by lying to men. Telling them the things they wanted to hear. *Yes baby. Like that baby. You're the best baby.* He shuddered imagining it all. Derek Ambrose wanted his women wet, willing, and brutally honest when they fucked him. Call him crazy, but he needed to know that when he thrust and they screamed it was for real.

No, he wanted London Sharpe, but as a man, not ever as a client. He wanted her to want him back. He didn't want to have to worry that she was faking anything between them. But he couldn't have that, so he sat around and fixated while sporting wood.

"That's the 'things aren't going my way' face," Kamal said from the doorway as he sauntered into Derek's office unannounced.

"I need to fire my secretary apparently," Derek answered, leaning back in his chair.

"Well, in all fairness I brought her flowers." Kamal sat in the chair in front of Derek's desk and grinned.

"If she lets everyone who brings her flowers into my office it will be the new Union Station," Derek grumbled.

"She is popular," Kamal answered. "Although a little young for my tastes."

"Mine as well. But not my brother's if I'm reading the situation right."

"Really? Marcus is interested in Renee?"

"He claims he isn't, but I can tell. I've been watching the kid chase skirts since he hit puberty. All the signs are there. I told him I'd kick his ass back to Penn if he doesn't stay away from her. It took me ten years to find a good secretary, I'm not going to lose her because my little brother can't keep it in his pants."

Kamal chuckled, then went for the kill. "And how about you? Can you keep it in your pants around our lovely Miss Sharpe?"

Derek glared at his oldest and best friend. "She's not *our* anything, and I'm not even going to justify that with an answer," he spit out.

Kamal put his hands up in the universal sign of surrender. "Just asking. I've seen you chase a few tails as well, and I'm not blind. You were enjoying the little ruse quite a bit at the press conference."

Derek sighed, a feeling of defeat washing over him. "You didn't see anything other than she's gorgeous, and I'm male. It's no big deal."

Kamal didn't look like he bought the brush off, but he let it pass. "I've got some information on who might have started the rumors with the press."

Derek sat forward, alertness sparking every nerve in his body. This is what he needed to get his mind out of his pants, the thrill of the hunt, the scent of blood. When he found out who had fucked with him he was going to tear them into a million tiny pieces and feed them to the White House press corps.

"Tell me," he instructed Kamal.

"Teague called in some favors with his firm's investigators, and Scott's had his ear to the wall at the Capitol. The two of them have heard one name in common during the last week."

"And?" Derek's nails dug into the desk in front of him.

"Ryan Williams, Chief of Staff to Senator Donovan."

"Donovan, who has been making noise about running for President, but hasn't announced yet?"

"Yes." Kamal shifted his weight and stretched his long legs out fully. "Williams has been talking a lot of crap about Melville, and also hired a firm to do a background report on him."

"And you think somehow in that report they found London?"

"If he had Melville followed, he could have seen the meeting between our Ms. Sharpe and the Senator, correct?"

Derek sighed and ran a hand through his hair as he gazed at the ceiling, wishing it held the answers he was looking for. When nothing appeared in the pristine paint he looked back at Kamal. "If someone were watching Melville really closely they certainly could have seen her go into his hotel room."

Kamal nodded. "How do you want us to proceed?"

Derek stood and paced the length of his ample office, five hundred-dollar dress shoes sinking into the plush carpet. "We need a way to get to Williams. What do we have on him?"

Kamal pulled out a folded piece of paper from his inside jacket pocket, obviously having anticipated Derek's question. "You should probably take a look at this." He handed the paper to Derek.

Derek scanned it quickly then looked at Kamal from under his brows, a devilish smile playing across his hard features.

"Well, well, well. Never thought the White House Christmas party would be of so much use."

Kamal chuckled. "Yes, finding Williams screwing his boss's wife in a bathroom stall was a true stroke of luck."

Derek leaned over the desk and tapped the intercom button on his phone. "Renee. Get me all the information you can on Ryan Williams. He's in Senator Donovan's office."

He leaned back against the solid piece of furniture, feeling like he had control of his life again for the first time in days. "Looks like we've got ourselves a lead," he told Kamal.

"Looks like Donovan's not going to be running for president," Kamal answered.

**

The event was cocktail attire, and Derek filled out his dark suit admirably. Washington was replete with men in suits, but few in London's memory looked as good in one as her new 'boyfriend'.

As she stood in the corner of the ballroom she watched him making the rounds, shaking hands with one man, kissing a woman on the cheek before laughing at something that had been said. He was everything polished and charming. And she was surprised at how much she wanted to pretend he was hers even though she knew full well he wasn't—and never could be.

She turned her attention back to the congressman's wife who was trying to recruit her help for a children's charity.

"I think you and Mr. Ambrose would make such striking ambassadors for the program," the stocky Mrs. Bunker said, smiling broadly at London.

"Why thank you," London replied, thinking about just how striking Derek would be in his red tie and very little else.

She gave herself a small shake and tried to concentrate. "If you'll give me your card I'll be sure to discuss it with Derek. I'm not sure what philanthropic events his firm is participating in this season, but I'll make sure one of us gets back to you."

Mrs. Bunker leaned toward London. "And I must tell you, dear, I'm so interested in hearing about your former profession. Just what was it like with all those—" The woman stopped and looked over London's shoulder. "Oh! Were your ears burning Mr. Ambrose," she giggled.

Derek gave London a peck on the cheek as his arm slipped around her waist. It felt entirely too natural and good. She gritted her teeth and fought the urge to shift away in self-preservation.

"What terrible things are you two lovely ladies saying about me?" He looked down at London with so much devotion she wondered if he'd been an actor in a previous life. She silently repeated the mantra, *it's only pretend*, before answering him.

"Nothing but the best, dear," she answered, playing her own role to the hilt. "We're discussing a possible charity activity. I have all of the information and I can give it to your office tomorrow."

Derek grinned and continued to small talk with Mrs. Bunker for a few minutes, giving London time to take a breath. So far she'd had three people mention her prostitution. Two had been like Mrs. Bunker, well-meaning busy bodies. One had been a minister who made sure to tell her that God approved of her new path in life. Things had actually gone better than she might have anticipated, and Derek treated her like a queen. He had to have taken acting classes in college, she almost believed he really was in love with her.

When Mrs. Bunker excused herself to go visit with the Ambassador to Venezuela, Derek turned his back to the room and pinned London with a bemused expression.

"You didn't tell me you'd studied how to be a political wife."

She laughed, noticing the way his eyes sparked as his gaze dropped to her cleavage for just a moment. A shiver of awareness ran up her spine. "Actually, I stay as far away from politics as possible," she answered.

"Well, you knew all the perfect things to say. I couldn't have asked for a lovelier date." His hand came up to her elbow and he caressed her arm briefly, sending her pulse shooting up even though she knew damn well it shouldn't.

Someone bumped into Derek from behind, causing him to stumble as his drink splashed onto the front of London's dress and down into her cleavage.

"Shit," he growled as he turned to see who had collided with him.

London's eyes see-sawed between her damp dress and the man behind Derek's shoulder as she tried to wipe the droplets running between her breasts. She immediately recognized the perpetrator and cringed. Congressman Frederick Foster was a well-known D.C.

face, and held the position of Minority Whip in the House.

Foster's eyes narrowed in on London. His face was red and puffy, and she could tell he was drunk before he even spoke.

"Ambrose! Sorry, didn't mean to knock you there," Foster slurred as he drew up and faced Derek.

Derek's smile was tight and his voice rough. "It's actually my date you owe the apology to Congressman, I imagine the dress you've ruined wasn't cheap."

Foster's face broke out into a leering grin. "Well, that makes sense, since I well know that she's not either..." he paused and gave her a very obvious once over, "but while my whiskey might not have done much for the dress, it looks like it made her even tastier."

London's whole body stiffened while gritting her teeth and preparing to set Foster in his place, but before she could open her mouth Derek's hand shot out lightning quick. The next thing she knew his fist was full of the front of Foster's shirt and he shook the smaller man hard once.

"What the hell did you just say about my girlfriend?" Derek snarled.

Foster shoved at Derek ineffectually. "Please Ambrose," he slurred, "you really going to keep up this charade? She's a whore. Whatever floats your boat, but don't try to act like she's a real date."

The words were barely out of the bastard's mouth before Derek's fist connected, and blood shot out of Foster's nose and lip.

"Derek!" London screamed as he grabbed the drunk again. Foster's eyes rolled back in his head, and Derek gave him another hard shake before shoving him away.

As Foster collapsed on his hands and knees to the floor Derek shook his hand. "Fuck," he hissed.

Several men, including Senator Melville, appeared as if from thin air, and London's head began to throb with what she knew was further humiliation on the way.

"Derek?" Melville questioned, looking at his campaign manager like he'd grown two heads.

A hotel security member stepped into the fray. "Is there a problem here, Senator Melville?"

Derek grimaced. "Not anymore, but could you please escort *this*—" he gestured with his foot at a mumbling Foster, "off the premises. He's had one too many." He looked up at the curious faces. "Sorry. My mother raised me to defend a lady's honor." He shook his hand out again and straightened his cuffs.

As the security staff hoisted Foster from the floor and half-carried him away, Melville smiled at the onlookers. "No need to disrupt your evening, everyone. Nothing to worry about. One of the guests had a little too much to drink. I guess my speech wasn't as entertaining as I'd thought."

The cluster of people chuckled and one of Melville's aides subtly began directing them away. Sweet relief flooded London's body as she watched the remaining gawkers move on.

"What the hell, Derek?" Melville hissed. "Decent recovery, but they all saw you lay him out. What's gotten into you?"

Derek threw Melville a dark look and shook his head. "It doesn't matter, just go back to the event. You need to press the couple from Chicago. They're about ready to commit, and he was talking a bonus donation if you get the nomination."

Melville's eyes flicked to London, and she gave him a tight smile in return. She could feel her face burning. All she wanted was away, as fast as she could get there.

"You're leaving soon?" he asked in a tone that indicated he thought it would be for the best.

"Consider us gone," Derek answered.

**

Derek's hand hurt like a bitch. He knew how to throw a punch, boxing for exercise and all, but he hadn't slugged anyone bare-knuckled since his days as a college soccer player.

He thought back to the look in Foster's eyes as he leered at London, and rage coursed through him again. Bastard deserved a lot more than he'd gotten. If Derek hadn't been at a formal function he wouldn't have stopped until Foster was in the back of an ambulance. He remembered the look on London's face when Foster insulted her and his stomach roiled again. She tried to cover it, but she'd been mortified, and hurt.

And since they'd reached the car she hadn't spoken. Not one word. She sat on his expensive leather seats and looked out the window, her face turned away from him.

"Are you okay?" he asked, his voice rusty and thick.

"I'm not the one who was in a brawl in the Grand Esquire ballroom," she snapped back. "Why wouldn't I be okay?"

He ran a hand through his hair and weaved in and out of traffic as he tried to avoid a slowdown heading into Georgetown.

"He insulted you. Some women would have been upset by that."

London huffed out a bitter laugh. "I'm hardly like the other women you know."

Derek glanced at her, taking in her long neck and elegant profile. "No. You're not," —*you're so much better*— "but that doesn't mean he didn't upset you."

"I'm fine. And the whole scene could have been avoided if you'd just let me handle it."

She couldn't seriously mean that? What the hell kind of man did she think he was? No way would he stand by and let a woman in his company be verbally assaulted by a drunken pig.

"I don't allow other men to insult my dates, no matter what kind of function I'm at," he responded.

She turned to him, and her face was flushed, her lips trembling. "I'm not a real date, Derek. Have you forgotten that this is a ruse? You don't even know me. And if you think that I'd rather have you defend my honor like some barbarian than handle the matter *quietly* myself, then you really need to get a few things straight. If you'd thrown a punch at every person who said something inappropriate to me tonight you'd have done nothing but that. I knew this would happen, I was prepared for it, and all you did was draw even more unwanted attention to me."

Derek gripped the steering wheel until his knuckles ached. As he reached London's townhouse he whipped the small car into a vacant space on the street.

Shifting it into Park, he turned to her, heat pouring through him. "How can you say that a man demanding people respect you is worse than one insulting you to your face? Whatever your job might be, you deserve to be treated with basic respect. If I'd had the slightest idea anyone was mistreating you tonight I'd have put an end to it immediately. There's only one way to deal with people like Foster. You show them who's the boss and send them on their way. You're too good for men like him, London. You're too good for all of it."

Her eyes rounded and her mouth fell open to a little 'o' of shock. She stared at him and he saw her throat work up and then back down as she swallowed.

When she finally spoke her voice was dry and quiet. "So that's what the fistfight was about," she whispered. "You think you can *save* me?"

She chuckled to herself, but there was no mirth in her tone. "I would never have pegged you for the savior type, Derek." She shook her head. "How did I miss that?"

"What are you talking about?" he asked as she opened the car door. He put his hand on her arm but she shook it off, exiting the car and heading to her front door. He leaped from the driver's side and jogged to catch up with her.

"London!" His voice was sharp, and for reasons he didn't fully understand, panic was welling up inside of him, adrenaline spiking in his chest.

She rounded on him, her beautiful eyes sparkling with moisture. Something inside of him tore, the pain shooting through places so deep he couldn't identify them.

"I don't *need* your help. I don't *need* to be rescued. This isn't a Julia Roberts movie. I'm a strong, independent woman. I chose my job, I chose my lifestyle, I take care of my own problems and I take care of people like Frederick Foster however I see fit. The last thing I need is an overbearing master manipulator catering to his savior complex by trying to make me into someone I'm not. I spent the first seventeen years of my life being manipulated and told I was someone I'm not, and I will *never* live that way again."

Frustration made it hard for Derek to think clearly. "I'm not trying to save you. You don't need saving. I just couldn't stand by and listen to that bastard talk about you like that. What was I supposed to do?"

"Why?" she asked, silence falling on the tail end of her question.

"What?" He clenched his fists at his side, on the verge of losing control completely. No woman had ever pushed his buttons like this one. She was the most ungrateful, confusing female he'd ever known.

Her chin tipped up and her eyes flashed with defiance. "Why couldn't you let him talk to me like that? He didn't say anything that wasn't true. In fact, he seemed to insinuate that I'm pricey as hell. It was actually quite a compliment. So why couldn't you stand to hear it?"

She cocked her head at him and pursed those luscious lips. His heart lurched hard once, and before he could think about it he had reached for her, yanking her against his chest.

"Because I kept picturing him touching you and I couldn't stand the thought of it," he growled before he brought his lips down on hers hard.

She tasted like champagne and cream. Smooth, rich, decadent. His lungs felt as if he'd just run a marathon and when she melted into his hold he plundered her like his very life depended on it. His tongue stroked along her teeth, her lips, her tongue. She nipped at his bottom lip and he growled in warning. He felt her smile against his mouth and he moved a hand to grip her ass and shift her up, pressing her against his raging hard-on. The need to sink into her soft, warm flesh clouded any other thoughts and wiped away all the events of the night.

"Jesus," he whispered as he moved his mouth to her silky neck, nipping and licking his way down the elegant column.

She clutched at the lapels of his suit jacket and moaned as he pressed her back against her front door and ground against her like a teenage boy trying to dry hump the prom queen. Then he heard her handbag hit the ground and something in the back of his head told him they needed that bag. It had the keys to the house, and he very much wanted to get inside that house so he could pursue getting inside of her.

"Keys," he mumbled as he palmed her full breast.

"Uhh," she breathed out, arching against him.

He moved his lips to the v-neck of her dress, licking along the edge of the fabric where it clung to the swell of her breasts. Skimming a hand down her side, he gripped her hip as he reluctantly let his lips part from her luscious flesh. He stooped and picked up the handbag just as his phone vibrated in his pocket. When he stood, she was staring at him with wide eyes, her hand clutching the front of her dress. As their eyes locked he felt her withdrawing from him. *No, no, no.*

He ran a finger along her jaw and leaned in to whisper in her ear. The damn phone in his pocket kept buzzing, but he intended to ignore it. Preferably until tomorrow morning sometime.

"I'm sorry I screwed up. Let me make it up to you. Why don't you invite your *boyfriend* in?" he whispered in her ear, eliciting a full body shudder from her.

"I don't think that's a good idea."

"Why?" he asked, resting his forehead on her shoulder, his dick aching with need.

She stiffened and gave him a gentle, ineffectual shove. Out of politeness he took a very small step back.

"I'm a prostitute, Derek. And now I know that's not okay with you."

Derek scratched his head, searching for a response even though he knew the answer but simply didn't want to say it.

"I have sex with men for money. Sometimes they're men like Foster," she persisted.

He pressed his lips together, his stomach lurching at the image.

"And I think I hate that," he finally replied, all the heat leaving him in a rush as icy cold seeped in to replace it.

She gave a small nod of her head, her lips pursed, her eyes dark and unfathomable. "Thank you for the ride home," she answered as she withdrew her clutch from his hand and fished out the house key. Before he could formulate a response she'd shut the door, leaving him alone outside in the rapidly cooling night.

**

"Hello?" London's husky voice came over the phone two days later, and Derek felt his pants tighten. Damn. The things the woman did to him.

"Am I forgiven yet?" he asked, settling back in his desk chair and smiling to himself as he remembered what it felt like to kiss her smart mouth.

"Since we're not actually dating I don't think that matters, does it?"

He sighed. She wasn't going to give him an inch. "I'd still rather not have you pissed at me every time we need to make an appearance."

"Fine." He could hear the smile in her voice and he suspected she wished she could control it. "You're forgiven. But we need to make sure that we keep some boundaries in place. This is pretend after all. No one is watching you drop me off at my door. They won't know whether you kiss me or not."

"So you're saying no more kissing?"

"And no more punching or rescuing either," she answered.

"Jesus, according to Alpha Life magazine fucking and fighting are mainstays of the modern American man. You've taken away my primary two occupations. What the hell am I supposed to do with myself now?"

London's laughter was like hot toffee sliding over his skin. Dark, rich, and sinful. He looked up at the ceiling trying not to focus on how the sound of her traveled through his ears down into his chest and then landed squarely in his groin.

After a moment she stopped abruptly, clearing her throat as if she'd just remembered she wasn't supposed to allow lightness into their interactions.

"Derek." She was quieter now, and very serious. He hated the sound of her serious. "This can't turn real. You realize that don't you? You said we'd do it briefly so that we took the focus off the rumors. How much longer?"

He bit back the part of him that was stung because she was in such a hurry to get away from him. "As long as I need in order to track down where this story came from in the first place. We're providing a great distraction in that regard. Whoever tipped off the press is trying to keep up with our spin now. We've got them disoriented, and we want to keep them that way until we can hunt the fuckers down."

"Bloodthirsty, aren't you?" she quipped.

"When it comes to my career, yes. I haven't made it this far by letting people get the best of me. I'm not about to start now."

"All the more reason to keep your association with me short. I'm not good for your business, Derek." She paused. "And you're not good for mine."

He refused to acknowledge the satisfaction the second part of her statement gave him. "Let me worry about my business," he said dismissively. "You worry about where you'd like to eat dinner tonight before we go to a reception I need to attend at the White House."

"A reception at the White House?"

"Yes, and I need you to be there with me. I would have called sooner, but it's a last minute request my friend Kamal had. He wants me to speak to the president about a treaty he's trying to negotiate with the U.N."

"And why do I need to be there?"

"It's a perfect opportunity for our relationship to get the tacit stamp of approval from the highest ranking official in the party. You being at the White House says that the president approves, even though she will of course have no idea that she's approving anything. But no one will believe that you had anything to do with Melville after the President has invited us to the White House as a couple."

"So will we have to continue to see each other after this? I mean, won't the press get tired of it once it seems so official?"

Derek knew that with the White House appearance the press corps would quit any digging they might have been doing. No one would think that the President of the United States was allowing a woman into the White House who might be the *paid* bedmate of Jason Melville, her heir apparent. Everyone would absolutely believe that

London was Derek's girlfriend, and hopefully fully reformed to boot.

But Derek felt a deep dissatisfaction at the idea that he might no longer have a reason to see London. They'd only been on one date—pretend date, whatever he was supposed to call it. He wanted more. She was whip smart, gorgeous, and difficult as hell. He loved nothing more than a challenge. He wasn't ready to give that up yet, whether it was wise or not.

"You're really not enjoying our little charade." He hated having to say it and hated the possible response even more.

She was quiet for a moment. "It's nothing personal."

"But you don't want any more fist fights or kisses?" Dammit.

"I want boundaries."

"Back to that." He sighed lustily. "Fine. No kissing. No fights. Nothing even remotely untoward. Will that make you happy?"

"Yes. Thank you."

"Good. I'll pick you up at eight. The attire is black tie."

"All right, I'll see you then." She still sounded unsure and it left him feeling unsettled.

"Maybe try to let yourself enjoy it a little. It's the White House after all, and some women have even enjoyed my company."

"I don't doubt that for a moment," she answered before she disconnected the call, leaving him to wonder why she couldn't seem to enjoy a date if she wasn't being paid to.

CHAPTER VI

The White House was lit up like a Christmas tree, chandeliers blazing, candles covering tables, and a fire popping in the giant fireplace at one end of the ballroom they were walking through. Derek had told London that the reception was for a mishmash of Middle Eastern and United Nations diplomats, members of the House and Senate foreign affairs committees, and oddly enough, the finalists in the national youth choir competition. She felt butterflies of excitement in her stomach as he led her through the various clusters of people, heading toward the center of the large warmly lit room.

"Madam President," Derek said as Jessica Hampton approached them from the other direction, her hand tucked under the arm of Kamal.

Derek raised an eyebrow at Kamal, who seemed to pointedly ignore the gesture.

"Derek." She smiled and put out her hand. He shook it, then put his other hand on the small of London's back to press her forward a step.

"Madam President, Kamal, I'd like to present my date, Ms. London Sharpe. London, I believe you met the Ambassador at our little press conference, and this of course is President Hampton."

London smiled, quelling the urge to curtsey or some such nonsense. Derek had assured her that aside from the formal address of "Madam President" there was no protocol she needed to follow, but she still felt as though she should indicate her obeisance to the nation's first female president.

But she opted for shaking the woman's hand instead. "Madam President," London said. "And Mr. Ambassador. It's so nice to see you both."

A waiter passed by with glasses of champagne and bite-sized desserts. Derek snagged a tiny key lime pie and two flutes of champagne while the President was waylaid by an aide. London couldn't help but overhear the quiet conversation between Derek and Kamal.

"You holding up okay?" Kamal asked as he leaned closer to Derek's ear.

Derek didn't respond immediately, taking a healthy gulp of his champagne first. "Why wouldn't I be?"

"You've been wound pretty tight lately."

"I want this thing settled," Derek snapped back.

"And it will be, don't worry. You have to trust us, we'll take care of it."

"I hate..."

"I know what you hate. Not being in control. Maybe it's good for you once in a while." Kamal grinned and Derek scowled. London tried not to smile and give away the fact that she was eavesdropping. Derek was definitely a control-freak after her own control-obsessed heart. She might not like the challenge of handling him, but she certainly understood him.

The President turned back to London with a smile. "I'm so sorry, I didn't mean to be rude. One thing about this job, I've got staff running out my ears, and they always want something. I sometimes think they make up work just so they don't have to worry about being laid off."

London laughed and the President raised her glass in salute before taking a large gulp of champagne.

"I hope the press haven't been giving you too hard a time," President Hampton said.

London felt her face heat but maintained her placid expression. "Nothing I can't handle."

The President smiled, her cheeks turning pink beneath her pile of pinned coppery curls.

"Well, I am sorry if they have been. The press operates by the theory of ask forgiveness not permission. They'll jump on anything with the slightest hint of possible scandal."

"It's very kind of you to be concerned. Luckily Derek is good at handling them so it's all fine." London frantically searched the room with her eyes for an idea of how to redirect the conversation. When her gaze landed on the oldest living congressman in office she knew she'd hit the jackpot.

"Is that...?" She gestured toward the wizened old man who appeared to be talking to a large fern next to the navy blue velvet armchair he sat in.

The President laughed. "Chase Jepson. Yes it is. And yes, I do believe he might be talking to that plant." Her voice dropped to a whisper. "But I only suggest it because he's from the opposing party."

"Does he—" London cleared her throat as she struggled not to laugh. "Does he do that often?" The President sighed lustily. "His Chief of Staff has been running many things for the last ten years, and I don't think his constituents care. They've reelected him twenty-two times." She looked around, checking to see who was nearby. "Rumor is that his staff turns his hearing aides off so that he won't get woken up during debate."

London slapped a hand over her mouth as the President grinned and pretended to glance around the room casually.

"What in the world is going on here, Madam President? Are you telling State secrets to my date?" Derek turned away from his conversation with Kamal and raised an eyebrow at London.

"Derek," the president said, casting one last smirk at London as she gestured toward the doors to the balcony. "I'd like to talk to you about this treaty that the Ambassador has his heart set on." She smiled prettily at Kamal, and London saw Derek scrutinize his friend, only to be completely shut out again. The Ambassador was a master at poker face.

"Will you be okay here with the Ambassador?" he asked London.

"Of course."

"I'll find you in a bit then."

London watched Derek and President Hampton walked away before she turned to Kamal.

"Shall we sit?" he asked gesturing to a nearby sofa.

"Yes, thank you," she answered before following him over and sitting down.

"How long have you held your post?" she asked politely.

"Long enough to know that a good Iranian girl doesn't end up as a high-class Washington escort without a very good story to explain it."

London froze, her breath catching. She hadn't expected a confrontation, but he clearly had one in mind. Kamal watched her, a pleasant smile on his face, but his eyes sharp, ready to dissect her every movement.

"I beg your pardon?" she asked to stall while she caught her breath.

"Of course you realize that we've had you investigated. No way we'd have set this whole farce up without knowing who we were dealing with."

She nodded, thankful that no response was required of her yet.

His voice was low and his eyes kept track of everyone who came and went in their general vicinity.

"I know you were raised in Georgetown. I know your mother is a professor at the University, I know that she has plenty of money and you're an only child. What I don't know is what made you up and leave that lovely red brick colonial with four bedrooms and a sunroom ten years ago and hit the streets alone at seventeen. What I don't know is who your father was, or why you seem to have materialized out of thin air at the age of two. But I can tell you that I won't stop until I find out."

London gritted her teeth and focused on staving off the panic. There was no way she was going to give Derek or his friends a speck of additional information about her past. Down that path lay nothing good. Down that path lay ugly secrets and a lifetime of lies. She'd hoped they would be satisfied with what they'd learned, but now she could see that Kamal at least was not. It was her nightmares come to fruition, and the worst part was, no longer was she only afraid of her friends finding out, now she was in danger of the world finding out—and Derek. Suddenly it mattered so much to her that Derek not find out.

"I don't see how that is any of your business, Ambassador," she snapped.

When he replied it was in Arabic, and London's chest clutched, an ache taking root and blooming as he continued. "I know when someone has secrets, Ms. Sharpe. I won't rest until I unearth yours, and if you so much as blink wrong at the man I consider to be my brother, I will stop at nothing to destroy you. I have resources you can not even begin to imagine. I won't hesitate to use them if it means keeping Derek safe from you."

When he finished speaking she swallowed once, nausea rolling through her like a tidal wave. Kamal Masri was a very powerful man, one who'd been raised on the edge of dark and dangerous things. His threats were more like foreshadowing, and his enmity was something no one in their right mind would court.

"London?" Derek's voice broke through her haze. She looked up to find him standing in front of them, concern written across his features.

"There you are. We were chatting about home," Kamal said smoothly, standing and offering his hand to her.

London stared at his expensive French cuffs, his neatly manicured fingernails, and the heavy gold watch that draped his thick wrist. Numbly she put her hand in his as she stood. He squeezed her fingers once before releasing her.

"Are you okay?" Derek asked. "You look pale."

She darted a look at Kamal, but his face was placid, open, warm. Only his eyes gave any indication of what he'd said to her. His eyes were sharp, distrustful, filled with accusations.

"No," she answered. "Maybe a little tired is all." She forced a small smile.

"How did your discussion with the president go?" Kamal deflected.

"Good," Derek answered. "I think I made some progress for you. She's agreed to meet with me to discuss it further this week."

"Excellent." Kamal slapped Derek on the back. London took a deep breath in an effort to lower her heart rate.

Derek put an arm around London's shoulders and smiled at her. "I think my date might have had all the hobnobbing at the White House that she can take for one night. I'm going to take her home."

"Well, thank you for coming," Kamal replied. He lifted London's hand and pressed it between both of his. "I'm so glad we got a chance to chat," he told her darkly.

"Yes," she answered. She could hear the stiffness in her own voice. "It was delightful to see you again."

"We'll talk tomorrow," Derek said to Kamal before guiding London away. When they finally reached the door she turned to look back. The last thing she saw was Kamal Masri lifting his champagne flute in salute, his eyes flashing a warning that she'd be a fool to ignore.

**

London was quiet on the way back to her townhouse. Derek watched her from the corner of his eye. She was such a mystery to him, bouncing from charming and graceful one moment to quiet and insular the next. His fingers itched to touch her, his chest ached to find out what was going on behind her beautiful eyes.

"I didn't hit anyone," he joked finally, hoping to lighten the mood.

She gave him a small smile. "You behaved perfectly. Thank you."

"As did you," he responded. "The president couldn't stop complimenting you."

"She's compelling. I can see how she became our first woman president. Are she and the Ambassador close?"

"They've always gotten along, but they seem to be spending more time together lately. I think it's all the work on this treaty."

She nodded and the conversation faded once more.

But Derek hadn't gotten where he was by giving up easily.

"Is something bothering you?" he asked as they reached her block and he started looking for a parking space.

"Why would you think that?" she asked dully.

"You're very quiet and it seemed that you and Kamal were having a serious discussion when I walked up. Was he speaking to you in Arabic?"

"Yes," she answered as he pulled into a space across the street from her dark red front door.

He nodded, not sure what to make of it all.

"Did he say something to upset you? If so I'll speak with him about it. He can be a little overprotective, he doesn't mean anything by it. He's been my wingman for so long it's become second nature to him."

She shook her head, but something about it didn't ring true to him. "No, no, he was just…it was nothing. I enjoyed hearing Arabic again. My mother used to speak it to me along with Persian. It's been a long time."

She looked out the window away from him and he felt the distance between them grow. He hated it.

She opened the door and he hurried to reach her side of the car before she could cross the street without him. He kept a hand at the small of her back as they went up the walk to her front door.

She took her keys out of her handbag then turned to him. He was crowding her, he knew it, but he didn't want to leave her this way. He'd already promised not to kiss her, but he didn't like whatever this was between them. Loathed the thought of her sad and alone in her house, while he was alone and frustrated in his own miles away.

"Thank you for the chance to see the White House," she said softly.

"Thank you for going with me," he answered, mesmerized by her lips in the soft lights from the street. He leaned closer, and heard her breath hitch.

"Derek," she warned.

He planted a hand against the door next to her head, leaning in casually and taking a deep breath of her spicy scent. "Yes?" His voice was gravelly and deep with want.

She shook her head slightly, her eyes pinned somewhere in the vicinity of his chin. "You promised," she almost pleaded.

"I promised no kissing." He rubbed his nose along her neck and she gasped softly.

Her hands flattened against his chest, but instead of repelling him they cupped him, her fingertips softly pressing into his flesh, searing him at every point of contact.

He took a strand of her thick hair between his fingers, stroking it gently. "I never promised to give up. You should know I'm not the type to do that."

She sighed, midway between exasperation and desire. He couldn't help but smile at the sound.

"Why would you want me? There's no future. I'll have to go back to work sooner or later, and everyone in the world now knows what I do. I'm about as far from girlfriend material as it gets. Maybe it's the conquest? You just want a one-night stand to see if it's different with a hooker?"

His heart skipped a beat and he moved incrementally closer, aligning their bodies from hip to shoulder. He felt her breasts give against him, her hands trapped between their bodies molding to his pecs through the thin shirt of his tuxedo.

"You know that's not it."

"I can't imagine what other reason you could have," she gritted out, her entire body stiffening as she tilted her head down, refusing to look him in the eyes.

"I want to know you," he answered, as if it were that simple when he knew it was anything but. "You're beautiful, smart, mysterious, and you fascinate me. I want to see the woman behind the perfect date."

Unable to control himself he planted a series of tiny kisses along her satiny cheek. She released a sigh, fragile and full of pain.

"You won't like what you find," she whispered sadly.

Anger jolted him out of his lust-induced coma. He pushed away, taking her chin in between his thumb and forefinger so she was forced to look at him. "Don't. Underestimate me," he snapped. "I make my own decisions about the people in my life, and I don't base them on superficial crap like conventional morals. I didn't get where I am by being a bad judge of character."

"And what have you judged about me?" She twisted her head, forcing him to release her. His fingers twitched from the need to touch her, but fear and anger, and something that might have been longing flashed in her eyes and he dropped his hand, resigned to the distance— for now.

"You're strong, and you may not abide by society's code, but you've got your own code and you adhere to it religiously."

"You're right," she answered. "And a big part of that code is not doing harm to others when I can help it. I *will* do harm to you, Derek. I will. The sooner you realize that the better. I'll admit it, when you suggested this farce I wouldn't have predicted that I'd like you so much. But even knowing that now, it doesn't change anything. My code says I have to keep this from being more than pretend. It's for your good as much or more than for mine."

He turned away from her, gazing out over the street softly lit by the antique-looking lamps. Hands on hips he took a cleansing breath, tamping down the frustration that knotted in his gut. Derek Ambrose didn't get told 'no' often, in business or in life. He was surprised by how much it pissed him off. Or maybe it was just that it hurt and he didn't want to feel *that*. Didn't want to think that any man with cash could have her—but he, standing before her with his regard, his respect, and his sincerity, would be turned away. It was insulting, confusing, and yes, if he were being honest, painful. And ultimately, it was more than enough to make him walk away. For tonight at least.

He took a step down her porch stairs before turning to look back at her. "No worries," he said stiffly. "I'll leave your code intact. I'll also get to the bottom of this leak quickly so you can get back to your life."

As he strode away he didn't glance back, but he never heard her door open, and he knew she watched him as he drove off down the street.

Unable to relax after being rejected—yet again—Derek drove around aimlessly for a time, stopped in at his office, and finally went to the twenty-four hour newsstand near the Capitol, to grab the earliest edition of the national papers. Often he'd work so late that by the time he left to go home it was after four a.m. and the papers were just being distributed. He hoped maybe one of the photos of he and London at the White House might have made the society page, adding to the credibility of their fabricated relationship. Tonight, or this morning as the case was, he arrived right as the delivery truck pulled up.

"Hey, Mr. Ambrose," the newsstand owner, Orlando, quipped as he grabbed a stack of papers tied in twine from the *Post* delivery driver.

"Orlando. Looks like I'm right on time," Derek answered, reaching over to snag the next stack that the driver handed out of the truck.

Orlando gave the driver a wave as the man slammed the back truck doors shut and hopped into the driver's seat before he roared off down the street.

"You do seem to have a nose for when these papers arrive," Orlando said. He gestured for Derek to set the stack of papers down on the small counter that ran along the front edge of the newsstand, then he placed his stack on top of those.

Derek took out his wallet and pulled a twenty-dollar bill from it. "And I can always count on you to have them when I need them," he said. "They say no news is good news, but in my experience *your* news is the good news."

Orlando chuckled as he clipped the string on the stack and peeled the top paper off. He handed it to Derek. "Just the *Post*, or you want all the big ones?"

"Let's go for broke," Derek answered as he handed Orlando the cash. "Give me one of each."

The sky was shifting from inky to gray as he slid into his car, and Derek sat for a moment looking at the still, quiet street, lights shining from upstairs windows where people in apartments were just waking to start their days. He loved the city. Watching it at times like these, when it was in that moment between the gritty, splashy nighttime and the bustling, mechanical daytime, was his favorite view of D.C. He'd been here for over a decade and still never got tired of the energy that hummed through the city twenty-four hours a day. Washington was the jewel that he wanted to possess more than anything. Melville in the White House was his way to grab that jewel.

He set the papers down on the passenger seat and moved to buckle his seat belt. As he did, his eyes grazed the headline of the *Post*.

Road to White House Paved with Sex and Lies: New Information Says D.C. Prostitute Was Having Sex with Senator Jason Melville.

CHAPTER VII

Derek held his bleeding hand against his chest, and leaned back against the tile wall of his office bathroom. He gripped his wrist tightly, hoping to stem the flow of blood from his knuckles and the meaty pad of his palm. Next to him the gaping hole in the plasterboard mocked the substantial pain that throbbed with every heartbeat.

"Here," his secretary said from the doorway as she held out a damp rag. "Wash up and then I'll get you something to eat and drink. Mr. Roberts is waiting for you."

"All right," he rasped, looking down at his wrinkled, bloodstained shirt and wondering if he should risk changing it yet or if he might find another way to bleed in the next few minutes.

As if she could read his mind, Renee said softly, "You'll be okay once you get cleaned up. I pulled out one of your spare shirts and a new tie. They're hanging on the doorknob of the closet."

She left quietly then, shutting the door behind her, and Derek stared at the tile wall for a few moments, his breath coming in slow rasps as the morning's headlines flashed through his mind yet again. Naturally he'd been furious when he saw the story break, but as five a.m. turned to six, and then to eight, as the leadership of the party continued to call him, demanding to know how he'd let this happen, and as Melville became increasingly despondent and began asking for Derek to draft a resignation speech, his initial anger turned to panic.

Derek Ambrose was a dedicated, tireless, cutthroat worker who had earned every good thing in his career, but he had also never been challenged like this. He'd had his politics questioned, his methods, his decisions, but he'd never had his personal credibility questioned. He'd never had anyone doubt his word. Today they were, and for the first time in his life, Derek didn't know what to do next.

A soft knock sounded on the door. "You coming out?" Teague's voice rumbled through the solid wood.

Derek cleared his throat. "Yeah. Be right there." He hoisted himself off the wall, feeling his stomach lurch as he did. After getting it under control, he rinsed the washcloth, rewrapped it around his hand, and opened the door to face the music.

"Yeah," Teague said from his perch on the leather sofa in Derek's office, nose wrinkled in disgust. "You're definitely going to want that clean shirt Renee put out for you."

"Sorry," Derek muttered as he walked to the closet door and began unbuttoning his wrinkled, stained blue dress shirt. After he'd replaced it with the clean gray version, he flopped down in the armchair that matched the sofa.

"Do you think you broke it?" Teague asked with deceptive casualness.

"I doubt it."

"I'd like to get someone to drop by and take a look at it anyway. You'll never forgive yourself if you let it heal wrong and you can't box at Spar anymore."

Derek nodded, conceding. "Did you guys draw straws?" he asked, leaning back his head and closing his eyes as the throbbing pain subsided to a dull, but persistent, ache.

"No, I volunteered," Teague answered. He took a sip of coffee and set the cup down before relaxing back into the plush leather cushions, one ankle cocked on the opposite knee. "It was either Jeff or I. Kamal is so pissed that the press has gotten more information in spite of all our efforts to bury it, he can't think straight, and Scott's scared of you, to be honest."

Derek propped one eye open and huffed out a breath of disbelief. "Bullshit. Scott's more likely scared to be seen coming into my office. The party might exile him if he gets caught."

"In all fairness, the President Pro Temp has drawn a one-mile radius around your office building on a map in his conference room and forbidden anyone on staff from entering the circle of doom."

Derek chuckled softly, grateful that even in the midst of all of this Teague could make him laugh.

"I've already filed injunctions against the *Post* and WNN," Teague continued. "It won't stop them in the longer run, but it'll get us access to exactly what information they have and where they got it. They'll also have to refrain from disseminating anything more until they've sent their guys to the courthouse and had a sit-down with the judge."

Derek cleared his throat. "Thank you. What does that buy us—a day or two?"

"That's about right. I asked for Judge Hopkins. He's on vacation this week, so if we get on his docket it won't be until Monday. That gives us two weekdays plus the weekend. That's best case scenario."

Renee walked into the room then, her high heels sinking silently into the plush carpeting. She set a tray down on the end table next to Derek, and poured a cup of tea from the pot before handing it to him.

"Make sure he drinks this," she told Teague. "Stress can make you dehydrated."

Teague nodded and gave her a small salute.

She placed a comforting hand on Derek's shoulder and gave it a squeeze before drifting back out of the room. Derek sighed and leaned his head back again, inhaling the steam from the tea. He appreciated the warmth, as everything inside of him had gone cold three hours ago, and remained frozen since.

Teague stood and walked to the built-in bar that ran along one wall of the office. He grabbed a bottle of scotch and returned, pouring a generous portion into Derek's teacup.

"Renee's very motherly," he said as he set the bottle down on the coffee table. "But she doesn't know shit about getting through a crisis of this magnitude."

Derek smiled wryly and tipped his cup at his friend before taking a big swallow of heat and alcohol. It landed in his stomach and burned for a moment before settling into the glow he was hoping for.

"Now," Teague said as he produced an iPhone from his pocket and began typing rapidly with his thumbs. "You've had your half hour to wallow—or self-destruct as the case may be. It's time to get to work. You'll obviously need to cut your losses and let Melville drop out, but if you want, we can continue to say the stories about her and Melville aren't true. I can start the paperwork for a suit of defamation of character. Both you and Melville could go that route. It'd probably never get resolved, but it would cast some doubt and maybe clean him up a touch. The other way to go is to let him sink for the prostitution, you say you lied to protect him, and I'll get you a publishing contract for a tell-all book. I can negotiate something pretty lucrative with that publisher that did the unauthorized biography on President Hampton last year. They love political stuff."

Derek felt his throat closing up at the words, 'drop out' and 'tell-all'.

"Jesus," he managed to choke out. "Isn't there an option three?"

If Derek didn't know any better he'd have sworn Teague smiled at that, but the expression was gone in a flash.

"Ok. What's option three?" His friend gave him a thoughtful look, waiting patiently.

Derek didn't know the answer. What he had known since six fifteen that morning was that not only did he not want to give up on the campaign, he didn't want to give up London. The moment Melville dropped out of the race all pretenses for spending time with her would be eliminated. Melville would go on, Derek would go on, and London would go on—separately—but to what? Would she go back to work? Undoubtedly she would be in high demand, now a world-famous D.C. escort. The very idea made him queasy, and even though she'd rejected him the night before, he wasn't ready to give up. And he sure as hell wasn't ready to give her the opening to go back to prostitution.

He needed more time—more time to think of options, more time to think of ways to spin it all, more time to figure out what his feelings for London might be, and if she could ever possibly return them. Derek Ambrose didn't quit. Ever. It wasn't in his nature, and he had no idea how to do it now. He'd set out to put a man in the White House, and then, unwittingly, he'd also determined to save a beautiful woman. He wasn't ready to give up on either goal, no matter how stacked against him the odds appeared to be.

"I don't know what option three is, but if I can get some time I'll figure it out."

Teague watched him thoughtfully. "So the question is, how do we buy you time?"

Derek nodded.

"As I said, the injunction gets you a couple of days." He looked thoughtful for a few moments. "If we file the defamation suit immediately, but don't put out any statements, it implies that we're saying the articles are false, yet you haven't *actually* said so. People will demand a statement from the campaign, but I suspect that we can get by for another two or three days with the speculation and theories that the suit puts into motion."

Thus, between the two legal maneuvers they had four days, five tops. He'd get less than a week to find some way to stay in business and keep London too. The press would flay him, implying that he was guilty of lying to them simply because he didn't respond immediately. He gave Teague a sharp nod. "Do it," he instructed.

"And you think she and Melville will agree to this?" Teague asked.

No. "I'll make sure they do," Derek answered.

"All right then," Teague said grinning. The man did love to file legal actions. "Let's get to work. Renee!" he bellowed. "Order up a car, I'm going to the courthouse."

**

It was all over. The truth was out. London was free. Why didn't she feel like it then? Why did it feel as though that headline had crushed all the hope in her world? Her messy bun shifting awkwardly on top of her head, London sifted another cup of flour into the bowl before stirring it thoroughly. She didn't have a recipe for the cake, but she didn't need one. She had watched her mother bake Persian love cake dozens of times over the course of her childhood. Persian cuisine didn't include many sugary items, but her mother's refrigerator had always contained a platter of baghlava, the Persian variety of baklava, and on special occasions, a Persian love cake was always on the menu.

She whipped the egg whites, her mind preoccupied by the tangle of emotions that raced through her. It was a relief in one sense, knowing that she didn't have to pretend at all anymore, that she could return to the life she'd built for herself over so many years. It could never be exactly the same, but she could survive it, and most importantly she would once again be in total control.

However, relief was only one side of the coin, because there was also fear. She'd lied to Joanna—again—and she was afraid even Jo couldn't forgive her this time. She'd persisted in telling Jo that Melville hadn't been a client. Now Jo knew the truth just like the rest of the world, and it would be rough going to justify this latest in a long list of untruths and half-truths.

But both the relief and the fear were awash in something entirely different—regret. Yes, London had to admit to herself that she regretted the fact that she no longer had a reason to be connected to Derek Ambrose. She'd rebuffed his advances, and she knew she'd done what she had to, but the man was addictive, and she could tell that she'd already been hooked.

She sighed as she folded the flour mixture and egg white mixture together. For those brief moments—on his arm at events, in his car in the dark of night, when his bare skin brushed hers—she'd had a glimpse of another life, a life she hadn't dared to dream about in a decade. Her heart hurt with the regret that a life like that would never be hers, and now she couldn't even pretend anymore.

Thirty minutes and a batch of homemade hummus later her doorbell rang. She brushed the excess flour off of her yoga pants and tank top and walked to the front door. Standing on her front porch was the man who'd spurred all of that regret.

"May I come in?" he asked, his eyes a deeper blue than usual to match his cornflower blue t-shirt. He was dressed more casually than she'd ever seen him, a pair of well-worn jeans hugging him in all the right places. All the right big, hard places. Her throat went dry as her eyes raked over him involuntarily.

She snapped her gaze to his face when she realized she was gawking. His lips quirked up on one side as though he was able to see exactly what she'd been thinking.

"Yes, of course," she finally answered, stepping aside so he could enter.

He smiled and her heart skipped a beat.

"Something smells delicious," he said.

"It's a cake," she answered as she led him to the living room. "I'd offer you some but it's still baking. Would you like a glass of water or a cup of tea, perhaps?"

He shook his head. "No, but I'm hoping we can talk."

She sat on the far end of the sofa from him. "Of course."

He leaned forward, leaning his elbows on his knees. "I'm sorry I didn't get in touch this morning when the news broke. It's been a crazy day, but I should have made the time to speak with you much earlier."

"I assumed that there wasn't much to talk about really," she said. "With everything out in public we're done with our little charade."

His eyes narrowed and his lips pressed together in a tight line. "And if I say no?"

She blinked in surprise. "What do you mean?"

He ran a hand through his hair, his brows drawn down. "I'm exploring options for the next few days. I don't want to give up on this campaign yet. I've never been in a spot this tight before, but I've been close, and I worked things out then, I'm not convinced I can't do the same here."

Those conflicting feelings churned inside of her again, but he continued before she could formulate a response.

"I know you haven't enjoyed this, the pretending and deception..." His voice faded away and he looked at her inquiringly.

Her cheeks heated and she dropped her gaze for a moment. "It's actually been better than I would have predicted. I don't like to lie, but the break from work has been nice I guess."

His jaw clenched before he continued. "Maybe you won't be opposed to a few more days then? I don't want to put anything out to the press. I've got my attorney working on some things—suits against the newspapers, trying to discover where they got their information. I've been talking to Melville most of the day and he's finally agreed to wait a few days before saying anything publicly. I'd like to ask you to do the same."

Her heart fluttered, and she remembered her mother's saying, *Be careful what you ask for.* Only an hour ago she'd been thinking how she would miss pretending to belong to Derek Ambrose, and now he was here asking her to do it for a few more days.

"But if everyone knows that Melville was actually involved with me, what purpose can it be for us to continue this pretend relationship?" she asked.

Derek looked uncomfortable, something that didn't happen often to a man so innately comfortable in his own skin. He rubbed the back of his neck and cleared his throat.

"I can't give you an answer to that yet, but I want to keep all of our options open until I figure this out." He looked at her earnestly then, his voice low, "Just a few more days. Please."

She knew there wasn't much logic at play in what he wanted. Wondered what his real reason was for asking her to hang around a bit longer. She also recognized a danger when she saw one. She'd feared the additional scrutiny of the press and what they would find out if she continued to associate with Derek. Her best bet at this point was simply to go back to her life and let the story run its course, which she doubted would take much longer. As soon as Melville officially withdrew the press would move on.

But now Derek was refusing to let him withdraw and on top of it he was asking her to sit around while the press chomped at the bit for more dirt, and it could very well end up being *her* dirt. The dirt that had ruined her life once already, and she'd sworn would never ruin it again.

As much as her chest hurt when she thought of never seeing Derek again, she knew it was utter foolishness to continue to be part of his world.

"I don't think that's a good idea."

"Why?" he asked, his expression not that different than a toddler having a cookie taken from them.

"I don't want to remain under scrutiny from the press. If we acknowledge that it happened—Melville and I—they'll move on and I can go back to my life."

He stood, frustration rolling off of him like heat off of a radiator. "And that's really what you want?" he asked as he paced across the room and stopped, facing the fireplace, his broad, muscular back to her. "You want to go back to sleeping with those men, hiding in the shadows, lying to the people around you?"

She lifted her chin, trying to fight the shame that burned through her at his easy dismissal of everything she'd built over eight years.

"No, I want to go back to my high-paying job, my privacy, and having the choice of what to share and with whom."

He was across the room and kneeling before her in seconds, hands planted on either side of her hips on the sofa, his eyes pleading, his face fierce with emotion.

"Don't," he demanded. "Don't tell me that you want those men to touch you again. Don't tell me that you'd turn me down, but let them—" His voice cracked and he swallowed. "All I'm asking is a few more days."

She could feel the burning behind her eyes, and steeled herself against the onslaught of feelings that threatened to burst out of her. Feelings that made people do and say things they could never take back, feelings that included hope, and joy, and other words that she couldn't imagine thinking, much less feeling.

"A few more days to save the campaign? Or a few more days to try to save me?" she asked bluntly.

He watched her for a moment, his face a play of exhaustion, desperation, and something else that she couldn't quite place.

"Both," he finally answered.

**

She told him 'no'. He was angry, he was exasperated, he was frustrated. He left, and she sat, immobile, on her living room sofa for what seemed like hours. She knew it was the right thing to do, there was no point in continuing their involvement with one another, but it left her cold, and unsure, and alone. She didn't realize that the game—the one where she pretended to be Derek Ambrose's girlfriend—had given her days a purpose that wasn't there before. For the first time in so long she'd had someone she was waiting to talk to, wanting to see, worried about knowing.

And then she'd sent him away. It was so simple and yet so incredibly complicated. He couldn't save her, she didn't want to be saved. And as she told it to herself over and over again the doubts chipped away at the conviction. But even if she did want him—his salvation, his companionship—she couldn't have it. How long did she have? Hours? Days? Maybe a few weeks if she was exceptionally lucky. Then the press would find out about her family and she'd be right back where she started, but even more disdained than she was now. And while Derek seemed as though he could get past prostitution if it was only in her past, she knew he'd never get past her father. Hell, she'd never gotten past her father and it had been ten years since she'd found out about him.

And that was the real reason why she'd told him she was done—he would never get past her father, and she couldn't bear to see that in his eyes. The way the warmth and affection would drain out, the disappointment, the disgust. A few more hours, or days, or weeks with Derek Ambrose and she'd be thoroughly absorbed by him, then thoroughly destroyed by him as well.

As the sky outside her front windows grew dark, London finally pushed up off her sofa, carefully stepping around the place Derek had kneeled when he asked her to be someone she could never be. She ignored the taut tug inside her chest, and went to remove the charred Persian love cake from the oven.

**

Derek stood on the balcony of the Powerplay condo and watched the city lights glitter in the night. He'd shown up here after the debacle with London, sickened by her refusal to agree to his timetable, unable to think about what he could possibly do to save the campaign, unable to *stop*thinking about her. He was now four double scotches the worse for wear, and his chest still ached like a bitch.

"You going to tell us what happened?" Kamal asked as he stepped out onto the balcony.

"When did you come in?" Derek asked, noticing that his words were slightly slurred.

"Just got here. I figured this is where I'd find you."

"Teague coming next?" Derek took the last swig of amber liquid from his glass before dangling it from his fingertips over the edge of the railing he leaned on.

"No," Kamal answered succinctly. "Seems like he's done plenty of damage for today by indulging your stalling tactics."

Derek spun around, his icy gaze landing on Kamal, who leaned against the wall, arms crossed, chest straining beneath his expensive dress shirt.

"What the hell does that mean?"

"It means that I don't buy you're doing this to save the campaign. I know you. You're a realist. You've never pushed a candidate to stay in a race when it was obvious he needed to get out."

"I've never had a candidate who needed to get out," Derek snapped.

"Is that what it is? You can't stand to lose that badly? So badly you'd try to jumpstart a candidate whose career is in ruins and a campaign that's a cold corpse beginning to rot? Or is it that you don't want to let the woman go?"

"I put eighteen months into prepping for this campaign," Derek said without answering Kamal's question.

"And now you're going to spend another eighteen beating a dead horse for a woman you hardly know, a woman who is a prostitute, Derek. She would do anything, including sell her damn body, to make a buck. She's not operating from a place of principles or a party platform of ideology. She's doing whatever it takes to make her next dollar, and I'm not convinced she didn't make some extra money by ratting out Melville to the press."

"Stop it." Derek's voice cut through the humid air like a knife through soft flesh. "What the hell happened to thinking it was Ryan Williams? He's by far the most likely culprit. Is it that you can't get any decent intel on him? You feel like you have to shift blame to someone else because you haven't been able to figure this out? I can assure you, that it isn't her. But it could very well be

Williams, and you're wasting valuable time chasing after the wrong person."

"I'm following up on Williams. I'm not an idiot. This is what I do, and I'm damn good at it. I've got information on him, just nothing definitive yet. What worries me a lot more than that is the fact that I don't have information on her. She's a blank card until she's two years old. There's something wrong with that picture."

"So she's guilty simply because you don't know anything about her."

"Neither do you," Kamal hissed back.

"How can you not see that this has damaged her as much or more than it's damaged me? She's been exposed in front of the entire nation. She'll go down in American history as a notorious hooker. She can never have a normal life again, and believe it or not, she had one before this."

"I don't believe it, because she was living a lie, and that's the proof of what an accomplished liar she is. She's taken you for a ride, my friend. I don't trust her, I don't trust that we know what we need to about her, and the longer you associate with her the bigger the risk that you'll be damaged more than you already have been." Derek gritted his teeth, restraining the urge to punch the concern off his friend's face. "It's all to save the campaign."

"Stop it." Kamal looked less than amused, shaggy hair falling down over one eye, turning him from an uptight international diplomat into a swarthy pirate ready to kidnap and torture the innocents on shore. "The fact that you think this campaign can be saved at this point is proof of how far gone you are. You had one path to follow here—have Melville drop out. But instead of following that path you've gone off-road. Far off-road. And it's because you're letting some part of your anatomy other than your brain do the navigating."

"Go to hell," Derek answered pushing past his friend and going inside. "I'll repeat myself—this isn't about some sort of hang up I have for London. It's about saving the campaign that we've spent eighteen months preparing for. Do I want to sleep with her? Yes. But that doesn't have anything to do with all of this. I'm able to separate sex from business decisions."

Kamal followed, shutting the door behind him and mumbling a string of curses that clearly communicated he was not convinced, which was no surprise, since neither was Derek. Not even close.

Before Derek could make it to the bar to refill his glass, the front door slammed open, and Jeff burst in, dressed in uniform, a military guard behind him on full alert.

"Jesus, you need to answer your phone," he snarled.

"Sorry. It's been a shitty day," Derek answered, glaring at the colonel.

"Well, it just got shittier," Jeff said, crossing his arms as the guard stepped into the condo and assumed a position of protection alongside the doorway. "Melville's been shot."

CHAPTER VIII

Derek shouted into his phone as the doors to the Emergency Room slid open before him. Jeff flanked him on one side, the military guard on the other, and Kamal followed close behind.

"I don't care what you have to do, Marcus," Derek commanded. "Make sure it's you who gets here first. The press are going to go ballistic over this and I need someone I can trust to get the information correct."

Jeff and the other two men elbowed people aside as Derek strode through the crowded room, unaware of anything around him, his focus solely on the admissions desk in front of them.

"I have to go," he spat into the phone. "Get here. Now."

"We're here for Senator Melville," Jeff said as they reached the admissions desk.

As Jeff dealt with the nurses to get information on Melville's location, Kamal put a hand on Derek's shoulder. "Breathe for a second. They got him here in minutes, it was a single shot. My bet is he's going to be just fine."

"He's got two little kids," Derek said, his brow wrinkled in distress. His gaze shot to Kamal's. "No matter what, I wouldn't wish this on anyone."

"I know." Kamal sighed. "I know."

"All right." Jeff rejoined them. "They can't tell us where he is, but they're taking us to the waiting room with the family." They started moving to the end of the adjacent hallway where the elevator waited. "And Derek? You need to know that she's okay, but his wife was standing next to him when it happened."

Derek and Kamal looked at one another before turning to Jeff. "This will not go unanswered," Derek said softly.

"I have people who can handle it," Jeff responded, his face impassive. "Don't worry. We'll find who did it and make sure they never do anything like it again."

**

As Derek entered the small waiting room that sat in a far corner of the Intensive Care Unit, he paused to take in the picture before him. Senator Melville's pretty blonde wife Angela stood, back stiff, as her father, famous trial attorney Winston Vandermeer, spoke to her rapidly. Mrs. Vandermeer sat to one side, pretending to read a magazine while her gaze skittered between her daughter and husband.

"Angela," Derek said softly as he strode toward the group. Angela turned and gave Derek a pained smile as he reached her and gave her a kiss on each cheek. He held her hand while saying all of the platitudes required of someone in such a circumstance, then he held out a hand to her father. "Winston. It's good to see you, though I'm sorry it's under these circumstances."

Vandermeer ignored Derek's hand and scowled at him. "Given your antics over the last few weeks I can't say the same."

Derek withdrew his hand, reminding himself to be patient with the older man. This was a stressful moment for everyone.

"I understand it's been stressful for Angela and the family," Derek answered diplomatically.

"I always thought you were one of the few good men left in politics, Ambrose." Winston's face flushed and his hand quivered as he pointed at Derek. "But after this sex scandal you've gotten Jason embroiled in, I can see I misjudged you."

"Daddy. Please," Angela intoned, placing a hand on her father's arm. "This isn't the time or place."

Vandermeer looked at her as if only then remembering that she was there. He nodded sharply once, then spun on his heel and stormed off to the far corner of the room where he took out his phone and began punching buttons.

"I'm sorry," Angela said. "He's just worried about us—Jason and I."

"Of course. As am I. I'm so sorry that you were there when it happened. And very glad you weren't hurt."

She nodded her head rapidly, and he could tell she was fighting the tears that threatened to spill down her cheeks.

"So what news do you have so far? Any word on his condition?"

"Just that he's in surgery," she answered.

"What can I do for you? The kids are okay?"

"Yes, they're fine. At home with the nanny."

"Let me get some security over there," Derek said, taking his phone out of his pocket.

"Thank you, but my father's already taken care of it."

"Good. I'll make sure someone's posted here—one person outside Jason's door and one to stay with you at all times."

"Thank you."

He looked around the room, feeling stifled by the hostility rolling off of Winston Vandermeer.

"In the meantime, why don't I see if I can get you an update on the surgery."?

"That would be perfect, thank you."

Derek nodded and turned to walk to the door.

"Derek?" Angela asked.

He looked at her and gone was the sad delicate woman waiting for news on her critically injured husband. In her place was a woman with steel in her eyes and danger on her lips, but the look was gone in a flash and Derek wasn't sure he'd really seen anything at all.

"It was kind of you to take on the whore for him," she said.

Derek stood stock still, unflinching, waiting for what she'd say next.

"Don't worry, I won't tell anyone. He thinks I didn't know, but I did. A wife knows when her husband does something like that. He used to come home with her smell on him. It made me wretch. I admire your dedication. It can't be enjoyable to have to act as though you'd really touch her. Next time though, you might want to consider whether the man you're covering for is really worth it."

She turned away from him then and walked to where her mother sat, taking a seat next to her. Derek could only leave the room, thinking that this truly might have been the single worst day he'd ever had.

**

London's hand trembled as she flipped on the porch light and leaned toward the peephole to see who was on her front steps at four a.m. Somehow she wasn't surprised to find Derek slouched against her door.

"What's happened?" she asked as she gestured for him to come inside. His tie had disappeared, his shirt was unbuttoned at the throat, the front tails untucked. His hair was sticking up in ten different directions, and his eyes looked so tired it nearly broke her heart.

"I'm sorry," he muttered as he shuffled into her foyer. "I didn't…" His voice drifted off. "I didn't know where else to go."

All of the sorrow and confusion London had fought with throughout the day, and taken to bed with her that night, dissolved as she looked at this ravished version of Derek. His exhaustion emanated from his very pores, and that soft part of London, the part that she tried so very hard to cover with efficiency, polish and a sophisticated shell, couldn't deny the wreck of a man in front of her.

"Come in," she whispered, as she took his hand and led him like a small child up the stairs. "Let's get you cleaned up, then you can tell me all about it."

In the bathroom London switched on the shower, then turned to Derek where he slumped against the countertop. Quietly, she stood in front of him and unbuttoned the remainder of his shirt, slipping her hands under the fabric to slide it from his shoulders and down his arms before letting it drop onto the floor. He sighed as her fingertips came in contact with his hot skin, and shuddering, he laid his head on her shoulder, defeat in every movement and gesture. Her hand flattened against his chest, the stiff hairs there prickling against her sensitive palm. Her other hand went to the back of his head out of instinct, and she caressed his hair, comforting him as she cooed sweet nothings into his ear.

When he finally lifted his head to look at her, his eyes were red, and the pain in them made her own chest ache in response.

"It's going to be okay," she told him, although she didn't know if that was true. "I'll leave a robe on the bed for you. Take as long as you need." She kissed him gently on the lips and slipped out of the room.

**

Twenty minutes later Derek joined her in the kitchen, clad in a white cotton robe that she'd picked up on a spa trip with Joanna.

"It's a good thing that's one size fits all," she quipped, eyeing the substantial slice of tanned chest that the wraparound terrycloth revealed.

"Yes, those clothes have been through a lot today. I'd have hated to put them right back on again." Derek gave her a small smile, and she could see that he'd revived somewhat.

"Would you like some tea?" she asked, pushing the lever on the electric kettle.

"That sounds good," he answered. "I imagine not even caffeine will keep me awake once I finally hit a bed."

She busied herself with the tea prep, trying not to wonder if his eyes were on her the whole time, sizing her up, dressing her down, stripping her bare. When she finally had the tray ready, she turned and set it all in front of him where he'd taken a seat at the kitchen bartop.

"Thank you," he told her, his eyes so serious that they made her want to cry.

"You're welcome."

He took a deep breath as he poured hot water over the tea bag in his cup. "I'm sorry—that I woke you and invaded your house like this."

"Don't apologize. I couldn't sleep anyway." She huffed out a wry laugh.

His gaze was sad, and he watched her in silence.

"So are you going to tell me what happened?" she asked.

He tensed, and she immediately wished she hadn't spoken.

Setting down his teacup, he planted his elbows on the counter and looked at her, steely eyes and determined lips wreaking havoc on her self-possession.

"There was an attempted assassination tonight." His voice was hard. "Someone shot Melville."

"Oh my God," she gasped, hands flying to cover her mouth.

"He's alive, but in critical condition. He was getting into his car with his wife."

London made a small choking noise, her throat feeling as though it might close up completely.

"As near as they can tell right now, the shot came from the third floor of an adjacent building. It was a planned, professional hit. A sniper."

"Who?" she whispered. "Who would do that?"

Derek sighed and stood from his stool, walking around to her side of the counter. He took her in his arms and held her, big palms splayed across her lower back, their heat seeping into her skin and then deeper, into her very soul. She sensed that the caress was as much for himself as for her, but in that moment she didn't care, only relished the feel of it, committing the sensation to memory for the moments later—after—when she would need to be apart from him again.

"Someone who wants to punish Melville. Maybe someone who thinks they're the moral police. Or, since he hasn't yet withdrawn from the race, maybe someone who simply doesn't want him to be President," Derek said softly. "But I will find them, and I will make sure that they don't get away with this."

He was the kind of man who made a woman feel safe. Even in his battle-weary state London had no doubt that he would make good on his vow. Standing in his strong embrace, his big body wrapped around hers, London could feel that he wasn't just powerful in influence and money. This was the kind of man who held power in his very body. He was big and confident and he could slay dragons for the right woman. Her heart hurt knowing she wasn't that woman.

He leaned away, looking down at her with such fierceness it frightened her. "I don't want you to be afraid. I've hired private security. They'll be here in a few hours, and they'll stay with you twenty-four seven."

"Me? Why? I'm not part of this any longer, and I'm sure as hell not a member of Melville's family."

He took her by the hand and led her to the sofa, seating them side-by-side and twisting so he could face her. He didn't let go of her hand and she felt her own tighten and twist to mold around his.

"Until we get whoever's done this, anyone who has been associated with the campaign and Melville in such a public way is a possible target. If this was some religious fanatic they could very well come after you next."

London's heart raced, and she couldn't stop her gaze from darting to the front windows, wondering what lurked beyond the curtains.

"I'm not willing to take the chance. So, for now—security. Round the clock. And that's not negotiable."

He'd anticipated her disagreement, and she scowled at him. It made her anxious to feel like he knew her somehow. No one had known the real her since she'd left her mother's home at seventeen, and she wasn't prepared for anyone to now.

"I haven't agreed to this," she said, firmly.

"You need to."

He touched her briefly, on the back of her hand. "It would kill me if I didn't do everything I possibly could to keep you safe. That's what matters to me now."

Her heart flipped like an acrobat through the air, and she caressed him with her eyes. Roaming over the planes of his face, his tousled hair, still damp around his neck, the stubble that seemed to always graze his jawline. She knew what she felt for him wasn't possible, that there was nowhere in this world for the two of them to be together, but she yearned for it, yearned with an intensity that obscured everything else—her self-preservation, her fears, her human decency.

"You can't do this," she protested one last time.

"It's my candidate who got you into this. I have a responsibility, London. Surely you realize by now that I'm the pinnacle of responsibility?" He gave her his trademark grin and she melted into a puddle of liquid sunshine, her brain turning to a lust-filled haze of desire and girlish worship.

As if he could see her thoughts playing across her face, his grin turned wolfish and he leaned forward whispering a kiss across her lips. "You threw me out earlier," he breathed into her mouth.

Yes. And she was tired of it. Tired of running from the world, and especially tired of running from him. If only he didn't make it so damned hard. She straightened her spine and put a finger on his lips just before he brought them down on hers again. "I can't. I can't do this part of it. You know that."

He shook his head, a lock of his unruly hair falling across his forehead, making him look even darker and more dangerous.

"Why? Because you think there's no future? Or because you refuse to let there be one? I've told you I don't care about the past, and I'm not worried about the future. I see this amazing woman in front of me and I want to know her—every way I can. The past is just that, dead and gone. The future we can manage. I've been managing candidates' futures for years, I can manage ours too if you'll let me."

She felt herself being carried away by the baritone of his voice, lulled into a cocoon of warmth and pleasure that she wasn't sure she could fight her way out of.

"I've never met a challenge I couldn't conquer, London. I can conquer the future too, you just have to let me." He brushed another kiss across her lips and she felt the prickling of his stubble around her mouth, smelled the hint of cinnamon from the tea on his breath, heard the hiss of her sigh as she dissolved into him.

He moved slower than he had in the car, nibbling on her tender flesh, running his tongue along the seam between her lips, stroking a single finger up and down her arm, murmuring about the silky feel of her skin. But her heart raced every bit as fast as it had the last time his skin was against hers, and she felt as aroused as if he'd been touching her darkest, most sensitive parts.

The battle between so much wanting and so much fear pushed her further into an abyss that she wasn't sure she could climb from. She clutched at his arms, afraid she was falling, knowing that while he was the one pushing her, he was also the only thing keeping her aloft.

His lips travelled down her cheek, then her neck and along her collarbone. He traced the curve of it with his tongue, gliding along the sweet bumps where the two halves met at the base of her throat. A groan rumbled through him, and she pulled him closer on instinct, wrapping her arms around his neck, digging her nails into his back through the thick terry cloth robe.

Then he was parting the silk of her pajama top, sliding the tiny buttons free as his lips followed his hands and he bared her breasts. She leaned in to his caress for just a moment, relishing the feel of his rough, hot hands on her delicate skin. She ached, she yearned, and then the alarms went off. Inside of her head warnings rang out, terror grabbed her in its clutches and squeezed her chest. She gasped, but it was panic this time, because she *felt*. God, she *felt*. And with feeling came everything, things that she could never allow, things that would break her into so many pieces no one would ever be able to glue her back together.

**

Derek knew it, the moment that her breathing shifted from lust to fear, but he was a man in the throes of passion, so it took his body a few seconds to catch up. By the time he pulled away to look her in the eyes, she wasn't able to breathe.

"London? Sweetheart, what's wrong?" he asked, as she clutched at her throat.

She continued to hyperventilate, her big, velvet eyes staring at him in desperation. He searched her face and neck for some sign of an injury or a mark to indicate what might be happening. Then he saw all the color leaching out of her face. Jesus Christ, what had he done to her?

"Does it hurt somewhere?" he asked, holding her shoulders so she had to look in his eyes.

She shook her head again, then nodded, tears ready to fall. Her breathing slowed some, and her face flushed as she dipped her head in what could only be interpreted as humiliation. He realized suddenly that this wasn't a medical emergency, but an emotional one. She was having a panic attack, and something he'd done had caused it. His heart clenched inside his chest and he grabbed her and pulled her onto his lap.

"Oh gorgeous, God, what did I do to you?" he crooned as he held her close, her head tucked under his chin.

He stroked her hair as she'd done his only an hour before, and settled them back on the sofa, enveloping her in his embrace. "It's okay," he said softly. "Whatever it was, I promise I'll never do it again."

A sob broke free, as if it had fought its way out of the very depths of her soul, and the sound hurt him more than anything he'd ever felt. Her anguish was so unsettling he wanted to leap to his feet and crush the invisible enemy in the room—even if that enemy was him.

As her breathing finally returned to normal and she relaxed in his arms, he hummed the song his mother had always sung to him and his brother when they were sick or had bad dreams. The song was as old as the hills, but to this day it comforted him and he owned five different versions of it on his iPod.

"You are my sunshine?" she asked in a small voice as she shifted so she could look up at him.

He nodded. "My mother used to sing it to us—my brother and I. Sorry. I'm not much of a singer. She did it better."

She gave him a tiny smile, and he briefly thought that he could make it his life's purpose to get her to smile fully. He didn't think he'd ever seen it reach her eyes. It was yet another warning to him that there were many things about this woman he didn't know. Things that could steal your smile—forever. Things that could break your heart and destroy your career. And yet, he stayed. He came to her here in her home, he stayed with her now when she hurt, he worried about her happiness, her safety, and whether she'd ever let him in. He saw the warning signs—he wasn't a fool—he simply didn't pay them any mind.

"It's nice. Your voice is nice." She sighed and wriggled closer into his arms. He shifted a touch to lean further into the sofa, her body like a soft, warm blanket over his aching muscles.

He slowly ran a hand up and down the silk sleeve of her pajama top, it still gaped open, exposing most of her breasts, but he knew that this wasn't that kind of moment, so he kept his eyes averted.

"Are you going to tell me what happened?" he finally asked.

She cleared her throat. "That's hard," she whispered.

"The important things always are."

She fiddled with the cuff of his robe, and he let her, holding his arm still while she picked at the threads.

"I panicked."

"Yes, that part I got." He gave her arm a little squeeze to indicate he was teasing.

"I never..." She swallowed audibly. "I mean I don't..." Her voice trailed off again.

"Take your time," he said softly. "I'm not going anywhere." And he meant it. Whatever waited out there beyond her front door could continue to wait. It was nearing dawn, his candidate was in the hospital, the press had outed Melville's sexcapades, and his friends were going to be looking for him to run damage control very soon, but none of that mattered as long as this one woman was coiled around him, her heart in so much pain that he could feel it through her skin. He'd sit here as long as it took to slay that dragon for her.

"Since I started my—job—" For the first time ever he heard disdain in her voice as she talked about her profession. "I haven't...*been* with anyone. Well, obviously the clients. But I haven't been with anyone *other* than the clients."

He nodded. "So no boyfriends, no relationships." It was twisted, but that information made something inside of him leap up and start high fiving the rest of him.

Her voice sounded like sandpaper as she responded. "Right." She paused again. "When I'm working, I do something, something I learned early on. I sort of turn *off.* I keep talking, keep doing the things I have to, but inside? Inside I turn something off, like a little switch, and that way I don't feel anything I don't want to. It's like part of me—the real me—isn't actually there, doing those things."

He sat silently for a moment, and every fiber of his being burned in agony. He'd never thought about it, not for one single moment. He'd seen this tough, sophisticated shell, and simply taken for granted that her inside was the same. The control, the steel under satin, he'd thought that was her. But in a blinding flash, he realized that it was all a façade, and that this real, soft, sensitive soul lay underneath the cold, hard outside. No woman could do what she'd done and not have it mark her. No human could be used by others that way and not suffer for it.

"God," he gritted out. "I hate that you've had to live like that."

She sniffed. "It's okay. It's been okay. Until now."

"Until I did something that reminded you of them… of the clients?" he asked, sickened at the mere thought he'd be anything like those men.

"No." She shook her head vehemently. "You don't understand. The switch I turn off when I'm working—it's not just that I don't think about what I'm doing or I don't feel anything for those men. It's that I don't feel *any*thing. Anything physical. It's all fake. Everything I do and say to them. All of it. I haven't felt anything with a man in years, Derek."

His mind raced trying to catch up. This beautiful, lush creature, who spent her working hours selling a world of sensuality to men was in fact devoid of any sensuality in her own life?

"Are you saying you haven't been aroused or had an orgasm in all that time?" he asked, astonishment saturating his words.

She nodded her head briskly, keeping her gaze down so he couldn't see her face.

He sat with that for a moment, listening to the sound of her breath, the big grandfather clock ticking across the room from them, his own heart pounding a touch too fast inside his chest.

"There hasn't been anyone? Anyone who made you...feel things?"

"No, and I've wanted it that way. It's how I survive. How I keep control."

His next question had them both holding their breath for a brief second. "And with me?" The rush of hope that washed through him was so intense he struggled not to shout it out.

"I feel too much," she whispered. "And I'm so scared."

**

There. She'd said it. She'd told him something she'd never told another human being in eight long years. Oh sure, there were a few girls at the escort service who she'd talked about work to, but she'd never admitted exactly how she got through doing it all. How she'd taught herself to deal with the realities of what she did to earn money. And she'd sure as hell never admitted to another soul that she was no longer able to have orgasms. Not if there was another person involved anyway.

The fact was, the few dates she'd been on over the years had never progressed beyond a good night kiss at the front door. She'd been fixed up with some very nice men, who had treated her well, been respectful and kind, but she'd never felt anything with them either, and she sure as hell had never wanted to be touched by them. After being pawed by her clients, the last thing London wanted was the touch of a horny man in her off-hours.

But with Derek, want had returned. And it was a fierce, uncontrollable want that scared her so badly she'd broken down in front of him. And now he knew it. The sordid, humiliating truth of just how broken she was. And so far he hadn't moved or spoken a word in response. In fact, she thought maybe he'd forgotten to breathe he was so shocked.

"I'm sorry." She struggled to stand from his lap. "I shouldn't have—"

"Stop," he commanded, pulling her close again. "Don't run from this again. From what's happening between us."

She stayed put, stiff in his arms, waiting in agony for what he'd say next.

He kissed her temple and tucked a strand of hair behind her ear. "I am so..." he paused, and she knew that if he said the word sorry, she'd never be able to move on, "thankful that you feel even a portion of what I feel when I'm with you."

Her breath rushed out in a whoosh, and the backs of her eyes pricked with unshed tears.

"I want to help you," he said softly, gazing into her eyes. "You deserve to feel everything that someone who cares for you can offer. You're a vibrant, beautiful woman, London. You deserve it all."

She shook her head, knowing that he was asking too much, asking for things she couldn't give. She hadn't survived all these years by letting the feelings in, and she wouldn't continue to survive if she did. This was temporary. Derek was temporary, only until the world told him who she was, and when he was gone, she'd be back to work, back to a place where feelings could break you and she was alone with no one to pick up the pieces.

"Shh." He put a finger to her lips, then slid it slowly back and forth, his eyes locked on her mouth. "Don't. Run." He cupped her cheek in his warm palm. "We'll go slow, focus on one thing at a time. One feeling at a time. I'm a patient man, London. And a determined one. I can do whatever it takes to help you feel the beautiful things you've given up. Let me show you. Give me a chance."

As she gazed into his crystalline eyes, she wondered how she'd ever thought they were icy. No, his eyes were clear, and deep, and you could practically see into his soul through them. They were full of passion and fire and they were anything but icy. He was anything but cold. They were the eyes of a wolf—a fierce hunter out in the world, but a devoted protector at home. He would protect her, she knew he would, except from the one thing he couldn't protect her from—himself. But in that moment, with his touch on her skin, and his voice in her head, she couldn't bring herself to tell him no again. The press, her past, her future, the thousand ways he could end up hating her—she wanted so very much to let it all go.

"I'll try," she answered. "It's so hard, but I want to feel. I want to feel it all—with you."

CHAPTER IX

Since Derek had left her at daybreak, both of them exhausted from the turmoil of the previous day and the confessions throughout the night, London hadn't left the house. She knew she should, that eventually she'd have to, but she couldn't manage to do it yet. The constant loop that played through her head was a jumble of questions—how had she ended up here? She'd sworn she'd never be exposed, she'd sworn she'd never let a man under the careful shell she'd constructed, she'd sworn that only she would control her life after she left her mother's house that day. And now here she was, violating every bit of it.

Everyone knew she was a prostitute, Derek had carved his way through that hard shell—she couldn't even leave her house because of the press, and the campaign, and the fear that the last dirty little secret she had buried would explode what few bits of her life were left intact. So, how had she gotten here? As much as she'd like to blame circumstances—Melville's bad sense, Derek's bad timing, the press's bad intentions—she knew that none of that was what had done it.

She was here because she had feelings for Derek Ambrose. Plain and simple. She couldn't resist him, and she was about to do something really stupid—get even further involved with him. Let him in deeper, entwine their fates more tightly. It would only end badly, of that she was certain. Either he'd break her heart by tiring of the novelty of dating a hooker, or she'd break his when he found out the truth about her father. Yet, even with that certainty, she couldn't make herself go away and stay away. She had money, she could leave town, go on a vacation and not come back until this had all blown over.

But she couldn't imagine it, couldn't imagine leaving Derek to deal with the mess that she was a crucial part of. She wanted him to come out of this intact—his career, his campaign, and his regard for her. She was fighting a hopeless battle, yet she was unable to leave it.

The phone vibrated in London's hand and she hit ignore before returning to staring out the window at her small backyard. It was the fifth time Joanna had called, in addition to the seven times she'd texted.

The phone chimed. Another text.

Please call me. I'm here for you.

London couldn't help but wonder if Jo was wrapped in some sort of denial that allowed her to send messages of support. In all the years she'd imagined what would happen if her separate life became public, she hadn't been able to fathom one half of the pain that she felt. What hurt the most, what really stung and kept her from answering that phone was the idea of the disappointment. The look on Joanna's face when she had to admit that she'd lied to her yet again.

Because for London, her friend wasn't only who she lunched with and gossiped with, and used for companionship. For London, Joanna was the closest thing to a family that she had. And no one knew better than she did how it felt to have your family disappoint you. She'd never once realized that by keeping so much of her life hidden, she was doing the same thing to Joanna and the other people she was closest to that her mother had done to her. The irony was almost too much to bear.

She stared down at the screen of her phone, the messages waiting icon blinking over and over. How had it happened? How had she managed to go and do the one thing that she'd sworn was a deal-breaker in a relationship—hiding who you were? Her mother had hidden such a crucial part of their shared past from London all those years. Gone so far as to create a false history to placate her impressionable daughter's need to have a father. And London had been devastated when she discovered the lie. Now she sat on the other end of the equation and she couldn't fathom that the people she loved, the friends who had taken her in, supported her and been her foundation all these years, could ever forgive her.

She wasn't Farrah Amid's daughter anymore, and there was no point in answering the phone, because eventually Joanna wasn't going to be her friend anymore either.

**

The remainder of Derek's day was spent on the phone, first with one media outlet then another. After the culmination of one disaster after another, he'd only known one thing to do, find the friendliest media outlets he could and deal with them. He'd stayed on message all day—the Senator's shooter must be found, and the campaign had no response to the further accusations of Melville consorting with hookers.

He'd taken that message, however uninformative it was, and he'd put out press releases, given interviews, appeared on WNN Mid-Day, given a European exclusive to the principal British news network, and finally, ended the circus on the Lexi Cornice show defending the campaign's handling of the situation, and explaining that sex scandals weren't of importance when a United States Senator had been gunned down next to his lovely wife in broad daylight. None of his spin had overcome the lack of family values grilling that he was enduring in a lot of the outlets, but at least he was able to spend the day with legitimate news sources who didn't have an ulterior agenda of skewering him in public.

Amidst the media storm he'd managed to keep in touch with Melville's wife, and get the news that the Senator was improving rapidly. The bullet had missed Melville's heart, tearing through one lung and shattering his shoulder blade on the way out. Luckily reconstruction had gone well, and the lung had been repaired.

He pressed send on the last press release of the day, updating the press corps on Melville's health, then sat back in his desk chair, rubbing a hand over the substantial shadow that had grown on his face since six a.m. when he'd left London's house with the promise that he'd return in the evening.

"Renee!" he yelled through his closed door.

He heard light footsteps approaching and swiveled toward the door as she popped her head in.

"You bellowed?" she asked, one eyebrow raised.

"Sorry, I'm too tired to press the intercom button."

Her brows furrowed and he could have sworn she looked guilty for a moment. "I'm so sorry you had to go through all of this. Do you think this was the worst of it?"

He swiveled his chair side to side, keeping his eyes on the desktop in front of him while his mind tried to sort through the morass of information and feelings that had collected during the day.

"I can't imagine how it can get much worse, but I feel like I'm inviting that bitch fate in if I'm too sure of it."

Renee grimaced and walked further into the room, standing in front of his desk, arms crossed.

"Well, either way, you need food and a bed right now. How can I get you to go home?"

He gave her a wan smile. "Do the same for yourself? I'm going in just a few minutes, so I want you to go home too. Have the security guy walk you to your car. I'll be fine here for ten minutes alone. The building's locked down tight. Get a good night's sleep and don't be here before eight a.m. tomorrow. Anything happening before then can wait until a civilized hour for your attention."

"Promise you'll leave too?"

"Scout's honor," he answered, holding up a strange V with his fingers.

"That's *Live Long and Prosper*." She chuckled.

He looked at his fingers in confusion. "What?"

Renee rolled her eyes. "You're too cool to even know. It's from Star Trek. Never mind, I get the idea. I'll see you in the morning, and I'll know if you didn't get enough sleep so don't go taking any work home."

"Aye, Aye, ma'am." This time he saluted her and got it right.

**

Forty minutes later Derek got out of the car driven by his security detail on the street in front of London's townhouse, and slouched to the front stoop where a security guard stood inconspicuously in the shadows. He'd been quietly thankful when she'd agreed to let him come back this evening after the dark discussion they'd had. In spite of the fact that most of the hell he'd endured during the day could be directly linked to London, she was still the only person he wanted to see.

He didn't have a clear plan for what he was doing with her, or where they were going to end up, but he knew beyond a shadow of a doubt that he wanted to be around her, wanted to protect her, and even cosset her a bit if she'd let him. He was spending hours each day fighting the compulsion to get in his car and go to London, wherever she might be. Just so he could stare at her face, hear her voice, smell her skin.

He hadn't even had sex with the woman and he was utterly obsessed.

"Good evening Mr. Ambrose," the big bruiser at her door said politely.

"Hi. Owen, is it?"

"Yes sir."

"Any problems today? Press find her?"

"No sir. Looks like we got lucky. Apparently the house here is listed under a different name in the property tax records so they can't find her address. Since she hasn't left the house and your driver is careful about being tailed, we might get another day or two of peace."

Derek gave a sharp nod. "Well, I guess we'll enjoy it while we can, and at least she gets a breather before it gets worse." He paused, looking out to the car he'd arrived in, now parked at the curb across the street. "I'll be here all night, so only one of you needs to stay, then I'll need a driver first thing tomorrow morning."

Owen nodded, clicking on the earpiece he wore to issue instructions to his colleague in the car. "We've got it covered, Mr. Ambrose," he said as he knocked once on the door then swung it open to admit Derek.

Derek walked into London's foyer and set his duffle bag down, letting his eyes adjust to the low lighting.

He squelched the urge to shout out, "Honey, I'm home" and opted for her name instead. "London?" He walked further into the house, turning the corner through the living area to find the small dining table set up for two, candles glowing, crystal sparkling.

"Hi," London said as she walked out of the kitchen, a large platter in hand. She gave him a small smile and set the dish down. "I thought you might be hungry after such a long day."

A rush of warmth and belonging washed through him at the sight. She was dressed casually in skinny jeans and a loose, cropped sweater, her long hair flowing down around her shoulders. Her dark eyes were warm like the flames in the candles, and somewhere in the back of his mind it occurred to him that he could come home to those eyes, that smile, this very scene, every night for the rest of his life and not tire of it.

"I knew there was something I liked about you." He reached out and caressed her cheek, a small gesture, but one he hoped gave her a clue as to how their night would unfold.

"Come sit down, it's all ready."

He removed his jacket and hung it on the back of a chair, then loosened his tie, sighing deeply as he sat.

London went to the kitchen and returned with two more dishes that she set on the table before sitting down herself.

"I didn't know what kind of food you like—"

"Anything that doesn't come from a paper bag," he joked.

"Good. I made you a traditional Persian dinner—koresh, which is the stew in that red dish, kuku, a soufflé with lots of vegetables, and nan. You've probably had nan at Indian restaurants."

Derek looked hungrily at all of it. "Show me how to serve it all and keep it coming," he said.

She laughed and began scooping rice and stew onto his plate.

**

Thirty minutes later Derek took the last bite of kuku and the last swallow of wine and leaned back in his chair. "That was seriously one of the best meals I've had in months. Where did you learn to cook like that?"

London's eyes shifted away briefly before she answered. "My mother loved to cook. She taught me."

He knew her family was a sensitive subject for her, but he'd decided that helping London rediscover her feelings of all sorts, on all levels, was his new mission in life, and that required some gentle prodding.

"She's a professor? Linguistics?"

"Yes. Last time I heard anyway."

"And you miss her." He stated it as accepted fact, because anyone who saw the look on London's face when she discussed her mother could see it in a moment.

"Sometimes," she answered quietly. "But then I remember the things she's done and I stop missing her at all." She gave him a look that challenged him to pursue the topic further and he altered course.

"So, in gratitude for the spectacular meal, why don't I do the dishes and make us a couple of nightcaps?"

She stood and grinned. "Be my guest. I'll be in the living room."

Once cleanup was finished, Derek grabbed the tray with the cocktails and the whipping cream he'd found in her refrigerator and went to her in the living room where she was flipping through a magazine.

"All right, it's late, I'm taking you upstairs."

She stared at him, eyes wide.

"Don't give me that look," he warned. "I've had one of the worst days of my life and about the only thing that got me through was thinking about being with you at the end of it. I told you we were going to work on your issue. Nothing you're not ready for, but I'm going to be the teacher and you're the student, and class is starting so get your pretty ass up the stairs."

London's mouth dropped, and for a moment she looked like a gaping fish. Derek laughed and reached out to grab her hand, pulling her from the sofa.

He wrapped an arm around her waist, balancing the tray in his other hand. He brushed his lips up the long column of her neck until he reached her ear where he nipped at the tender little lobe. "Come on gorgeous, let me show you that feeling things isn't all bad."

She gasped and arched her back, pressing into him harder. He spun her and smacked her on the ass. "Move it. Now."

She looked back at him over her shoulder, smirking before scurrying up the stairs. He followed chuckling.

**

London landed on the bed with a bounce, Derek's big frame following her down until she lay flat under him as he hovered over her, his arms and knees creating a cage that trapped her, willing detainee that she was. His eyes sparkled as he took her in, and she felt her heart rate pick up at the heat in his stare.

He kissed her softly on the lips before pulling back. "Nothing you can't handle. Only good stuff, and if you start to feel like things are going too fast you just say so, right?"

She nodded, itching for him to touch her, because even though it was frightening, it was also intoxicating.

He blew softly on her neck and cheek, licking the same earlobe he'd nipped a few moments ago. She felt her entire body turn to hot liquid, her center beginning to burn and ache.

"But first things first," he murmured. He stood, leaving cold air washing over her. She felt bereft immediately. He walked to the corner of the room where he'd put a duffle bag at some point earlier in the evening, and after rummaging in it for a few moments, emerged with a blindfold.

Her eyes widened. "Mr. Ambrose, I would have never guessed."

"Hush," he said, grinning evilly. "This is all in the name of your instruction." He strode back to the bed. "Off with the top."

She sat up and watched the expression on his face as she slowly removed her sweater, leaving on only a lacey pink bra.

Derek's eyes grew hungry. "Pink," he murmured. "Perfect." He handed her the blindfold. "Put this on."

She took it, but before she could slide it into place Derek began unbuttoning his dress shirt and she paused to watch, her mouth watering when he revealed all those muscles covered in smooth skin and a light dusting of golden hair.

"Blindfold, gorgeous," he rumbled.

She pouted but pulled the blindfold down over her eyes.

"Now, lie back, cede some control to me and let me make you feel all the best things."

London lay still, waiting in heightened anticipation for what might come next. She heard rustling, and then Derek's hands were unbuttoning her jeans. She stiffened.

"Shh. Just getting you more comfortable, nothing you don't want, I promise."

She relaxed as he peeled the denim from her legs leaving her in the matching bra and panties set.

"Jesus you're gorgeous," he rasped out. He ran his hands up and down her legs, his touch whisper soft, on the outsides of her legs only, stopping when he reached her hips. Over and over until she felt a thousand tiny sparks dancing along her skin and her breathing hitched.

"Do you feel that?" he whispered in her ear. "It's electric, this thing between us."

She sighed, melting into his touch, and then he was gone. She writhed, needing to feel him there with her again. Then she heard it, a hissing sound, and the smell of vanilla wafted around her. Something cold danced over her belly and in its wake she felt hot, rough flesh stroke along with the coldness. The whipped cream. He was licking the whipped cream off of her skin, and it was so much feeling she nearly came off the bed.

"Derek," she hissed.

"Shh," he hushed. "Breathe, let your mind turn off. I'm just having some dessert, all you need to do is lie here and enjoy it." He chuckled and she couldn't help but smile imagining what he must look like, bare chest, rippling muscles, dress pants, with a nearly naked writhing, sticky woman underneath him.

He deftly unsnapped the front clasp on her bra, then the can made another whooshing sound and she felt the cold whipped cream surround her nipples. His tongue followed, licking slowly in circles around her areolas, then closer, almost to her nipples but not quite. Her breasts ached, almost painfully, as the rough flat of his tongue rubbed along her skin. When she thought she'd die from the want, his lips closed over one nipple and he sucked. Painful pleasure radiated from the point he was focused on straight to her core, and her inner muscles clenched.

"Oh, oh God," she moaned, canting her hips, craving pressure and relief. One of his hands swept along the curve of her waist while the other plumped her breast as he continued to suck and swirl her nipple in his mouth. She needed to touch him, and one of her hands found a fistful of his silky hair while the other clawed at his back, trying to pull him closer.

But he didn't comply, letting her pull and scratch at him as he leisurely moved on to the other breast, lavishing the same attention on it. When he finally released her second nipple, she heard him shift positions, as he sat back on his heels, his knees straddling her hips. The new position provided weight and pressure exactly where she craved it and she gasped in relief and agitation, pressing her pelvis against him as she writhed.

"Mmm," he groaned. "We're not there yet, gorgeous." She felt his stubbled face brush against her cheek as he planted tiny kisses along her jaw while his hands palmed her waist, holding her steady. Then his lips found hers and he thrust his tongue in her mouth as his hips rocked, pressing down on her clit, rubbing the fabric of her panties against the swollen, tender skin. She wanted to spread her legs, take him inside of her, then his chest brushed against hers, his hairs scraping her overly sensitive nipples, and she felt a shock of electricity run through her.

As if she were a glass of water and someone had just poured over the rim, it suddenly became too much. She knew she was close, an orgasm to end all orgasms hovering just beyond the next touch, kiss, thrust. And she couldn't do it. Couldn't let herself go. Her heart raced, and she wasn't able to catch her breath. Dammit. No. Not like this.

In a moment Derek's lips were gone, his weight disappearing, and his voice rumbling in her ear. "It's okay. It's okay. We'll stop. You don't need to be afraid. I'm right here, but no pressure. Just breathe."

She reached up and ripped the blindfold off, blinking for a moment in the low light of the dimmed nightstand lamps. Derek hovered over her on his hands and knees, so close, but not touching, his face full of nothing but concern and empathy.

"I'm sorry," she sobbed, turning her head to the side in humiliation. She wasn't a crier, wasn't much for emotional outbursts of any sort, but she was frustrated, embarrassed, and longing for something that she was starting to fear she'd never have.

He cupped her cheek as he shifted and sat next to her on the bed. Forcing her gaze to his as he stroked her skin with his thumb. "Don't be sorry. You did fantastic. You're beautiful, and I love being with you. It's not going to happen overnight. You have a lot of years to overcome. But I know we can do it. I know you can learn to trust me. If you want to?"

She leaned in to his touch and kissed his palm as he slid down and lay next to her. "Yes. I want that more than anything."

"Then we'll make it happen. You don't need to worry."

She took a deep breath and looked into his beautiful eyes. How had she ever gotten so lucky to find a man like him? She knew she didn't deserve him, and she could only hope that he never realized that.

"I'm just so…" Her voice trailed off, not knowing what she wanted to say.

"Horny?" he asked, grinning.

"God yes, that too." She wiggled as if to verify that everything below her waist was still on fire.

He ran one finger along her torso, pausing briefly to caress the soft skin around her belly button.

"Are you able to do it yourself?" he asked quietly.

She swallowed. "You mean…?"

"Do you get yourself off?"

She nodded, feeling her face flush. That she could be embarrassed by talk of sex after the last eight years of her life was nothing short of amazing.

"Then do it," he said, his voice rough with desire. "Right now."

She rolled to her side and looked at him silently. They breathed in unison and she felt a sense of being in sync with another human being that she'd never experienced. Their breaths, their heartbeats, the energy of their want, all of it circled around them, swirling in and out of the cocoon that they existed in for that moment.

She leaned forward the two inches between them and placed one perfect, butterfly-light kiss on his lips. "You too," she whispered. He nodded before taking her hand and gently moving it to the waistband of her underwear. She slid her fingers under the elastic and further until she felt the slick skin of her sex. She looked in time to see him unzip his pants and shove his boxers down enough to bare his cock. It was dark and smooth, swollen and shiny with precum. It made her throb and she released a small moan as she stroked her clit, circling it with one finger.

"Watch," he rasped. "Look at what you do to me."

She kept her eyes glued to him as he fisted himself, spreading the moisture from the tip around the head with his thumb. He began to move his hand up and down in firm steady strokes, his breath increasing in speed as his hand did.

London pressed on her clit, then circled and pressed it, pausing to dip inside her channel every so often, touching her g-spot briefly before moving back to her clit. The intense ache that was already burning in her gut worsened, and she squeezed her eyes shut, waiting for that wave of ecstasy to pour over her.

"Eyes on us," Derek commanded roughly and her eyes popped open as she looked down again, finding him thrusting into his hand rapidly, his body straining, muscles flexed, face tense.

She pressed her hand against her pelvis, pushing hard on her clit. "Oh, oh, God," she cried out.

"Come for me, gorgeous," he growled, and she did. Her eyes snapped shut and the waves of pleasure rolled through her. Her muscles spasmed and released over and over as she gasped for breath. At some point she realized that she heard both Derek's voice and her own as she cried out and he roared his release, her name on his lips like a curse and a benediction all at once.

As the orgasm slowly subsided she moved her hand aside, letting her panties shift back into place. She felt sticky warmth on her hip and looked down to see Derek give himself one final stroke before he released his cock, groaning in satisfaction. His entire body melted into the bed as he flopped onto his back in exhaustion.

"I'll get you something to clean up. Just give me a moment. I'm not sure I can move right now."

She giggled, the relief making her giddy. Derek rolled back toward her and kissed her on the lips. "That was the hottest thing I've ever seen in my life," he said quietly. "How do you feel?"

She smiled shyly at him, butterflies dancing in her chest at his words and the feel of his lips on hers. "Really good," she admitted. She paused, amazed that it was true. She felt like a weight had been lifted from her soul. There was a lightness that she'd not even realized she was missing.

He hoisted himself off of the bed and went to the bathroom, returning with a damp washcloth. Tenderly he wiped her hip clean, then his cock, before tossing the cloth back into the bathroom. Then he peeled his pants off, leaving his boxers on and picked her up, as she laughed, struggling in his hold. "Be still, woman," he bellowed. He flipped back the covers and deposited her on the cool, smooth sheets before climbing in next to her.

He turned her back to him, banding an arm around her waist and grasping one of her breasts possessively. He nuzzled the back of her neck, breathing in deeply with his nose in her hair. "Mmm. Now go to sleep," he mumbled. "We've got a big day tomorrow."

London smiled in the darkness, completely surrounded by his big body, bossed by his big mouth, and the happiest she'd been in years. Just for that one brief moment, she let herself bask in the warmth, the glow, the sensation of being cared for. She ignored the fears that lurked in the dark corners of her mind, turning a deaf ear to the warnings that whispered through her head. For that one night, London Sharpe let herself be happy, and it was better than any dream she had after she drifted off to sleep in the arms of the man she was rapidly falling in love with.

CHAPTER X

It was almost seven when Derek woke the next morning. He was usually up before six, but even he had to admit it had been a stress-filled few days. He spent the first few minutes watching London sleep, her face and hair lit up by the weak sunlight streaming through the gap in the curtains.

God, he hadn't known what to expect with his little experiment the night before, and he had to admit that it had gone better than his wildest imaginings. He was no therapist, but he had a gut instinct that told him if he could ease her into the physical feelings the rest would follow. And he had to admit that he wanted both kinds. He wanted to fuck her senseless, and he wanted her to care about him. He'd have never expected it, but this damaged, fragile, beautiful woman had turned his heart and mind inside out, and now all that mattered was how to get her to want him as much as he wanted her.

He quietly put on the running clothes he'd brought with him the night before and tiptoed downstairs. Outside he met up with the security detail who had arrived to accompany him throughout his day. London's house was still blissfully free of press, but the security guys told him that his Georgetown brownstone had been overrun with media, all waiting for him to show back up.

"We're keeping them at the requisite fifty feet from the property line, but they're not going anywhere for now, Mr. Ambrose," the guard who'd replaced Owen said.

"That's fine," Derek answered. "I'd rather they be there than here bothering Ms. Sharpe. I'll make an appearance at home later today to keep them interested. I want to keep them away from here as long as we can."

"Yes, sir."

"You ready for a run?" Derek asked.

"Looking forward to it, sir. Let me go tell Charlie to come up to the house." After Charlie was in position at London's front door Derek and the other guard went for a short run to Hamilton Park. Derek put in his headset and dialed Kamal before putting the phone into his armband.

"Any more news on Melville?" Kamal answered without preamble.

"He's sitting up and eating according to the text Angela sent this morning. I'll go see him as soon as I finish this run and grab some breakfast."

"Good. You'll put out another press release once you've seen him?"

Derek's feet pounded on the concrete as he turned the corner onto Harlow Street. "Yes, I want everyone to know that he's going to be fine, and whoever did this to know they didn't succeed."

"And I've got some news on that," Kamal said, his voice deadly serious.

"Really? The cops couldn't tell me a damn thing when I last talked to them. What are you hearing?"

Kamal was known for his less than savory contacts. As the son of a prominent Egyptian businessman he was acquainted with a wide variety of people, including members of the Egyptian underworld.

"It appears that someone contacted Melville's office last week asking for the Senator's campaign schedule. Naturally they were only given his public appearances, but the campaign worker said that shortly after that phone call a man stopped by saying he was interested in volunteering. She went to get him the paperwork to fill out and when she got back he'd wandered into the conference room where you've got the Senator's events with times and dates shown on the map."

"So that he could have seen where Melville would be leaving the private meeting at the Carpenter's Hall Union where he was shot, and at what time." Derek cursed under his breath. "Which worker was this?"

"Denise," Kamal answered.

"And did she remember what the guy looked like?"

"Yes, we've got a good description, and interestingly it matches Ryan Williams, the Senate aide who was having Melville investigated."

Derek took a deep breath and shook out his hands, reminding himself that clenching every muscle in his body while he was running wouldn't help him out any.

"You've got to be fucking kidding me."

"There's something else," Kamal said.

"Okay, might as well hit me with all of it."

"It appears that our man Williams has fooled around with more than just his boss's wife. Eighteen months ago he was involved with Nick Patterson's wife as well."

Derek nearly stumbled he was so shocked. Patterson was one of his bigger competitors in the political consulting business. A good guy, they periodically met for drinks to discuss things if they wanted an outsider's input before taking on a new client.

"I had no idea Nick and his wife were having problems. And why the hell would she take up with a slimeball like Williams?"

"I'm not sure of that yet, but we've gotten reports that Williams and Nick have been seen together twice in the last few weeks, Derek."

No. This made no sense whatsoever. Nick Patterson was a good guy. Not the success Derek was, but no slouch. A consummate professional and a devoted family man. There was absolutely no way he'd be involved in destroying Derek's career and Melville's campaign. Not to mention an assassination attempt.

"Where the hell are you getting your information, Kamal? I don't believe for one second that Nick would ever involve himself in a mess like this. He's a good man. Ethical almost to a fault. And if what you've heard about Williams and Nick's wife is true, I'd think they'd be the last two men on the planet meeting up with one another unless it was in a back alley with brass knuckles."

Derek's security guard gestured to the left, indicating he wanted Derek to round the corner, away from the denser sidewalks of the main thoroughfare that were rapidly filling with early morning commuters.

Derek complied, simultaneously trying to pick up his pace which he'd slowed as he talked to Kamal.

"You know I'm not going to tell you who I've talked to," Kamal scolded. "I'm able to get you this kind of information because I promise them complete anonymity. But they're solid sources, Derek. Could it be that Nick was meeting with Williams about something completely unrelated to Melville's campaign? Of course. Maybe Williams was talking to Nick about consulting on Donovan's possible presidential run. Maybe they were discussing the affair, albeit in a lot more civilized fashion than you've suggested. But why wouldn't they have met at the office for that? We don't know at this point, but we need to find out. Even though it involves someone you respect."

Derek knew his friend was right. He knew that with Melville's life threatened, his own career circling the drain, and London's life torn apart there was no way they could afford to skip any possible suspects. But damn it hurt to think about Nick involved in something like this.

"Okay," he answered gruffly. "Do what you have to do."

"I'll tell Jeff. Call me tonight if there are any updates on Melville's condition."

"Will do." Derek paused. "And Kamal? As long as you're looking into the Pattersons, find out if Nick's wife is okay. She's not the type to cheat. Something's gone very wrong there. It may be none of my business, but I'd like to know more about it."

They ended the call, and Derek turned back toward London's townhouse, a sudden need to see her taking over any noble ideas of self-improvement that might have started his morning off with a run.

**

London woke with her skin tingling, her heart racing, and her mind a delicious mixture of images, smells, and sounds. The memory of Derek's tongue across her skin, his deep, raspy voice in her ear, the hard shiny head of his cock as he leisurely pumped it into his big fist. Her sex throbbed and she stretched luxuriously before turning to find the rest of the bed empty.

Dammit. She might like a repeat of last night. And maybe, just maybe, she could get comfortable enough to let Derek take her there instead of her own fingers.

She sat up, looking around the room for some clue as to where he might have gone. He was nothing short of amazing. She'd never known a man who would go to so much trouble to help a woman feel comfortable. That he'd forgone actual sex just because she had such outrageous hang-ups was astonishing to her, and made her feel more than a little warm and squishy about him.

She noticed his work clothes draped over an armchair in the corner, and his big duffle bag still sitting on her floor, so he couldn't have left for work yet. Maybe he was downstairs getting coffee? The man did love his coffee.

Five minutes later, hair brushed and teeth clean, London wandered downstairs in one of her many silk kimonos, following the smell of strong coffee and the sounds of something she'd never experienced before—a man cooking in her kitchen.

She turned the corner and came to a standstill. There he stood, bare chested, athletic shorts hanging loosely off of his narrow hips, hair mussed, and scruff covering his face. He had a spatula in one hand, a cup of coffee in the other, and he was cooking what smelled like the world's best bacon—or maybe she was simply hungrier than usual. She sighed, disbelieving that this was her very own kitchen. She felt like she must have wandered into someone else's life.

As if he had a sixth sense that told him when she was near, Derek turned and looked over his shoulder at her, his expression growing hungry the minute his eyes dropped from her face, slid slowly down her scantily clad body, and back up again.

"Good morning," he growled, carefully removing the pan from the stovetop and setting it aside. He stalked across the kitchen to where she stood and set his hands on her hips before yanking her against him and lowering his mouth.

"You're looking exceptionally delicious today," he murmured before crushing his lips to hers.

London's body flared to life, need slamming into her like a velvet hammer to her midsection. She moaned and opened her mouth to him as he thrust his tongue inside, his hard cock pressing against her stomach.

His hands slipped around to her backside and he clutched her ass, yanking her up against him tighter and higher. Then he bent his knees, licking down her neck and pressing his erection against the perfect spot between her legs.

"Damn, woman," he growled. "I should have never gotten out of that bed this morning."

"God, no," she gasped. "Whatever possessed you to leave?"

He chuckled, slowly nibbling back up to her lips, softly pressing a kiss to them before he released her.

"Unfortunately I can't play hooky today. We've got a shitstorm to tame, and a candidate in the hospital."

London's lust-induced haze cleared as Derek turned back to the stove, and she was reminded about the disaster of her life outside this house.

As if sensing the crashing mood, Derek walked to her, a plate of eggs and bacon in hand and gently maneuvered her to the bartop. "Sit," he commanded with a smile. "Have some food, I'll get you caught up with everything, and you can tell me what you need today so that the security detail can take care of it."

**

Forty-five minutes later, London was fed, she'd looked over the newest press releases Derek's office had drafted, and she was sitting on her living room sofa with a cup of coffee listening to him give instructions to the security staff about where she needed to go during the day.

While she bristled at the idea of a security detail, as well as Derek parceling out permission for her day's arrangements, she knew that at this point it was necessary. If she were to brave the outside world on her own right now she would be assaulted by press, curiosity seekers, opportunists and bullies. Everyone would want a piece of the most notorious hooker since Heidi Fleiss and it wouldn't be pretty. She knew she didn't have what it took to face down the hordes alone.

"Excuse me!" a familiar voice rang out from the foyer. "I don't give a damn if you're the secret service, I *will* see her this minute if you know what's good for you!"

London leaped off of the sofa as she heard Derek's voice intercede. "It's okay Michael, I've got this...Hi, I'm Derek Ambrose, London's boyfriend, can I help you?"

"I know exactly *who* you are," Joanna snapped back. "*What* you are to London is a whole other issue. I, on the other hand, am her *best* friend, and I'm coming in to see her right now, or I'll call the police and say you're holding her against her will."

Derek chuckled then and London couldn't help but smile herself, even as her heart beat double-time in trepidation.

"No need to call D.C.'s finest," Derek replied. "She's right in here, you're welcome to see her."

Joanna's heels tapped harshly against the hardwood floors as she burst into the living room, Derek ambling behind her, what could only be described as a bemused expression on his face.

"London, oh thank God, you're okay." Jo vaulted to London and grabbed her in a hard hug. London looked over Jo's shoulder to find Derek smiling benevolently at them.

"You okay?" he mouthed.

London nodded and he went back out, his voice and those of the security detail receding as they walked out of the house and shut the front door.

Joanna pulled back and set London away, clutching her shoulders and giving her the once over.

"You're all right?" she asked gently.

London smiled at Jo's theatrics. "Yes, he's taking very good care of me. The security is to keep others out, not to keep me in." Although her gut reaction was to feel confined anyway—but she didn't need to tell Joanna that.

They sat down and Jo turned to her, concern etching her sweet, porcelain features.

"Why won't you return my calls?"

London sighed, guilt clawing at her insides. "Why would you call in the first place?"

Joanna shook her head before reaching out and grasping London's wrist. "When are you going to get it? I love you. You're the sister I never had, you are my family, and I'm yours. It doesn't matter what you do, I won't abandon you."

London's eyes swam with tears, and she choked back a sob. "But I lied to you—again. And I'm a prostitute—"

"I knew this you'll recall."

London sniffed. "But now you know that I'm a prostitute who's had sex with a married politician you supported. I've seen pictures of his wife. He's got little children, Jo. I've never known that about a client. We don't ever...I've never..."

"Shh," Jo shushed. "What you did yesterday or the day before that doesn't matter to me nearly as much as what you decide to do tomorrow. Am I pissed? Damn straight. You lied to me. After we had that discussion about the prostitution, after you told me how you got here and why. You still lied to me. And it hurts. It makes me feel like you don't really trust me, even after all these years, after I found out the things you've been hiding and I forgave you. You still don't trust me."

"I'm so sorry, Jo. I do trust you. I think I've just spent so many years hiding and lying that I don't know how to do anything else. I don't know how to be anything else. I'm a liar."

"Stop it," Jo admonished. "You're not a liar, you're someone who has lied. But you're at the bottom now. There's no way to go but up, and it's going to be a fantastic ride. You need to put this whole double life behind you and let me help you find the real London. She's here, she just needs some encouragement."

London grabbed Jo and hugged her hard. "The way you forgive me no matter what is the most encouraging thing in my world. And I'm so sorry that you had to find out about Melville like this."

Jo nodded solemnly, her lips pursed. "So he isn't quite the guy I thought he was."

"I'm sorry, Jo." London meant it for so much more than Melville's mistakes. If she could turn back the hands of time to give her friend at least a presidential candidate to admire she would.

"And you and Derek? I don't understand. You said you were dating, but now you're admitting you were seeing Melville. Was Derek only a decoy for the press? It looked a hell of a lot like he spent the night here."

"It's complicated."

"Was he a client too?" Jo looked somewhat pale when she asked.

"No!" London's stomach twisted at the very thought of Derek paying her for sex. "He would never. He's a really good man, Jo."

Joanna finally showed a sign of her usual spark. "So you *are* seeing each other?"

"He's...different...than anyone I've ever known."

Joanna's face broke into an enormous grin. "You like him!" she crowed in delight. "You're really dating him. Oh, London, I'm so relieved."

London rolled her eyes. "Don't go planning a wedding. This is temporary. We started the whole thing as a ruse to keep the press from knowing that Melville had been seeing me. But now we're stuck because of the assassination attempt. Derek doesn't feel that anyone publicly associated with the campaign is safe right now."

Jo grinned. "What a convenient excuse."

"Again, don't go getting any ridiculous ideas."

Joanna stood and walked slowly to the fireplace where she ran her finger along the mantle while she talked. "He obviously likes you. I saw the way he looked at you, and he made a point of referring to himself as your boyfriend."

She paused before turning to face London, her face much more serious now. "He's wealthy and powerful, London. If you continue to be involved with him he could help you get out of...your job. Maybe he could help you pay for school or start a business. There are all sorts of things you're good at, I'm sure you could figure out something that interests you."

London's chest tightened at the imaginary future Jo described. Her friend meant well, but didn't understand half of what lay under the surface of the arrangement with Derek.

"I know it looks that way from the outside, but it's not that simple."

"Why?" Jo asked, a stubborn set to her chin. "Why can't you have a fresh start out of all of this? I can help you, Brian and I already talked about it. You don't have to live like that anymore."

London's first response was, as always, to bristle, cloak herself in indignation and tell Joanna to go run someone else's life. But she knew Jo meant well, and she also knew that Jo's reactions were based on incomplete information. A situation that couldn't be rectified.

"I appreciate it. You and Brian are the most generous people in the world and I love you both very much." She took a breath, trying to conquer the tension in her neck and chest. "I'll think about it all. I promise." There. That was the easiest way to placate Jo for now. She didn't need to know that as soon as Derek had the campaign rumors under control it would be back to life as normal for London.

Jo smiled and rushed over to hug London where she sat on the sofa. "Those are the best words I've heard in two days. Now, don't ever make me find out something about you that way again. No more secrets, okay?"

London nodded, too overcome for a moment to speak.

"I love you," she answered, neatly sidestepping any promises or commitments. Dissembling came easy to her. She'd spent the better part of a decade perfecting the art.

CHAPTER XI

London should have looked at the phone more carefully. She didn't recognize the number, it didn't show a name, and she was in the middle of a media feeding frenzy, so it should have made her cautious. An anonymous number, an unknown caller. But before her mind could get her body to exercise caution she'd swiped the screen and answered, "Hello?"

The line was silent for a split second then London heard an intake of breath. Somehow, from that one tiny noise she knew, and the voice that followed the breath rolled over her like a familiar old coat.

"London, please don't hang up," Farrah Amid's sultry voice begged.

London clenched her teeth together, her eyes stinging. She was breathless for a moment, her vision wobbled and she collapsed against the wall she stood next to.

"How did you get this number? And what do you want?" Her own voice was barely above a whisper.

She heard Farrah swallow, and even though she'd never seen the woman cry, she sensed that it was a sob she shoved down deep into her throat.

"I needed to know you're okay," Farrah answered. "I saw the news weeks ago, and was finally able to get one of the reporters to track down your number. I had to hear you myself, to know if you're all right?"

London's gaze went to the window. The press had found her house this morning, and each time she looked out the window there were more of them, like vultures waiting to pick a carcass clean. Then her eyes drifted to the newspaper on the table nearby, its headlines screaming about the assassination attempt on Melville.

"I will be if everyone will leave me alone," she answered, "but I don't think that will be happening anytime soon."

There was a pause then, a moment of negative space, where nothing was said, no one breathed, and London and the woman who had given birth to her existed, in each other's presence, for the first time in ten years. If pain could travel through invisible waves in the air, it did in that moment, and London felt it. The crushing weight of grief, and regret, and sorrow.

"Is it true?" Farrah asked. "The things in the paper." London's stomach lurched and she squeezed her eyes shut against a vicious flash of pain that shot through her chest.

"Which part? That I'm a hooker? Yes. That Jason Melville was one of my clients? Yes. That I'm dating Derek Ambrose? It's complicated."

"Habibi," her mother said, using the Arabic term of endearment from London's childhood.

London broke. The tears coursed down her face and she bit her lip to keep from making any sound, but deep in her chest a wail began to rise, pressing hard against her ribs, screaming to be released, set free, liberated after ten long, hard years.

"My heart hurts for you," Farrah continued. "Please let me help you somehow. Let me take this burden from you. Whatever happened in the past we can figure it out later. For now, let me help. I can give you money, I can hire lawyers, I can take you away from all of this. We'll go on a vacation somewhere. Anything you want."

London could feel it all breaking wide open—the tremor of it as the foundation of what she'd thought was cast in concrete, a permanent wall around her heart, began to split in two. It was terrifying, and yet she craved it as if it were a drug.

"I don't think so, Mom," she gritted out around the mass in her throat. "I can't. Not now."

Her mother made one of those tiny breathy sounds again, and when she spoke her voice cracked. "Okay. I understand. I won't push you. Ever. I'll never push you to do something you don't want. But can I call again? In a few days maybe? Just to see how you are. Will you take my call? Please." Desperation exploded from the single word, as Farrah made a sharp, pained sound on the other end of the call.

That sound was the straw that sent London's self-control over the edge. She sobbed once, the tears coming faster, catching her breath nearly impossible. "Yes." She nodded her head emphatically, even though no one could see her. "Yes. Call again. I'll pick up. I have to go now." She needed to end this before it ended her.

"Okay, Habibi. I will talk to you soon. Please take care of my daughter."

London choked on another sob and disconnected the call, collapsing on the floor in a flood of tears and pain that had built over a decade. And in the back of her mind, she wondered yet again how she'd allowed any of this to happen.

**

The summons from Melville came at nearly five p.m., and Derek had to shove down the irritation that it was going to extend his day away from London by at least two hours. As he stood in the hospital elevator he couldn't help but think that the Senator might have timed it to minimize the press pursuit. The nightly newscasts were live at dinnertime, and the day and night reporting staffs were still switching off shifts. There was a lull, and in fact only two reporters were stationed outside the hospital and neither of them seemed to have noticed Derek coming in.

When he reached Melville's room Derek showed his ID to the secret service agents stationed outside the door. The Department of Homeland Security had assigned the early protection for Melville within hours of his shooting. The agents approved Derek's entry and he looked through the window in the door to see Melville sitting up in bed with a TV remote in his hand.

"Knock-knock," Derek called out as he stuck his head inside the doorway. "You ready for a visitor?"

"Derek. Come right on in," Melville answered.

Derek walked to the bed and shook Melville's hand. "You're looking much better today. How do you feel?"

"Better. Nowhere near a hundred percent, but better. Grab a chair, let's talk about what comes next."

Derek nodded and scooted an armchair closer to the bed as Melville turned the television to mute.

"The doctors are saying I'll be out in a week."

"That's great. What's the recovery look like from that point?"

"They've said if I hold it to three or four hours a day I can work from home the first couple of weeks. Then they'll reassess but they're expecting I can go back fulltime at that point."

"Okay. That's all workable. Do you want to talk about schedules and what we can plan from that point out?" Derek asked, feeling like his head was back in the game for the first time since that gunman had taken aim at Melville.

Melville shifted slightly on the bed, wincing in discomfort as he did.

"Derek, I think we need to talk bigger picture than that first."

"Okay. Are you rethinking the bid for office? It would be perfectly understandable if you were, but I'll tell you that I still think we can win this."

Melville sighed. "And I appreciate that. You need to know that I have the greatest respect for your instincts and your talents. I wouldn't be making this run if it weren't for you encouraging me."

Derek knew what was coming, even as the blood rushed through his head and the adrenaline spiked in his extremities. "But."

Melville leveled a look at him. Both men knew what needed to be said and neither of them wanted to have to do it.

"I've been talking to my friend who runs the polling outfit. He's run some quick and dirty surveys for me, and we've discovered that the shooting has actually swept a great deal of the negative image from the sex scandal away. If I apologize profusely, with Angela at my side, get counseling, that sort of thing, I think I can continue this campaign now, whereas before the shooting I don't think I could have."

Derek opened his mouth to agree wholeheartedly, but Melville raised his hand to silence him.

"But I think your affiliation with London has become too damaging." As Derek began to snarl a response, Melville held up his hand again. "Just wait. I realize you only have an affiliation with her because of me." He cleared his throat. "It was ill-advised on my part, and I know that none of us would be in this position if I'd kept it in my pants. But the fact is I can't change that now."

"So instead you'll have me take the fall for you then dump me?" Derek gritted out.

"No. I'm hoping that since you've only done this to protect me you won't have any problem dropping her. It's time, Derek. Cut her loose, tell everyone how sorry you are for lying about her, then take me on to the White House."

Derek stared at the man he'd thought could be President of the United States and blinked. He might not have breathed for a full minute before his lungs finally kicked back into action.

"And what happens to her?" he asked quietly when he'd regained his voice.

Melville shrugged. "I assume she goes back to her life. I'm not sure I really understand the question."

"We've blown up her life. I realize you didn't know this, but she's had a double life. She's been an upstanding, lunch and volunteer kind of woman. She had friends and colleagues who had no idea she was an escort all these years. Now everyone knows. She's been outed and she can't go anywhere without people recognizing her, in addition to the fact that until the police catch whoever shot at you she might not be safe."

Melville looked marginally uncomfortable. "I'm sorry about that, but I'm not sure how continuing to be involved with us helps that. I mean sure, we can give her some security for a bit while the police figure this shooting out, but other than that? You can't be seen with her anymore—I mean Jesus, Derek, they have a shot of you leaving her house at seven o'clock in the morning."

Derek stood and began pacing. "If I'm around she's got my protection in more ways than one. I can keep security on her, go places with her if she needs it, and continue to impress on the public that she's no longer working as an escort."

Melville shook his head. "I admire your chivalry, and believe me, I know she's gorgeous—"

Derek's fist clenched and his eyes narrowed.

"—but you're not lifting her up. *She's* pulling *you* down. And when you sink, the whole campaign sinks with you. It's time to cut our losses. You can salvage your career and the campaign, but only if you disassociate yourself from her for good."

"No."

"Come on, quit being so damn honorable. It's not like she's really your girlfriend. Did you start fucking her or something? I can't blame you if you did, but seriously, there are plenty of other women—women who won't destroy both of us—for you to sleep with, plus they won't cost you a dime. I'll introduce you to some. Angela's got lots of single friends who are plenty friendly."

Derek went cold, from head to toe, a frost that spread, from his ice chip eyes to his leaden feet. He walked back to Melville's bed and leaned down, inches from the Senator's face. His voice was soft, but deadly, and he saw the spark of fear that crossed Melville's eyes.

"You don't need to worry about firing me, Jason. You can consider this my resignation. I'll expect my full severance pay within the next thirty days per the terms of our contract."

"Shit. Derek, come on…"

Derek was already halfway to the door. He stopped and turned to look at Melville over his shoulder.

"For what it's worth, I've never paid her. Never had to. And you won't find another man in the country who can say the same. It's a very exclusive club."

"Goddammit, don't do this, Derek!" Melville yelled as Derek walked out of the room.

By the time he reached the elevator he had his phone out and speed dial number one punched.

"Hi. Can you call everyone? We need to have a meeting."

**

Kamal slammed a hand against the wood paneling of the Powerplay condo. The entire wall shook, and Derek thought briefly that it was lucky they didn't have anything hanging there, it would have never survived.

"Are you out of your mind?" Kamal shouted.

"Take a breath friend," Teague admonished mildly.

The instruction was meant for Kamal, but Derek followed the advice himself, breathing deeply before he answered.

"No, but I'm also no one's patsy. I let Melville dictate to me like that and I've lost all credibility. Everyone knows that you don't hire me to be your yes man. I'm a *consultant*, not an employee. No one tells me what the strategy should be, I tell them, and while I work with them on it, ultimately I decide. Or I walk. Which is what happened today."

Scott rested a hip against the pool table and casually sent a red ball careening against a yellow one before stuffing his hands in his front pockets, adopting a very nonchalant pose. He looked like he could be a model in a men's magazine, his blonde hair mussed, lean physique displayed to dapper perfection under his expensive dress shirt and designer tie.

"Obviously Derek feels strongly about this, Kamal. He's a big boy, if he thinks Melville was pushing him in an untenable direction then we need to respect that."

"Thank you." Derek nodded sharply at Scott before turning back to Kamal. He hated fighting with his best friend, but if Kamal didn't get his Egyptian spoiled rich kid under control things weren't going to end well.

Kamal jabbed a finger into the air while glaring at Derek. "You're daring to bring up your credibility? You've now told the entire world that you're dating a hooker, that you lied to the American people, and that you'd abandon a candidate you purported to believe in while he's lying in a hospital after an assassination attempt. And somehow you think by doing all of that you're protecting your credibility? I repeat, have you lost your fucking mind?"

Teague, lounging on the sofa, both arms spread across the back, gave Derek a look of concern. "When he puts it like that…"

"Shut up," Derek snarled. He knew Kamal had a well-reasoned argument, and his gut clenched at hearing it all laid out like that. But his heart knew that he'd do it all over again. He'd take any hit, endure any insult, quit any job, if it meant protecting London. That fact scared the shit out of him. And took the wind out of his sails.

He shook his head, feeling suddenly exhausted and sluggish. He just wanted to go to bed. Preferably with London.

"Okay, yes, when you put it like that. But I still can't do what he wanted me to. I don't think it's the right thing, for the campaign or for me, and definitely not for London. If it were to get around that I'd let a client dictate to me like that I'd be fighting these types of battles for the next decade. My success depends on the candidates thinking I'm the expert. I lead, they follow, it's as simple as that."

Kamal leaned against the wall, arms crossed, expression mutinous.

Teague stood and walked to the pool table where his jacket lay, picking it up and donning the perfectly tailored item.

"I agree. I'm in a similar business, Kamal, and you can't let the clients start running the show, it's like turning the asylum over to the inmates. So what's done is done, and there's no point crying over spilt milk. The press has a very short attention span. When they hear that Derek's no longer with the campaign they'll raise a fuss for a few days then move on. You—" he pointed at Derek, "are the one who'll have to deal with the fallout from this, and it'll be three months from now. I think you know that. I think you realize that you're not going to have a waiting list for clients the way you have. You're going to have to convince the party that you're trustworthy again, and that might take some time."

Scott grunted in agreement, and Derek nodded. As much as it hurt, he knew Teague was right. It was the price to be paid here, so he'd pay it.

"In the meantime, I'll get with Melville's attorney to make sure the contract terms are fulfilled. I've already contacted him to insist we issue a joint press release so that they can't spin it in their favor. If I have to get Judge Fries to issue an injunction to prevent them from speaking to the press until we've settled the details then I'll do that."

"Thank you," Derek told Teague. "But before you go, I've got something else."

"You realize you're being incredibly needy this month?" Scott asked, grinning.

Kamal scoffed from his corner where he continued to pout.

"Yes, thank you," Derek answered. "But this matters, to all of us. It's a point of pride, and also some insurance for the future." He began to pace. "We still have the issue of who leaked all of this to the press, and we're in possession of some really strange information about Williams. I don't want to let that go. For one thing, Melville was shot. If this is related to that in any way we need to know. The police need to know. I don't want the little fucker walking around the capital thinking he got away with bringing me down, or worse, trying to kill a United States Senator."

Kamal pushed off the wall and moved to the bar where he poured himself a generous glass of vodka. "Finally, some sense." He took a swig.

"Ah, the scent of revenge," Teague joked. "Nothing wakes up your inner Ghazi like the blood of an enemy, huh?"

"My inner Ghazi might decide to take a little blood from you if you're not careful," Kamal snarled before turning to Derek. "We have too many threads leading to Williams for it to sit right with me. I think we need to make sure we know exactly what's gone on or it may come back to bite us later." He paused. "And I also think we should look into London again."

Scott and Teague both groaned at the same time Derek went off the rails. "Goddammit! We've been over this and over it. She's not a threat, she didn't sell out Melville. I've offered her money, she turned me down. We're not going to waste everyone's time chasing after something that doesn't exist."

Kamal scowled, but kept his mouth shut.

"So, Williams," Derek continued, rolling his neck to one side as it made a loud cracking sound.

"Why don't I get one of my interns to stalk him?" Scott suggested. "I'll tell him it's part of an inside game, have him follow Williams around for a few days, see where he goes, who he talks to."

Derek nodded, that would keep track of Williams for a few days while they followed the link between Nick Patterson and Williams. "That's great. And I'm going to go directly to Nick. Sit down and simply ask him what business he's got with Williams. No point in beating around the bush, and I've suddenly got some extra time on my hands."

Teague opened the door before turning to face the rest of them. "As usual we're leaving one of Derek's meetings with plenty of extra work." He winked. "Now, I don't know about the rest of you assholes, but I've got a date, and she's a lot more interesting than all of this."

Derek grinned, and his mind flashed to an image of London sprawled naked in bed. "Meeting adjourned," he barked before striding to the door right behind Teague.

CHAPTER XII

"Shall I park here, ma'am?" the security guard asked as London sat in the back seat of the car he drove for her.

"Yes. I'm not going in, I just, um, need to sit here for a few minutes."

"Whatever you need ma'am. Take your time. I'll get out and stretch my legs a bit."

London silently thanked her obviously savvy guard for his discretion as he exited the car and leaned against the driver's door, alert but also relaxed.

She looked across the street at the two-story townhouse with its ornate ironwork fence surrounding the front yard and the generous porch. Iron also formed a sweet Juliet balcony on the second floor. London looked up at the French doors that opened onto the balcony and remembered standing there in the evenings, watching people walk their dogs, children playing on the sidewalk, workers coming and going to the nearby trendy commercial district. It was a narrow residential street, but connected two larger thoroughfares so it got a fair amount of foot traffic.

The leaves of the small ornamental maple tree in the front yard had turned red and were beginning to fall to the grass beneath. London could almost smell the pumpkin bread that her mother used to bake in the fall, full of the traditional spices as well as cardamom—

Farrah's Middle Eastern proclivities surfaced in her baking. The smell of the spices used to fill the house and when London would come home from school her mother would have left a warm loaf waiting for her, always making sure London came home to something welcoming even when Farrah herself had to be at the University working.

There was a shift in the light and the glass door in the center of the porch opened. London's breath caught and she leaned toward the window of the car, feeling like there was a cord attached to her midsection pulling her toward the brick house.

Farrah came outside, going to the mailbox that hung from the porch railing. Her dark hair had small streaks of gray in it that hadn't been there ten years ago. But it was still thick and shiny, tendrils falling around her face where they'd slipped the clip that held it into an upsweep in the back.

London looked at her mother with what could only be described as hunger. Her eyes roamed over every inch of the woman who had devoted a life to her daughter for seventeen years. Farrah's face was still beautiful, nearly unlined, but there was a tightness around her mouth that said she hadn't smiled much in a long time, and a shard of guilt pierced London's chest, creating a pain so sharp she had to catch her breath before she could move to rub at the spot with the heel of her hand.

Farrah wore the loose flowing silk pants that she'd always donned for work, a fine knit sweater clinging to her curves that were so very like London's. Around her neck was a vibrant scarf, a swirl of pinks, purples, teal, and black that gave the ensemble a flair uniquely Farrah's. London put a hand to her mouth trying to contain the sob that waited to pour forth when she realized that she had given that scarf to her mother on the last Mother's Day they had celebrated together when London was a junior in high school.

Farrah stood, one foot on the top of the porch steps, and one a step lower as she shuffled through the mail. London realized that one of her own hands was pressed against the cool glass of the car window, and her entire body had moved inches closer to the door, that cord tugging ever tighter.

"Mom," London whispered. "Why did this have to happen?"

As if she could sense her daughter's presence, Farrah's head shot up and she looked sharply at the car across the street, her gaze landing firmly on the window out of which London watched. London recoiled for a moment, but then she reminded herself that the car windows were heavily tinted and there was no way Farrah could have seen into the interior. She noticed the security guard shift so that he was turned sideways to the car, resting his arm casually along the roof and simultaneously blocking any view of London in the back seat. A cell phone had appeared in his hand and he looked as if he was one of a thousand hired car drivers in the city, waiting for a client. His act was obviously convincing, because Farrah turned back to her mail, going inside the house a few moments later.

As soon as she was gone, the guard opened the driver's door and slid in behind the wheel.

"Mr. Ambrose is waiting for you, ma'am. Are you ready to go?"

London wasn't sure that she could speak, her heart was so fractured, pieces spearing into her chest wall and rubbing against one another at the same time. The pain was visceral and incapacitating. She nodded once and that seemed to be sufficient for the guard as he started the engine and pulled out onto the street. They drove away from the house that had once been London's safe place, and she could only think that maybe it was time to go home.

**

London was surprised to find that the guard took her to the back of a brownstone in Georgetown rather than her own house.

"Where are we?" she asked, not sure if she should be worried or merely irritated.

"Mr. Ambrose's home."

Before she could process that, Derek was at the door of the car, reaching in to take her hand.

She got out of the car and looked at him, one eyebrow raised, arms crossed.

He smirked and leaned down to whisper in her ear, "Don't pout, this is one of your lessons. You can't always be in control, gorgeous. Now that there are reporters at your house too there's no reason to spend all of our time there."

"It would have been polite to ask. What if I needed something at my house, or had plans of some sort?"

"Did you?" he asked as he took her hand and started to lead her toward the open garage that took up the back of the house.

"That's beside the point," she snapped. She knew he was right, but she didn't have to like it.

Derek led her past his Porsche as well as a vintage motorcycle, chrome gleaming beneath its black leather seat and saddlebags.

"Do you belong to a gang?" London joked, pointing to the bike.

"As a matter of fact…" Derek let the sentence trail off, and suddenly London had a memory of his friends at the press conference he'd arranged when he announced he was dating her. She opened her mouth then closed it again, not sure what exactly she meant to ask or say.

"I'll tell you about it some other time," Derek said, before opening the door to the house and leading her into a spotless and obviously unused kitchen.

As soon as the door closed behind them Derek had her in his arms, his lips pressed to hers. London felt any residual irritation at being 'handled' melt away beneath his hot and heavy assault.

His lips crushed hers and his hands clasped her waist, his fingers squeezing her hips with a pressure just short of pain. He bent his knees to grind his semi-erect cock against her pelvis and groaned as his tongue snaked out and stroked hers.

Her mind whirled in a dizzying mixture of sounds, sensations and feelings. There was heat, aching want, the scent of his desire and his citrus cologne. His hands wrapped around her waist and he lifted her onto the cool granite countertop, sliding between her legs so that her core was against his now very erect cock.

He pulled away briefly. "I had the worst day I can remember ever having, and I don't want to push you past where you're comfortable, but I need you so badly I feel like I'm being torn in two."

She stroked his cheek, feeling the five o'clock shadow that had sprouted there. "I had a bad day too. And I hurt." She placed his palm against her breast over her heart. "Right here. But when I'm with you, it all goes away. I want to be here for you like that."

He tilted his head into her touch, his eyes closing in surrender. "Don't let me hurt you."

"You would never," she answered quietly.

"I don't want you to shut me out—not like the others." He swallowed uncomfortably and her stomach turned at the thought of Derek and her clients in the same moment.

"Don't," she told him, placing a finger against his lips. "I can't *not* feel when I'm with you. When you touch me it's like a fire tears through me. That's what's scary. I feel *so* much, and I can't control it, and I'm not used to that. You could never, never be like those other men, Derek. They weren't even men to me, just machines, and I was the mechanic sent to give them a tune up. You're flesh and blood and heat. You're everything human and male and you make me feel things I've never felt. Not even before…" She arched into his lips and the next words came out on a breathy sigh. "Before all of this."

He skimmed his hands under her top, caressing her skin with feather light touches while his mouth fused to hers, teeth and tongues and lips crashing against one another. He nipped and licked and sucked until she was utterly breathless, and all the while his fingertips explored her bare skin, seeking, learning, memorizing.

At last he pulled back and tugged her top over her head before unhooking her bra and sliding it down her arms. His eyes were flaming as he took in her naked torso, and she realized that no matter how much lust men had looked at her with over the years, she had never seen one look at her like Derek did.

As if he could read her mind he said, "It's because I want *all* of you." She watched him, not sure what he was trying to tell her.

"The reason you *feel* with me—it's because I want all of you. Not just your body. I want your mind—your thoughts, your dreams. I want your soul—your fears and cares. I want *all* of you, London Sharpe. And you can feel it, how badly I want every piece of you."

And in that moment, London became his. He was the dream she'd never dared have, the fantasy she hadn't been able to entertain. He was the future she'd given up at seventeen, and the hope she'd tucked away in a secret drawer, hidden from even her own eyes. And now, as her heart disobeyed every instruction she'd given to it over the last decade, and her soul fluttered against the bars she'd trapped it behind, her mind told her that this wasn't possible. *He* wasn't possible, *it* wasn't possible, because London held on to something deep and dark in that same secret drawer, it was the lock that kept the drawer closed and it was something that ruined men like Derek.

But she didn't have the strength to turn away from him. She couldn't bear the idea of being alone again, not after feeling so much. She wanted every piece of him too, and though she knew she could never really have him, she desperately wanted to pretend for just a bit longer. She shoved the truth away, tamped her conscience down harder, and gave herself over to the feelings—the butterflies in her stomach, the heat curling in her core, and yes, even the piercing pain in her chest.

"I want you to make love to me," she gasped. "I don't want to be afraid anymore. I want to feel it all."

His breath was hot and heavy and he dug his fingers into her hair and tugged her head back to look into her eyes. "Are you sure you're ready for that?"

"No, but I need you anyway."

"I'll go slow. If you want me to stop, say so. Just like last time."

"No." She knew that wasn't what she needed. She wanted him too badly, and their time was too short. He could be gone at any moment for so many different reasons she couldn't list them all, and if she lost him before giving him every part of her that she could, she'd never recover. "You have to push me harder. It's a physical reaction not an emotional one, I want to be with you, there's no question in my mind. I want you to do it."

He made a small choking sound and pulled back from her. His brows drew together before he turned and took a step away. "What are you asking me to do?"

She breathed deeply. "Fuck me no matter what I do or say."

He faced her, fierce heat pouring from every inch of him. "Absolutely not." He stepped back to her and took her chin in his fingers, his face inches from hers. "I would never do that to you. I'm not a goddamn rapist, London."

Her face heated and she felt such shame she broke their gaze. "That's why I'm asking you to push me harder. I know you'd never hurt me, but if you don't force me I'm not sure I'll ever be able to finish it."

"No," he said again, his eyes softening now, pain seeping through the anger. "I don't care if you never get there. It doesn't matter. We'll do what you're comfortable with, nothing more. You're far too precious to me to risk hurting any part of you—your mind, your heart, or your body."

Her eyes prickled with tears of frustration. How could she make him understand? This might be the only chance she ever had to share it with him. Sooner or later it would all have to end and she would regret it for the rest of her life if she didn't take this one fleeting shot at something real.

"Please," she begged. "Please help me, Derek. I want to be with you so badly it hurts everywhere. I don't think it'll stop hurting until I've given you everything. Take away that pain."

He sighed, gently brushing a strand of hair away from her face.

"A compromise then…"

She nodded rapidly.

"A safe word. I won't stop unless you say the safe word."

The breath left her in a rush of relief. "Yes. Yes, it's perfect. Thank you." She leaned forward and pressed a soft kiss to his lips, her heart lodging in her throat and her entire body trembling in anticipation.

**

Derek was a tangled mess of want and shock. Force her? Fuck no. He had never touched a woman who wasn't begging for it. Even as a teenager, he'd known to look for the signs that a girl was not just tolerating it, but an enthusiastic participant. He had no interest in doing things *to* a woman, he wanted to do them *with* her. Nothing turned him on as much as his partner being turned on. The breathy moans, the questing hands, seeking tongues, and writhing bodies of women were what did it for him. And men who didn't give a shit about a woman's wishes deserved to be strung up by their balls from the nearest tree.

But what the hell was he supposed to do with a woman who said what she wanted most was for him to force her? He was torn in two. Unable to hurt her—either by denying her something, or by forcing himself on her.

"Pomegranate," she said softly.

He blinked at her. The safe word. They were going to do this, and he was going to force things until or unless she said, pomegranate.

"Really?" he asked, unable to keep a small smile from his lips in spite of the seriousness of the moment.

"It's my favorite fruit and definitely not a word that's said normally during such activities."

He chuckled and shook his head. "Pomegranate it is then." He brushed the backs of his fingers across her downy soft cheek. "Please don't hesitate to use it. There have to be other ways to work on this. We could do some research—"

She thrust her breasts against his chest and wrapped her legs around his hips, wiggling closer to his erection. "This is what I want," she whispered. "Now quit talking and fuck me."

Derek was a prince among men, but he was still a man, and when a half naked sexy as hell woman twined herself around him and asked him to fuck her, he felt obligated to comply. He lifted her off of the countertop, locking his lips to hers at the same time. His minimalist décor made walking through the house while ravishing a woman relatively easy, and he quickly navigated them to the living room where he lowered her to the Flokati rug in front of the fireplace and kneeled over her, stripping off his own shirt and tie before peeling down her leggings and panties.

She was laid out like a buffet beneath him, her golden skin glowing in the low light that spilled in from the adjacent kitchen. Her breasts were full and tipped with dusky nipples, her waist narrow and her hips perfectly rounded before dropping to those long, slender legs.

"It was your legs," he said, running his hands along her thighs.

"What?" she gasped, squirming a little as his touch tickled her.

"The first I saw of you was your legs. They were the best looking pair I've ever seen—and I'm a leg man, so I know about these things." He leaned down and kissed high on the inside of one thigh.

"But I'm also a breast man..." He licked around one nipple, then took it in his mouth, sucking it for a moment before releasing it and moving on to do the same to the other side.

Her breathing was rapid, but he could tell it was from arousal and not panic. He leaned down, a mere whisper from her swollen lips. "Then you turned around and I saw that ass."

His voice was husky with want, and she opened her eyes to watch him, her tongue darting out to wet her lips. "Now I think I'm an ass man too."

She chuckled and raised her head to kiss him hard and fast. He rubbed his cheek against hers, and she shivered, her hands going to his ass and palming him through his pants.

"I'm going to lick that beautiful pussy of yours now," he whispered. "And I'm going to make sure that you enjoy every wet, slick, second of it."

If her moan was any indication, she was convinced.

He grasped both her ankles, placing her feet flat on the floor and spreading her open. God, she was so wet his cock throbbed in anticipation. Heart racing, he wrapped one arm around her thigh and lowered his hand to spread her open so he could lick up her juicy center. She tasted tart and sweet at the same time, and he licked her again, circling her clit with the tip of his tongue.

Her breathing grew erratic and he could feel the muscles in her legs tense.

Lifting his head he growled, "Are you okay, gorgeous? Do you need me to stop?"

"No...don't...stop...please," she gasped between breaths. Her face and jaw were set and he could see she was struggling, but he let her have the say, and went back to business. And what a business it was. He sucked on her clit, licked along her center, alternately thrusting inside of her with his tongue and his fingers. He could feel that tiny rough patch of skin in her channel, and he stroked it, noticing the way her hips canted in rhythm with his thrusts.

His thumb pressed down on her clit, and two of his fingers were inside of her as he nibbled along the world's softest skin at the apex of her thighs, when suddenly she sat up. He bolted upright with her, his hand still between her legs. She was gasping for breath, her eyes wide, pulse racing under the delicate skin of her neck. He tried to move his hand, prepared to back far away until she could calm down. But then her own hand shot down between her legs, her fingers closing over his to hold them in place, and she managed to gasp out a strained, "no" before her entire body froze for a split second, and she tossed her head back, screaming out her release as she throbbed and pulsed around his fingers.

Derek stayed inside her while the soft, swollen flesh contracted around his fingers, and his dick surged with need, the drive to fall on top of her and start thrusting an overwhelming urge. But then London's sobs brought him out of the haze of lust, and he sat back on his ass, pulling her onto his lap as she collapsed in a slick, soft heap.

"Shh, shh, shh," he hushed, his own eyes stinging with an ache for her pain. "Don't cry, gorgeous. Don't cry. I won't ever push you again. I'm so sorry. I should never have agreed. It's going to be okay."

Her head bobbed up and down against his chest and her breaths came in little hiccups like a child who'd cried too hard.

His heart hurt. Worse than it had when he played the soccer game against Dartmouth in college, worse than it had when he found out Melville's affair had been exposed. No, this was a pain that went deeper than his heart, it went to his very soul, and he thought that this time the pain really would kill him.

She finally tipped her head up, and even though her face was wet and pink, and she was still hiccupping, she was also smiling, grinning really.

"I know it's going to be fine. I did it, I made it through. And I'm still here. The world didn't collapse, you didn't get up and walk away, and it feels so good. You feel so good."

"You're okay?" He looked at her in disbelief.

"Better than okay," she said, her voice husky from the tears. "I was panicking, but I didn't stop, I didn't let it conquer me. *You* didn't let it conquer me."

He gazed at her, and the relief surged inside him. "You...happy?"

She threw her arms around his neck and kissed him over and over. "Yes. These are tears of joy, tears of gratitude. Thank you, thank you."

He finally relaxed, his whole body warming under her enthusiasm. Chuckling, he took her cheeks between his palms. "Slow down, gorgeous. Let me absorb this and catch up here." He ran his thumbs across her lips as they curled into a smile. "You feel better? You're fine?"

"So much better than fine," she whispered, her gaze tender.

He brought his lips to hers, and kissed her, knowing that he'd just handed something to this woman that he'd never get back. But he'd given it willingly, and he trusted her to keep it safe. He believed in what she and he could do together, in what they could be together. And he was going to enjoy the hell out of showing it all to her.

**

London's heart beat a tattoo as Derek's kisses grew exponentially hotter and harder. But this time it was a tattoo of excitement, arousal, and anticipation. She was high off the triumph of conquering the panic. She'd gotten all the usual signs—the fluttering, squeezing heart, the inability to catch her breath, the dizziness and head rush—but then she'd thought of Derek, the way he was gentle when she was scared, protective even if she fought against it, the way he'd been so patient with her when she couldn't do the most normal of things—have sex with a man she cared about.

And when she thought of him, and she felt the things he was doing to her body at that very moment, the feelings took over the panic, and she was finally able to stop thinking, stop running. The way he made her feel—his touch, his kiss, the heat in his eyes—her fears crumbled, and the pleasure took over, washing through her like a tsunami that left a new landscape, one where Derek stood tall in the center, and her heartbeat was the only sound that mattered.

Now she felt it all building again, the arousal, the aching need, but not the fear, and she knew that she was ready. And she also knew that it was time to show Derek exactly how he affected her.

"You're still far too dressed," she whispered, licking up his neck and coasting her palms over his muscled chest.

"I can fix that," he groaned, gripping her ass and pulling her closer to him.

She pulled away and crawled to her knees, her hands going to his belt buckle. He rose onto his own knees to give her more leverage as she undid the clasp, sliding the leather from his pants and dangling it above her head. "I know something very interesting to do with this." She grinned at him.

He licked his lips, an evil gleam in his eyes. "I'm all yours. And I don't even need a safe word," he growled.

"Take those pants off first."

He complied, taking a condom out of his wallet at the same time and laying it on the hearth before lowering himself to the rug in front of her.

"Now what, boss?"

Her heart soared realizing he was going to play along with her. This was different than the kind of control she had when she serviced clients. That control was all about making them *feel* like *they* were in control, like they were amazing sex machines that she couldn't resist. This was the polar opposite, her taking the symbolic control when she knew damn well that Derek wielded the real control. He was ceding it to her because he cared enough to want her to be happy, but he already ruled both her body and her heart. It was thrilling and sweet all at once. A lethal combination.

She looked at him thoughtfully then said, "I think I want you on your back. Right about there." She pointed at the rug, near one of the end tables that flanked the fireplace. He chuckled and lay down on his back, folding his hands over his terribly tempting abs.

She grasped his wrists and wound the belt around them before raising his arms over his head and buckling the belt around the leg of the end table.

"Comfortable?" she asked, running her eyes down to his hard cock that rested against his belly, the tip shiny and swollen.

"Not in the slightest," he answered, his voice gruff and needy. "Why don't you help me with that?"

She muttered, "Gladly" and straddled him as she put her tongue to good use on all that beautiful muscle he must exercise like a fiend to build. She laved his nipples, eliciting a set of moans from him that were gratifying. Then she stroked down his abs, making sure to put her tongue into every bump and groove of the six-pack that led to paradise. She let her hands roam, feeling his taut quads, his thick pecs and those glorious biceps that she could curl her fingers around over and over again.

When her lips reached the trail of hair that led to his cock she skated them over the skin and rubbed her breasts against his thighs, her hands resting over his pecs.

"Holy hell," he gasped and the table he was tethered to jerked, sending a vase crashing to the floor.

"Behave," she admonished.

"I'll buy a new one," he gritted out as her tongue finally reached his cock and she licked up the side like it was a lollipop.

She grasped the hard, thick shaft in one hand and pressed her lips to the tip, swirling her tongue around the head, tasting salt and something dark and rich that was all Derek.

"Fuck, I want to touch you," he complained as his hips canted up toward her mouth.

"Not yet," she answered, infusing her voice with as much school teacher as she could while she ached so much for his touch.

Then she took him deep in her mouth and he nearly shot off the floor. She couldn't help but smile as he groaned in suffering. If there was one thing London knew how to do it was give a blowjob, and she proceeded to prove her skills to him as she set up a rhythm with both her mouth and her hand, stroking up and down in wet, hot synchrony until he was so tense beneath her she knew he was about to snap.

She grasped his balls in her free hand and suddenly there was a crash as the end table that held her captor captive went tumbling over. Within seconds his hands were digging into her hair and he was pulling her up his body. His wrists were still strapped together but it didn't seem to hinder him in any way as he tugged her across his chest and crushed his lips to hers, his breath coming fast and hard. She moaned when his tongue invaded her mouth and he devoured her.

In a flash he had them flipped and she was on her back under him, one of his knees wedged between her legs. He thrust gently against her thigh, chuckling as he took one of her nipples into her mouth.

"Sorry," he muttered between sucks and licks, "I'm better at being in charge."

"Oh yes." She pushed shamelessly into his mouth. "That works too."

He planted open-mouthed kisses along her smooth abdomen, then sat up on his haunches, wiggling one hand out of the belt, then pulling the whole strap loose and tossing it aside. Watching her with dark eyes he reached to the fireplace hearth and grabbed the condom, tearing it with his teeth before rolling it on and stroking himself up and down with his large fist.

"You good with this?" he said in a low voice.

"Better than good," she answered, watching him and thinking that he might be the most beautiful man she'd ever seen.

He slowly lowered himself between her legs then and gently, smoothly slid inside of her. She lay quietly then and let herself feel every tiny sensation, every point of pressure, every tingle and ache. It was something she hadn't done in so many years she couldn't recall the last time. Because with clients at this point she would have shut off, moaning on cue, letting them thrust and pant, as she recounted the grocery shopping or lunch appointment she'd planned for the next day. Because if she let down for even a moment she would never have been able to stand it. The invasion, the reality that she was only a vessel, not a person, the possibility that she might inadvertently be aroused when she didn't know, much less like, the man. She had steeled herself against every bit of it, and now, she was free.

Finally free.

Free because she wanted to be there with Derek no matter what, wanted to experience every moment with him, as part of this thing that was bigger than either of them alone.

"You with me?" he whispered in her ear before he kissed her cheek gently.

"Yes. I'm here."

"Good. Because this is us, remember that. Derek and London."

"So good," she gasped, as he pressed even deeper into her.

"Fucking spectacular," he answered before he pumped harder, while he looked down into her face. She couldn't turn away from him. His blue eyes held her gaze with such devotion and heat her heart nearly burst out of her chest.

He hooked his arm under one of her knees, his hips pistoning against hers over and over. The change in position allowed him to sink deeper into her and the pressure in her core built quickly.

"You make me feel like I've died and gone to heaven," he told her, his gaze roaming over her features.

Her eyes slid shut and she shifted to get greater friction against her clit. "Close," she whispered.

He bent his head down, grazed his lips across hers, and she exploded. Behind her eyelids the world was covered in a spray of stars and fireworks as her deepest parts clutched at him and sucked him in until he was crying out her name, his breath hot on her neck and his big body shuddering above hers.

When the last wave rolled through them, Derek collapsed on top of her, his lips pressed to her neck, his hands wound into her hair. Her heart beat strong and hard inside her chest and she briefly thought that if she died tonight she wouldn't regret it because she had finally done something right with her life.

CHAPTER XIII

Derek felt like a teenage boy who'd just discovered sex. All he could think about was London—sex with London. He made love to her three times before they finally collapsed in front of the fireplace and slept for a few hours. When he woke at nearly four a.m. with a stiff neck from sleeping on the floor, he scooped her up, carried her to his bed, and made her scream his name one more time.

Now it was nine o'clock, the latest he'd slept in years, and he knew Renee would wonder where the hell he was, but he didn't give a damn, he just wanted to get inside of London again.

"You're staring," she mumbled without opening an eye.

He nuzzled her cheek and growled.

"And you're thinking very dirty thoughts Mr. Ambrose."

"How do you know that?" His hand slipped beneath the sheets and he found the sweet curve of the underside of her breast.

She moaned and wriggled. "I think the first clue was that large package pressed against my hip." He chuckled. "Not so subtle, hmm?"

The sound of his phone ringing interrupted her response.

"Hell," he muttered, taking a deep whiff of the spicy scent in her hair. "I've been dreading this."

She rolled over and snatched his phone off the nightstand before handing it to him. "I'll go make some coffee," she whispered before she climbed out of the bed and pulled on one of his discarded dress shirts. He watched her walk out the door, phone still ringing in his hand, a grin on his face. When he finally looked down at the screen his smile melted away like chocolate in the hot summer sun.

"I wish I could say 'good morning', but I know it won't be if you're calling already."

"Considering you jettisoned your whole career yesterday, not to mention a presidential campaign eighteen months in the making, I find it hard to believe you would have had a good morning no matter what." Derek stood and went to the dresser to get a pair of sweats, donning them commando as he held the phone between his ear and shoulder.

"If you only called to bitch about my choices, we may as well hang up right now."

Kamal sighed deeply on the other end of the call. "No, although you do need to hear some sense about throwing away fifteen years' worth of work for a woman you've known a month."

"Kamal," Derek warned.

"I have new information on Nick Patterson's wife." Derek walked into the adjoining bathroom and spread toothpaste on his toothbrush. "Give it to me," he said around the toothbrush he shoved in his mouth.

"It appears that she might have a gambling problem."

Derek spit, wiping the back of his wrist across his mouth. "What? That can't be."

"It sure looks that way. She was visiting the Bel Air Casino several times a week for the last year and a half or so."

"And I'm guessing she lost."

"A lot."

Shit. Derek ran a hand across his unshaven jaw. "So now the question is whether her gambling is somehow mixed up in all of this?"

"Exactly. On the face of it there's no reason to think it's all linked, but you and I both know that you have to follow every lead no matter how unlikely."

"Okay. I've got lunch with Nick today. I'll see what I can find out from him."

There was a pause on the other end of the call, and all Derek could hear was Kamal's breath and the background noises of staff talking in the embassy offices.

"I assume she's there with you?" Kamal asked, his voice low.

"Not in the room, but in the house, yes." Derek felt his blood pressure rise as he prepared to battle his best friend. It seemed that lately that was all they did.

"I want to run a deeper background check on her mother," Kamal said briskly.

"That's not necessary." Derek's response was sharp.

"Yes. It is. We know nothing about them before they landed here in the States. London was only two years old, but her mother had a life in Iran. We need to know what that life was. We need to know who she was before she immigrated. If you're going to throw it all away for this woman at least find out who she is first."

"Goddammit. How many times do I have to tell you that I know everything I need to? I know her. As she is today. And I trust her and care about her. That's enough for me, it needs to be enough for you too."

"It's not."

"Well get over it," Derek snapped.

The line went silent again, but this time it was Derek who broke the standoff. "I understand that you think you're helping. But you're not. This is hard, but it's not half as hard as it would be for me to leave her behind and move on as if she didn't matter. She matters. What Melville and I have done to her matters, what I feel about her matters. I appreciate your help with all of this. And I want to find out who created this mess as much as you do, but I will not make London into the enemy. If you can't accept that then maybe you need to take a step back."

"Maybe I do," Kamal replied. "Because I really can't see continuing to help you ruin yourself, and I know that's what you're doing here. You've never been self-destructive, but I'll tell you, you're doing a fine job of it now."

"Enough!" Derek finally roared, his head pounding with frustration.

"You're right, it's more than enough," Kamal snapped back. "I'm done."

"Yes," Derek answered, a burning sensation filtering into his gut. "We are."

He stabbed at the screen and ended the call. As his eyes drifted to the tangled sheets he'd made love to London on, he wondered why someone—anyone—couldn't be happy for him, because what he'd felt in that bed last night went far beyond a good screw, and he wanted to keep on feeling this way for as long as she'd have him. He was well and truly head over heels for the woman who'd just torn his world to bits.

**

Settling into the overstuffed leather armchair, Derek looked around the room, enjoying the anonymity the secluded corner afforded him. He'd quickly realized that if he sat in the center of the restaurant the way he typically did, he'd be the focus of stares and unwanted attention for the entire meal. He'd seen more than one camera phone pointed his direction as the Maître D' had led him through the room.

The Hampshire Pub had been a favorite eating spot for Washington's elite politicians and political professionals for three decades. The upscale Old English décor, complete with a long polished bar, leather club chairs, and dark wood paneling, drew congressmen, diplomats, and consultants, as well as the occasional political spouse or visiting Governor.

Normally, Derek would be in the center of it all, holding court, greeting officials of his own party, trading barbs with those of the opposing party, but today, he hid. He didn't like it, but he also didn't feel like having his every move documented by gossipmongers.

"Derek." Nick Patterson held out his hand as he reached the table. "It's good to see you."

Derek stood and shook Nick's hand before they both sat. The Maître D' took Nick's drink order and slid away, his features carefully neutral and polite.

"It's good to see you, Nick. Thanks for meeting me."

"Of course, you know I'm happy to see you anytime."

Derek took a sip of the bourbon he'd ordered when he arrived. "Well, you're running the risk the party bosses will chastise you for associating with me at this point."

Nick scoffed. "That's one of the benefits of being a consultant—I don't have to listen to the party. I don't work for them, and they don't control my business."

Derek knew that the party could, in fact, discourage candidates from hiring Nick, but he appreciated his old friend's bravado on his behalf.

"So how are you holding up?" Nick asked as the waiter delivered his scotch and soda. "I'm sure there's more to all of this than the press is telling."

Derek sighed, running a finger around the cold, damp rim of his glass. "A lot more, and I can't elaborate on all of it, but suffice it to say that someone's after either Melville or me."

Nick nodded. "We can all tell there's someone feeding this crap to the press, do you have any ideas about who it might be?"

Here was the point of the meeting with Nick, and even though Derek had prepared for it, that didn't mean he liked it—putting Nick on the spot, treating him like he might somehow be involved with all of this—it didn't feel right.

"So far, one name keeps coming up over and over—Ryan Williams, Donovan's Chief of Staff."

Nick's face went pale, then turned to stone, his jaw set, his eyes shuttered. Derek had hit a nerve of some sort, the only question was, did it have anything to do with the efforts to derail Melville's campaign?

"You've obviously done some of your famous research," Nick bit out, raising his glass in salute to Derek.

"Not really. Williams' name kept coming up, so we were looking into him. When we found he'd been meeting with you, something about it didn't seem right to me. So I'm here to ask you directly. I respect you, Nick. I think you're a good man, and I wanted to give you the chance to tell me if you know anything about Williams that might be of interest to me."

Nick's square jaw relaxed a touch, but the haunted look in his dark eyes remained, and Derek's gut sunk with the foreboding that he wouldn't like what came next.

"I don't know of anything directly related to your problems, but I can tell you that if there's a man in town who is evil enough to try to take down a U.S. Senator and the mighty Derek Ambrose, it's Williams."

Nick shook his head, dropping his gaze to the tabletop.

"What's he got on you?" Derek asked softly. "And what's he making you do?"

"A couple of years ago Marlene lost her job."

Derek nodded in sympathy.

"We didn't need the money, so I told her she should go ahead and take some time off, spend it with the kids, just enjoy life for a while. But you know she loved practicing law, and the mess that got her fired really stuck with her. She couldn't shake it off, and spent all of her time rehashing what she could have done differently."

"I'm sorry."

"Well, don't be yet. It gets worse. A lot worse."

Nick paused when their server arrived to take their order, picking the story right back up again when he'd gone.

"About six months after the firing, Marlene started to gamble. Online stuff at first, then she discovered the track, and the Bel Air Casino in Maryland." Nick's expression was tortured as he looked Derek in the eyes. "I didn't know about any of it, I swear. I was working on the New York Governor's campaign at that point, travelling all over the state, plus prepping my guy in

Massachusetts for his State Senate run. She was at home, she managed the family accounts. I had no idea what was happening."

"So she got in too deep?"

"She got addicted, and she was running out of cash, she'd run through most of our credit, used up the savings, and was onto the home equity line when she met up with Williams at the casino one night."

Derek's stomach churned.

"He started giving her cash, a grand here, a grand there. Not much, but enough to feed her habit for a night or two. And there were always strings attached. In the beginning he'd ask her to wheedle some sort of information out of me—"

Derek snarled, the idea so dirty and repugnant it made him want to scrub his hands.

"Nothing that he asked for was very important, so she justified it to herself that way. But next he moved on to sexual favors."

"God." Derek's face got hot and he automatically reached out a hand to Nick, grabbing his wrist and squeezing it hard once before letting go.

Nick's eyes grew even colder. "She was so far gone that she did it—started an affair with him."

"Son of a bitch. How is he still standing?"

Nick shook his head in disgust. "Because he's smart. He kept track of every penny he gave her, and then he took videos of them..." He stopped, clearing his throat. "Of them in bed. And he brought it all to me."

"What did he want?"

"Half of my business."

"What?!" Derek jarred the table in his shock, sending a knife clattering to the floor.

"He's tired of life on the Hill. Wants a cushy spot in an established consulting firm. Luckily, he doesn't want any public involvement, just the authority, the income, and the assets."

The waiter cleared their plates, although neither man had eaten much, and Derek knew his appetite would be ruined for the remainder of the day. However, they both asked for refills on their drinks.

"I didn't have a choice, Derek. He was going to release the video of Marlene plus send an enforcer after her, claiming that all the money had been loans, even though she'd paid him back in other ways. She's the mother of my children. I couldn't let her be hurt like that. I signed the partnership papers about three months ago. I got Marlene into treatment for the addiction, but we're done. I filed divorce papers as soon she finished rehab. I sold off the house to pay Williams the hundred thousand because there was no way in hell I was going to give him anything else to hold over us. Then I got Marlene and the kids a townhouse in Arlington. I've been staying at the office until I recoup enough to get an apartment."

Derek's breath left his lungs in a rush. "Jesus, Nick. I don't know what to say."

Nick chuckled as he took a healthy slug of his scotch and soda. "I'm a chump?"

"No. Never that." Derek looked at his friend, admiration filling his words. "You're a man, in the truest sense of the word. You protected your family, at your own expense. You put them first, you made sure your kids and their mother are safe and taken care of, and you sacrificed yourself and your career to do it."

"Well, you're the very first person to hear the whole story, but if there's any chance that Williams is involved with what's happened to you and Melville I wanted you to know what he's capable of."

"And I know you're taking a big risk telling me this. I also want you to know that I'm not going to let you continue this arrangement with Williams."

"That's noble of you, but I really don't think there's much you can do. Trust me, if there'd been anyone who I thought could help I'd have gone to them."

"I have resources that you don't know about," Derek said, his eyes narrowed in thought. "If you'll trust me to talk with a select group of people I know, we can help you find a way out of this. My friends are absolutely discreet. I'd trust them with my life."

Derek could see Nick weighing the options. Nick wasn't the kind of guy to go hat in hand to anyone. He'd already been crushed and humiliated, having that humiliation exposed to more people wasn't going to be high on his list of things to do.

Finally he gave one sharp nod. "Okay. I guess I don't have much more to lose."

"Good." Derek stood, peeling a hundred dollar bill from his money clip and placing it on the table. "I swear to you, I won't let this stand. There are too few good men in this town, Nick. You're one of them, and I stand behind the good men. Always."

Nick stood as well and shook Derek's hand, his firm grip a sign that Williams might have bruised him, but he hadn't defeated him.

"Thank you, Derek. And please let me know if I can help with your issue. I don't know the real story, but I hope you'll tell it to me someday when it's all over."

Derek nodded and turned to leave.

"Derek?" Nick called.

Derek turned around and was surprised to see his friend grinning.

"She really is gorgeous," he smirked.

"You have no idea, my friend," Derek answered with a grin of his own.

**

London hadn't seen Margrite in weeks. Ever since she'd taken a leave from work in order to become Derek's pretend girlfriend. And after making love to him, the first man she'd really allowed into more than just her body in eight years, she felt the need to visit with her mentor. Margrite had worked in the business as a call girl for several years before starting her own service and becoming the Madam. She'd also had a steady lover for years, and London figured if anyone could understand what she was going through it was Margrite.

"Darling!" Margrite greeted her as she walked into the store.

A pair of wealthy women speaking Spanish—probably diplomatic wives—were perusing the racks of the lingerie shop, and Margrite whispered to the girl she employed to manage the shop before she gestured for London to follow her to the back office.

"You look gorgeous," Margrite said, pouring her a sparkling water and topping it with a lemon before they took seats on the small loveseat.

"Thank you."

"Your time off obviously agrees with you."

London's face heated at the memory of the previous night in Derek's arms. "It does have its perks," she murmured.

Margrite looked at her thoughtfully. "So have you come to give me your notice? You know all I want is for you to be happy." She smiled at her favorite employee.

"I don't think so. I've been spending time with Derek. Quite a bit—it won't last, but if you're willing to give me some more time off I might try to just enjoy it a while longer."

Margrite's lips pursed. "You don't think it will last? He seems terribly fond of you. You can't get more romantic than an 'I don't care if my girlfriend was a prostitute' press conference."

"He's wonderful. And if it were only the job..."

"But you have other secrets don't you, dear?" Margrite's eyes were sympathetic.

She plastered on a small smile. "You're a very wise woman, have I told you that?"

"I am, which is why I'm going to say something to you, and I want you to listen carefully. I love my life, darling, but don't ever be fooled into thinking that I haven't missed certain things along the way. I've traded away love, a family, children, and respectability. When I was younger I was so damaged from the abuse that my stepfather poured on me I couldn't imagine ever wanting to have babies or one man to love me above all others." She took a sip of her mineral water.

"But decades later, I have to admit that I did long for those things, I simply didn't know how to have them— and more still, I didn't think I deserved them." She picked up London's hands in hers and squeezed them gently. "You remind me so much of myself at your age. You're strong and in control on the outside, but inside you're still confused and filled with remorse. I don't know all the demons that haunt you, but I know that every woman in this job has some, and many of them are so great that *this*," she swept her arm around the room, "is all those women will ever have.

"But that's not you. Whatever it is, you *can* get past it. You're simply too intact not to. And you deserve to have the things that I can see you want. I've watched you around children, I've heard the sound of your voice when you talk about your charitable projects. I see the look in your eyes when we discuss Mr. Ambrose. You need more than a way to earn a living. And this could be your chance for that. Don't throw it away."

London's mind filled with Margrite's words, and a fantasy wove itself around her heart. More nights in Derek's arms, more events where she was his partner in the light of day. Her cooking him dinner in the evenings, him bringing her breakfast in the mornings, dinner parties with Joanna and Brian. She could envision it so easily, and yet a few days ago she wouldn't have been able. Already being with him was changing her, and it hurt. It made things quicken, a feeling of the world and all its possibilities rushing at her so fast she was sure the impact would be violent and painful.

She realized that this was what she'd feared all those years. If she'd allowed her body to respond then her heart and her mind would as well. And now here she was, sitting in Margrite's office, imagining a future—with Derek. She shook her head, trying to force the visions away.

"The thing I'm hiding," she said, looking at Margrite with desperate eyes. "It wouldn't ruin me, it would ruin him. He could never be with someone who's hiding what I am. It's a violation of everything he's been, everything he represents. Derek is..." She paused, searching for the right words. "He plays on a field of manipulations and strategy, but he's the most committed, ethical, genuine man I've ever known. He knows how to play the game, but he's in it for real. Do you understand what I mean?"

"You admire him."

"Yes, and so does anyone who knows him. He can play with the best of them, but his heart is so pure, he's always playing for an end game that's the right thing, the good thing."

"And how would your past hurt him?" Margrite's brows furrowed as she tried to understand what London wanted to communicate.

London looked at her glass, watching the bubbles rising to the surface like so many soldiers marching to their deaths.

"My past would put his character in question...I'm from Iran, Margrite. It's a country with a strong history of Islamic fanaticism. Derek operates in the American political system. There are people connected to me..."

Her dear friend took in a quick breath. "Oh my dear."

They stared at each other for a moment, a thousand words being exchanged without a sound.

"What if you came clean? Told him everything? Maybe he'd have a way to hide whatever it is?"

London shook her head. "He would know though, and he would be horrified. He's the epitome of the American dream. His world is one where your loyalty cannot be questioned. A sex scandal is one thing, being affiliated with foreign enemies is an entirely different issue. I don't think he could know about my past and still care for me."

"Shouldn't you at least give him the chance?"

"No," she answered concisely. "I couldn't stand the hope."

Because hope was the most dangerous threat her heart knew, and it was far too close already.

**

"What the *fuck* have you done, Marcus?"

Derek stood looking at his baby brother with his pants around his ankles, hips wedged between Renee's very bare thighs. He'd made an unplanned stop by the office, and was now wishing he could unsee the train wreck in front of him.

"Jesus, Derek," Marcus growled, pulling Renee against him so her half-clothed torso was hidden from view. "Can you give us a second?"

Derek whirled around putting his back to them. "I'll step out. Let me know when I can come back in." He walked out to the hallway and leaned against the opposite wall, his head tipped back against the cool marble. Christ. As if he didn't have enough on his plate. How could Marcus do this to him right now? He'd told him in no uncertain terms that Renee was off-limits. Marcus never went back for seconds, so now Derek would have to figure out how to keep Renee from getting her feelings hurt when his brother disappeared. God forbid Renee quit, he desperately needed his office to run smoothly in the middle of the mess he was in, and Renee was able to do that.

The door opened and Marcus started to step out.

"Listen," he said, "this is all on me—"

"You're damn right it is," Derek snapped, jabbing his finger in Marcus's chest. "My office. Now." He strode past Marcus, finding Renee standing stiffly in the middle of the reception area, her hair tangled, tears tracking down her face.

"Sit down," he told her, his voice sounding harsher than he'd intended. "We'll talk in a few minutes."

Thirty minutes later he was still yelling at Marcus, and he was certain that his blood pressure must be off the charts at this point.

"She could make a case for sexual harassment and take both of us to court. I can't believe you would do something this irresponsible. There is no woman in the world worth destroying a career over, Marcus. Jesus Christ." Somehow in the back of his mind the irony of this statement wasn't lost on Derek, but he was too angry to address his own inconsistencies. He just wanted to hit something—or someone.

Derek turned away and shoved his hands in his pockets, struggling to maintain control. He felt betrayed, by the one person he relied on to have his back. He'd given Marcus everything a kid his age could possibly want or need. And all he'd asked in return was loyalty. Now Marcus had gone behind his back. It hurt, and the timing was about as bad as it could get.

Marcus ground his teeth audibly. "She's not going to sue us for sexual harassment," he muttered.

"And you know that how?"

"It wasn't like that."

"You were fucking her in my office lobby. Exactly what wasn't it like?" Derek roared.

Marcus stood, his face red, and his hands shaking. Derek was so far gone in his own pain that he couldn't see the warning signs. "That wasn't fucking. It wasn't like that. Don't you get it? I *care* about her. She isn't some fuck to me, and I don't want you referring to her like she is."

Derek laughed harshly. "Oh please. You don't do some woman on a countertop in an office and then get all high and mighty about how people are referring to her."

Marcus snapped, rage washing over his face, and in a mere second he was across the room, his fist wrapping around Derek's shirtfront.

He gave Derek a shake and snarled, "What happens between Renee and me, where it happens, and when it happens, is none of your business."

Derek was shocked by his brother's vehemence, but he recovered quickly. When Marcus tried to shake him again Derek held fast, his larger body like an immoveable boulder. They stood, eye to eye, staring each other down and a rumble started in Derek's chest. He could feel the adrenaline rush through him, and his control waned with each passing second.

"Get your hands off of me or this won't go well for you," Derek warned.

"Fuck you," Marcus spat.

The punch was an uppercut, and Marcus didn't even see it coming. It didn't have much power because they were already on top of one another, but it was enough to propel Marcus back into the corner of the desk behind him. He struggled to catch himself before he fell, and in the process knocked over trophies, papers, a laptop, and assorted other items on Derek's crowded desktop. The noise of things hitting the floor was nearly as loud as Marcus's oaths as he stumbled.

"What the *fuck* is the matter with you?" he shouted as he regained his balance. He stepped forward, fists balled and ready to strike, but Derek was already looking beyond him to where Renee stood, her face white with shock and horror.

Derek's anger dissolved as quickly as it had risen. "Oh shit..." he whispered.

Marcus whirled in time to see Renee before she turned and ran from the office.

"Dammit!" he croaked as the front doors to the office slammed. He looked back at Derek.

"Go," Derek said, as his head throbbed and regret coated his tongue. "Go stop her."

After Marcus left, Derek collapsed into his office chair and buried his head in his hands. What the hell was happening to him? He'd just punched his brother, and not for fun at Spar, but seriously. He'd hit him. He'd never hit Marcus—he was eight years older, and had known from day one that his job was not to bully or compete, but to protect and mold. He'd spent the better part of twenty years watching over Marcus, keeping him safe, guiding him toward a brilliant future. He'd celebrated Marcus's successes, bragged about him to anyone who would listen, and felt his own heart swell with pride whenever the kid reached a new milestone.

And now he'd yelled at him, berated him, and fucking punched him in the face. This simply wasn't the way Derek's life worked. Ever since he'd reached adulthood his life had been about gaining—power, influence, prestige. Now it seemed that all he was doing was losing—his friends, his clients, his family.

But then he reminded himself that he'd gained the greatest prize of all, London. The rest would be fine. He'd get it all back on track. Kamal, his career, Marcus. They were his, and while he might have hit a rough patch in the road, he'd never lose what was his. He was Derek Ambrose. He'd have it all, he wasn't about to give it up.

CHAPTER XIV

It was after ten p.m. when Jeff, Scott, and Teague arrived at the Powerplay condo.

"You do know I was on a date?" Teague bitched as he threw himself down on the sofa.

"You're always on a date," Derek answered, handing him a beer hoping it would mellow him some.

Jeff took up his usual position by the pool table, and Scott appropriated the most comfortable armchair. Derek remained leaning against the bar where he could watch the group of them easily.

"Kamal coming?" Jeff asked, his gaze sharp on Derek.

"No," Derek answered succinctly.

"So he was telling the truth when he said you two are on the outs?" Jeff asked.

"What? How the hell did I not know this?" Scott asked.

"I only found out because I gave Jeff a ride over here," Teague interjected.

Derek sighed. As much as he liked his friends, they gossiped like a pack of old women. "Look, we're not seeing eye to eye on some things right now, but it doesn't matter. We've got more important things to deal with."

Jeff scowled. "You two need to fix this. The rest of us aren't going to choose sides you know."

Derek shrugged. "You don't have to choose. I'll stay out of his way and he can stay out of mine."

Teague snorted and Scott muttered, "Yeah right." Derek glared at each of them in turn.

"Can we just move on?" he demanded.

"Fine. For now," Jeff answered as Teague and Scott both nodded reluctantly.

"I got some very interesting news from Nick Patterson earlier." Derek relayed the story of Nick's wife and Ryan Williams. When he was done with the story all three of the other men in the room were tense with displeasure.

"What kind of a sick bastard comes up with a plan like that?" Teague shook his head, incredulous.

Outside a siren's wail broke through the relative quiet inside the high-rise condo unit. Derek watched the lights of the neighboring buildings for a moment before he turned back to his friends.

"I won't pretend to know what motivates a guy like Williams, but if he's sick enough to do this to Nick, he's not above much, including trying to assassinate Melville, and discrediting him in the press."

Scott stepped to the bar and grabbed a beer from the fridge unit. "But Nick said the reason Williams wanted the income from the firm was that he's tired of life on the Hill. Why would he get mixed up in the presidential race if he's not going to be there to benefit from the results?"

"He raises a good point," Teague said. "Wanting to have an interest in a private sector consulting business seems to be the exact opposite direction of a grab for a White House position."

Derek scratched his head. Yes, it had occurred to him, but he'd been so focused on finding out who had messed with Melville's campaign and his own reputation that he'd dismissed it from the equation.

"I don't know. But I don't feel like we can ignore this since we know he's been sniffing around Melville. I also promised Nick that we'd find a solution to his problems with Williams. He's a good guy, and one that I can't stand by and watch be exploited like this."

Scott nodded. "Agreed. And I can make sure that Williams never works on the Hill or anywhere in politics again. But what do we do about the fact that Nick's signed a partnership contract with the bastard?"

Teague scoffed. "You're joking, right?"

Derek smirked. He knew what was coming next and he loved to watch it.

"I've never met a contract I couldn't break," Teague boasted. "I'll have Nick send me a copy first thing in the morning and I'll have him out of it by the afternoon."

"And the videos he's got of Nick's wife?" Derek asked.

"Let me handle that," Jeff answered. "I've got some guys on retainer who can find those videos, and also…" he paused, "provide a large disincentive to Williams ever setting foot near Nick or his wife again."

Derek saw Teague and Scott's eyebrows rise just as his own did. They were all smart enough to know that they shouldn't and wouldn't want to hear the details of whatever Jeff was going to set in motion. However, they also needed to find out once and for all if Williams was involved in taking down Melville.

Derek framed his remarks carefully. "And when this disincentive is being explained, would there be room to ask some questions about what's happened with Melville?"

"That can be arranged."

Derek saw Teague struggling not to grin.

"You handle things more directly than Kamal generally does," Derek remarked.

Jeff shrugged. "He likes to play spy games. Use his secret informants, see if he can manipulate people to give up information. I just need to know what the bottom line is and then I'll fix it. I'm a problem solver, he's a chess player."

"Yet normally you let him play chess, and now we're all wondering if things could be done much faster if you just handled them," Teague opined.

Derek and Scott nodded in agreement.

Jeff cracked a small smile, something rare and fleeting. "It gives him purpose and allows me to save my influence for when it's crucial. I could have simply had Williams approached when we first suspected him, but he hadn't done anything wrong that we knew of at that point. It would have been overkill, used up my resources unnecessarily, and run the risk of complications that you all don't want to know about. By letting Kamal continue to dig and hypothesize, I saved the big guns for when we actually found something significant. It all worked out like it was meant to."

Derek grinned at the quietest and most self-effacing of the Powerplay members. Jeff was a soldier through and through. He never sought to do things for himself, always worked as part of the team, filling in wherever he was needed. But now Derek could see that it paid not to underestimate the man. He was perhaps smarter and savvier than the rest of the members gave him credit for.

Teague stood and walked to Jeff, slapping him once on the back before picking up his drink and downing it in one gulp. "My man, you scare the shit out of me, so I'm glad you're on our side."

Jeff rolled his eyes and Scott chuckled.

"We'll have this settled in twenty-four hours," he told the group. "We'll know once and for all if Williams did this."

"Once and for all," Derek echoed. "We'll finally know."

**

London had just stepped out of the shower when she heard her phone ringing. She was hoping it was Derek. He had worked late the night before and had an early morning meeting, so he'd elected to sleep at his office. When she looked at the caller ID, however, she saw it wasn't him, but even without a name she knew exactly who that number belonged to.

She hesitated before answering. "Hello, Mom," she said quietly, her heart beating at double speed.

"Habibi," Farrah said. "I can't tell you how wonderful it is to hear your voice."

London nodded silently.

"How are you feeling today? Are you somewhere safe where those horrible reporters can't bother you?"

London sat at the dressing table and set the phone on speaker on the tabletop as she towel dried her hair. Somehow by not touching the phone she felt a little distance between herself and Farrah. Distance that helped her maintain emotional equilibrium.

"I'm fine, Mom. Derek Ambrose has hired security to keep the press away from me. They stay at my house and take me where I need to go. Who'd have imagined me with bodyguards?"

She regretted saying it almost immediately. It was too easy to slide back into informality with her mother, as if all the years hadn't passed, as if she should be bringing up things that reminded them both of what they might have imagined she'd become.

But Farrah didn't catch the implications, or was far too smooth at passing over them. "I'm very glad. Mr. Ambrose is good to you then. You said it was complicated with him?"

London watched her own dark eyes in the mirror as she ran a comb through her long, thick locks. "Maybe not as complicated as I thought. He's...we're involved."

This time there was a hesitation. And London knew exactly what that hesitation was. Humiliation washed over her, and she dropped her gaze from the mirror, unable to see the shame in her own eyes.

"He's never..." She cleared her throat, and pinched the bridge of her nose so she wouldn't break down. "He's never paid. It's not like that, and I'm not working now. I'm taking some time off. Maybe thinking about what I should do...differently."

Farrah cleared her throat as well, and when she spoke again, her voice trembled.

"This is good, habibi. You are still my beautiful girl and you deserve to have someone who cares about you and is good to you. You deserve to be whomever you choose to be."

London couldn't possibly have missed the subtext of the words—after having discovered that Farrah had hidden the truth of who London was for her whole childhood, who she *chose* to be mattered—deeply. At seventeen she'd been so determined to *have* the choice that she'd given very little thought to *what* the choice was. Now, confronted for the first time in a decade by people who cared about her—Joanna, Derek, her estranged mother—she was starting to think that the quality of the choice mattered just as much or more than the having of it. As much as she had painted her mother as the demon in the history of her life, London couldn't ignore Farrah's words and the understanding they imparted—you deserve to be whomever you choose to be. Was it possible, she wondered, that her mother understood her so much better than she'd ever given her credit for?

Farrah continued, "I want to ask you something. I have tried to think of how it would be best to ask, but I cannot pretend to know what you are thinking or feeling now. And I'm afraid that if I push too hard you will leave me when we have just found one another again. But I also can't bear not to at least ask."

Farrah paused, obviously waiting for London to respond. "Okay," she said, her voice weak.

"Would you be willing to see me?"

That was all. Not a question really. A statement, but one to which London needed to respond. And the last time she'd seen her mother face-to-face came rushing back to her in all its vivid and horrid detail.

She was a senior in high school, studying world affairs. Terrorism hadn't entered the American consciousness the way it would after 9-11, but Iran, Iraq, and Libya were all included in the curriculum in her class.

The unit was about the Iran-Iraq war, which had ended the year London was born. As her teacher discussed the important figures in Iran following the war, he projected photos and biographical facts about each on the screen at the front of the class.

"Mohammad Rouhani," the teacher had said as the image dissolved from one man's face to another. "This man is the principal advisor to the Supreme Leader in Iran. He's held that position since 1989, and is considered to be one of the most dangerous war criminals in the world. Rouhani was the Commanding General of armies that conscripted children, slaughtered tens of thousands of civilians, and violated the Geneva Convention protocols for prisoners of war."

As the teacher moved on to other key individuals, London had looked at the image of Rouhani, unable to take her eyes off of it, something about his face tugging at a thread in her memory.

"Hey, L?" her friend Monique had whispered. "Do you have any relatives in Iran? Cause that dude looks just like you."

When she'd gotten home at the end of the day London needed to know more about the man in the picture at school. A lump had formed in the pit of her stomach as she logged in to her mother's computer and began by searching his name. And after an hour she didn't know much more, but he had definitely been in Iran when her mother was a university student and London was a baby in Tehran.

She had a large picture of Rouhani up on the screen when Farrah arrived home from work. She walked into the room chattering about the dinner she had planned. She busied herself hanging her jacket, setting her briefcase down, and it wasn't until she finally turned and saw the image on the monitor that she stopped talking.

Her gasp was audible, and the weight in London's gut sank further.

"Where did you get that?" Farrah demanded, her face pale. Her hands shook as she walked toward the desk where London sat.

"Who is he?"

"Where did you get it?" Farrah repeated.

"We're studying him at school. But you know him, I can tell."

Farrah reached the computer and her hand snapped out to click the power switch off.

"Mom!" London shouted.

"He's a very bad man. I'm sure they've taught you that in school, and it's all you really need to know."

"I'm not five, Mom. You can't just say he's a bad guy and expect me to be satisfied with that. You obviously know him. How? When?"

Farrah exhaled a shaky breath. "I knew him when I was a university student before you were born."

"How? He looks older than you. Was he one of your professors or something?"

Farrah sat down in a nearby armchair. "Please don't make me do this, London," she pleaded.

Later London would wonder why she'd persisted. Maybe it was as simple as teenage antagonism, but if she were honest with herself it was more a premonition, a strong instinct that there was something crucial there she needed to know. Whatever the root cause, the result was that in that moment she could no more drop the line of questioning than she could have sliced off her own hand.

"Tell me, Mom. I have to know." Her voice dropped to a mere whisper. "I deserve to know."

Farrah gave one sharp nod and then admitted that everything she'd ever told London about her father, her origins, and her immigration to the U.S. was a lie. Farrah Amid was a twenty-year-old student at university in Tehran and a member of a radical student activist group who opposed the regime that had taken control of the country after the Islamic Revolution in 1979.

The group used any means necessary to infiltrate the highest levels of the government, feeding information to groups outside of the country who they hoped could help overthrow the Supreme Leader, the Ayatollah, who had spent nearly a decade purging the nation of any Western or Non-Islamic influences.

Tears trickled down Farrah's cheeks as she described to London that she was assigned to foster an involvement with Rouhani in order to get secrets about the Iran-Iraq war and the Iranian military.

"It was made clear to me that I was to use any means necessary to get close to him, London."

London's stomach soured and her eyes burned. She shook her head sharply from side to side. No.

"They selected me because of the way I looked. Once they'd arranged an introduction for me I made it clear to him that I was looking for someone who could help me pay for school and that I would trade sexual favors for that help."

"Mom," London sobbed.

Her mother stood and trembled with emotion. "You wanted to know. As long as we've gone this far you need to hear it all. You need to understand."

Farrah walked the length of the room, her arms hugging her stomach as if she was straining to keep her insides contained.

"We started an affair. He wasn't distasteful and I was the darling of the rebellion, willing to give up my very virtue to serve the cause. I gained valuable information and everything was going smoothly...until the day I discovered that I was pregnant."

At that point London broke into sobs. She'd known. She'd known it was coming, but it was still the most painful thing she'd ever experienced in her young life. Since she was a tiny child and had first asked why she didn't have a father like the other children, her mother had told her that her father died when she was a toddler. Farrah had given London an imaginary family, a father who watched her birth, loved her deeply and was killed tragically in an auto accident before London was old enough to remember him.

For London to hear that she had in fact been the product of an arrangement that didn't involve love in any form, a trick her mother had perpetrated on a man who was known throughout the world for his horrendous humanitarian violations, a child who was a mistake in every sense of the word—it destroyed her.

"I ended things with him," Farrah continued, the story spilling from her as if it had been ready to overflow for seventeen years. "And I went into hiding. I had you and I found a job to support us. My family helped me out as much as they could although they didn't have a great deal of money and an unwed pregnant daughter was a terrible embarrassment to them.

"You were about to turn two when the life I'd created for us fell apart. I was working in the little sundries store that hired me right after you were born. The owners were a very sweet older couple and I told them I was a widow, so they had taken me under their wings, even allowing me to bring you to work with me.

"There was a terrible rainstorm outside that day, and a group of men came into the store to get shelter. The store owner could see that they were very important men, so he told me to ask them if I could get them something to drink while they waited. I had already reached them, with you on my hip, when I saw him. Your father has done many horrible things to many people in his life, but he is not stupid. He took one look at my face, then at you, and he knew immediately.

"I was terrified, but all I could do was act as if everything was normal. I got the men coffees and tea, and kept you with me. I wanted to run, but the storm outside was fierce, and I walked to and from work. There was no way I could take you outside in the winds and the rain. But Mohammad didn't spare me another look, and a part of me began to think maybe he didn't know—or better yet, didn't care.

"When the rain slowed, the men prepared to leave and I tried to be inconspicuous, praying that they would go and I could disappear yet again so that he couldn't find me a second time. But as the others walked out the door, he came back to where I stood behind the counter. Quietly he told me that he was going to send someone for you—you were his property—and since I'd hidden you from him I was not invited to join you. Legally, in Iran, I had no recourse. It was why I'd run in the first place. I couldn't bear to give you to a man like him."

London stared at her mother, her heart beating like a wild animal struggling to break free.

"I took you that night and ran. I used my contacts with the rebel group to get out of the country and get help abroad. We went first to London where I changed your name, then we gained asylum here in the U.S."

London's mind snapped back to the present, and the woman on the other end of the call waiting for an answer to one of the hardest questions London had ever been asked.

"I think so," she finally said, deciding that after so many lies over so many years it was time for raw honesty. "This is hard for me." She pressed her lips together, searching her heart for the right words. "I left because you had lied to me, you had hidden who I was—from me. That destroyed me. That the one person who I trusted most in the entire world had kept part of me hidden away. And when I found out the truth, I was ashamed of who I was, and whether it was fair or not, I blamed you. You broke my heart."

Farrah's voice was small and sad. "I know."

"But I'm beginning to see something. I chose a new me, but I haven't been proud of her either. And I've made the same mistake you have. I've kept part of me hidden from the world the way you kept part of me hidden. I traded one version of me that was dark and secret for another."

"Oh my love," Farrah crooned, "it isn't your fault. It's mine. It's all my fault. Forgive yourself and place the burden on me. If you need to be angry with me for another ten years then do that, only promise me that you will stop being angry at yourself. That you will stop punishing yourself for things that you had no control over. It was me who made the choice to sleep with him. Me who made the choice to lie to you about him, me who created an alternate reality that gave you false hopes. You didn't do anything wrong. Your father did. I did. You didn't.

"But you are young and beautiful, and you don't need to hide in the dark with secrets anymore. You have your whole life ahead of you. You can do anything you want, and I would love nothing more than the chance to help you, to watch you become brilliant."

"Oh Mom," London cried. "I've been so unfair to you. All these years I worked so hard to hate you because I was selfish and hurt and stubborn. You made mistakes, but you did it all for love—the love of your nation and the love of me."

No more words were said for a long time as London and her mother cried the tears of a decade. But when they were done, London agreed to visit her mother, and she knew deep in her heart that it was the first step on a long road back to who she might have been.

**

Derek hadn't seen London in two days and he was losing his mind. His head hurt, his chest ached, and his dick was at half-mast all damn day. He'd never known another woman who could turn him on simply by answering his texts. But he'd been putting out so many fires trying to make up for the abrupt exit of his secretary that he barely had time to sleep, much less visit his erstwhile girlfriend. He'd spent two nights at the office sleeping on the sofa, and the only reason he was going to leave tonight was because he'd run through the supply of clean clothes he kept there for emergencies.

Teague had finished the negotiations with Melville's attorney and the joint press release had been issued. Melville had agreed to wait a week before announcing his new campaign director, but it didn't matter much to Derek, he knew Melville would never get the nomination without him. It was vanity on Melville's part to stay in the race, and Derek doubted he'd last more than another couple of months.

But none of that changed Derek's desire to find out who was behind the destruction of his reputation and nearly of Melville's life, and now Jeff was arriving with the information he'd gleaned from his *contacts* who had paid a visit to Ryan Williams.

"Mr. Ambrose?" The voice of his temp secretary was nasal at best, and grating at worst, which seemed to be the case right now.

"Yes?"

"A Mr. Thi-be-dough is here to see you."

My God he missed Renee. If he could ever get her or Marcus to speak to him again he was going to offer to double her salary. Hell, he'd let her screw his brother in the reception area too as long as she promised to wait until after five p.m. to do it.

"Please send him back," Derek instructed. He walked to the bar and took out two bottles of water. If it were Teague he'd have grabbed the scotch, but Jeff was military. No drinking on duty.

"Who the hell is that at your front desk?" Jeff asked as he walked into the room.

Derek rolled his eyes. "The temp agency sent her."

"Where's Renee?"

"Don't ask."

Jeff shrugged. "Well, I liked her better in any case."

"As did I," Derek muttered.

They sat down, Derek behind his desk, Jeff in an armchair facing him.

"I've got some information for you, but I doubt you're going to like it."

Derek ran a hand through his hair. "I haven't liked anything I've heard in weeks. No reason today should be any different."

Jeff nodded in understanding, his hazel eyes sharp, but kind. "I'll start with the good news. The videos of Nick Patterson's wife and Williams have been destroyed."

Derek breathed a sigh of relief. "Thank you. Teague had the contract voided yesterday, and Williams has been removed from every account and piece of paper Nick's firm owns. He is free and clear, and so is his wife. She made a huge error, but they didn't deserve any of that."

"I agree. And now for the other news. Williams swore, under some substantial duress I might add, that he had nothing to do with leaking the information about

London and Melville. He said that he, in fact, didn't even know about the affair before the news exposed it. He did, however, have a hypothesis about who might have."

Derek snorted. "Not sure I trust him enough to give it any credence."

"I think you may want to reassess that. See, Williams had Melville investigated at Senator Donovan's request just as we initially thought. Donovan was thinking about making a run for president. The investigators didn't find out about London and Melville, but what they did find out was that someone else was having Melville watched."

Derek's pulse raced. "Who?"

Jeff paused, one eyebrow raised. "Winston Vandermeer."

**

"Mmm," London moaned. "That feels amazing."

Derek dug his fingertips into her scalp again, massaging the shampoo into her long tresses. She squeezed his thighs in ecstasy and he chuckled.

"If I'd known you'd make noises like that just from getting your hair washed I'd have done it sooner," he joked.

She pressed back against his hard cock that was wedged in between their bodies as she sat in front of him in his large bathtub.

"You're terribly hard for a man who just helped bust open an attempted assassination investigation," she pointed out.

Derek caressed one of her nipples before he poured a cup of warm water over her hair, rinsing away the shampoo. "All in a day's work, beautiful."

She snorted. "Really, though, do you think the police would have figured out it was Winston who tried to have Melville killed if you hadn't discovered he was having him followed?"

"I'd like to hope that eventually they would have, but there's no telling."

"So you told the police about it, then what?"

He ran his fingers through her damp hair absentmindedly. "They didn't have too much trouble tracking down the P.I. that Vandermeer had hired, and he crumbled like a stale cookie. He also admitted that Vandermeer had him send the information about Melville's affair with you to the media. Apparently the old man was so pissed that Melville had cheated on his daughter he decided to ruin the guy."

"He certainly had a lot of faith in the assassin he hired. He had his darling daughter standing right next to the intended target."

Derek huffed out a bitter laugh. "I'm not sure if that's trust, stupidity, or a man who's not playing with a full deck at this point."

"It's really all tragic. I feel sorry for him."

Derek nibbled on her shoulder and she giggled. His hands roamed, squeezing her breasts, sliding over her slick skin, caressing her core.

"He was a very angry man," he whispered in her ear. "His daughter was complaining that her husband wasn't making her the center of his universe. He didn't like to see his darling neglected."

"Uh huh...but you would never neglect a woman?"

He licked her earlobe. "I intend to make you the center of everything I do from now on."

Her heart throbbed with the delicious thought of it. Maybe, her mind whispered, *maybe*.

Maybe he wouldn't find out about her father. Maybe he wouldn't care. Maybe she could be something other than a prostitute. Maybe there was a happily ever after for someone like her. Maybe.

"Stand up, we need the shower to get all that soap out of your hair," he said.

They moved to the big separate shower that took up one corner of the room. He adjusted the water until it was steaming, a soft spray falling from above them and mist coming from three sides. London felt warm, pliant, and full, her skin flushed and tingly. Derek took her in his arms and kissed her, gently at first, his lips and tongue learning their way around her mouth as if he had all day to explore.

She languidly wound her arms around his neck and rested her slick breasts against his chest, relishing the feeling of his stiff hairs against her nipples.

As Derek's hands slipped under her ass and he lifted her higher and closer to his erection, she speared her fingers into his hair, pulling it taut and groaning at the ache building in her center.

"Turn around," he panted.

He spun her and she planted her hands against the wall to catch her balance. He bent his knees and she felt his thick shaft push through her folds to slide along her clit.

"Oh, oh yes," she gasped, resting her forehead against the tiles.

He planted one palm on the wall next to her arm for balance and wrapped the other around her breast as he began to slide forward and backward across her tender clit.

The slippery friction was delicious, and she rocked against him shamelessly, moaning with the sensations.

His pace increased and he grunted as he thrust back and forth. When she was so wound up that she thought she might explode from the anticipation, he moved his hand from her breast to her clit and pressed, circling it three times.

She tipped her face to the ceiling, her head resting on his shoulder behind her, and cried out her release, as his cock and finger continued to stroke her firmly. He helped her come down slowly, his hands relenting, his hips stilling. She was left panting and ready to melt into a heap on the floor.

He spun her in his arms and kissed her on both cheeks.

"See?" he said, a wicked glimmer in his eyes. "You're the center of everything."

She reached for the body wash on the shelf next to her and popped the top, pouring a generous dab on her hands and rubbing them together. The scent of citrus mixed with the steam and made her think of lemon pie and her mother's special orange cookies. As she looked at Derek's big broad chest and six-pack abs she thought that he might be every bit as delicious.

"You know I was always taught that turnabout is fair play." She rubbed her hands up and down his chest, then found his cock, sandwiching it between her palms as the silky body wash coated him.

"Somehow that doesn't feel as good when I do it," he murmured, watching her with hot eyes.

She let the spray rinse the soap off, then began kissing her way down his chest, bending her knees as she got closer to his waist.

He slipped his hand under her elbow and lifted her up, flipping off the water at the same time.

"Derek—" she protested.

"Nope," he grunted. "I want to be inside of you, and I'm not going to last much longer. We need a condom and we need it now."

He scooped her up and carried her out of the shower as she laughed. They were both so wet she was afraid he'd slip and hurt them, but he made it to the bedroom and stood her next to the bed. Then he reached into the nightstand drawer and removed a condom, donning it in record time.

"Now." He kissed her lips like a man denied his favorite dessert for years.

"Inside," she moaned.

He released her and turned her around, pushing her gently. She crawled on all fours onto the comforter, knees bent, with her elbows tucked under her.

He came down over her, wrapping one arm around her waist, then he took one of her legs and straightened it, his free hand palmed her ass as he ran his nose along her spine, planting kisses along the way.

She arched her back, her nose filling with the scent of their arousal. The partial splits she was in stretched her muscles in just the right way, a gentle burning spilling through her body. She felt the pressure of his cock at her core, and he pressed in so slowly she thought she'd go insane.

"You're so tight like this," he growled, his breath coming fast and hard. "Please tell me you're close." He pumped in and out a few times, and she gasped loudly.

"More, please. Harder," she demanded.

He complied, shifting to get better leverage, and slamming into her over and over. The burn started in one point and spread out in rays until it peaked and the convulsions ripped through her. She screamed his name and his entire body stiffened as he jerked against her one last time before pouring everything he had into her. When they were done he pulled out, disposed of the condom and lay down sprawled halfway across her, his heavy leg on top of hers, his big arms wrapped around her small waist.

And before they both fell into a deep sleep he whispered in her ear, "I'm in love with you, London Sharpe. Utterly in love."

CHAPTER XV

"He said what?!" Joanna's yelp could be heard across the room at the small tea shop they sat at in Georgetown.

"Shh," London admonished. "You don't need to announce it to the people across the street."

Joanna apologized, but her grin was a mile wide. "Sorry. I'm so happy for you I can't stand it."

London took a bite of her chocolate croissant, and breathed deeply. The smell of fresh-baked bread permeated the shop, and even with the croissant in front of her she was imagining big slices of fluffy, white, French bread. Mouthwatering.

"Don't go getting a bunch of ideas. There are so many things for us to overcome still."

Joanna rolled her eyes. "Must you always be glass half empty? He knows about your past, he accepts you for who you are. He's given up everything for you, London. How can you not see that?"

London's stomach soured and she put the croissant back on the plate.

"I'm painfully aware of that. He's lost his presidential campaign, half his business, his best friend isn't speaking to him, and he got into a horrible fight with his younger brother the other day too. How long can it be until he starts to resent me for making him lose everything he cares most about?"

Joanna reached over and snatched London's croissant, taking a large bite before she replaced it.

"See? Glass half empty," she said, licking a bit of chocolate from her fingers with her own mouth half full.

"I'm being serious—"

"So am I," Jo declared. "He. Loves. You. I know that doesn't fit with your view of yourself as so terribly unlovable, but that doesn't make it any less true. He's given those things up, of his own free will, because you're more important to him. You didn't force him, he wasn't coerced, he *chose* you."

London's eyes filled and she had to look away, biting her bottom lip to stem the well of emotion.

"I know, but there are still things, things he doesn't know…"

"So you'll tell him, and he'll get over those things too. It's not finite."

"What isn't?"

"Love," Jo said as she took another, smaller bite of the croissant that lay forgotten on London's plate. "It's not a cup filled to the brim and when you've consumed it all it disappears. Love is a well, dear. It refills constantly, it's there for you to drink from. It's what keeps us all alive."

London nodded quickly, swallowing down her fears.

"Did you say it back?"

"No. I pretended I'd fallen asleep. I was so scared, Jo. I'm still so scared."

Joanna reached across the table and patted London's hand. "I know you are, darling, but it's time to grow up, to stop running. You're ready, and he's the right one. Just go get him already, will you?"

London's fears turned to laughter, and once again, that little seed of hope grew larger, ready to sprout, ready to flourish and bloom and turn London's heart into a garden.

If only a deadly weed weren't laying in wait.

**

"Fuck," Derek muttered as he hung up the phone. It was the third time in as many days he'd tried to reach Kamal and been rebuffed. His cell phone went straight to voicemail and calls to his office met with the brick wall that was the Embassy secretary. No, the Ambassador wasn't available. Yes, the Ambassador received his last three messages.

And he wasn't having much better luck with his brother. Marcus was talking to him, but barely. The kid was miserable, Renee wouldn't see him, and he was heartbroken. Derek had to admit that he'd gotten it entirely wrong. Marcus was in love with the sweet girl, and Derek had severely underestimated Marcus's capacity to commit to someone. He had to believe that all of this would work out, but it was tough when he felt so isolated.

Since coming to D.C. Derek had lived a hustle and bustle life. He was in the middle of the action, snapping up new clients, making political deals of one sort or another, hiring staff, building up the Powerplay club, helping Kamal set up the Embassy as a new Ambassador. He'd always been surrounded by people, people who could give him something, people who wanted him to give them something. Now, overnight, he was alone. No one banging on his door, no one needing his advice, no one caring one way or the other about him.

He sighed and looked around his desk. It was clean. And the only reason for that was because the eight clients he currently had were small state level candidates whose campaigns were managed by their local staff. His role was as strategist and policy advisor. The irony wasn't lost on him at this point—he was too important to get personally involved in those small campaigns, but no longer important enough to be hired for the bigger ones.

His phone dinged with a text.

London: Are you still coming to my place to meet my mother?

Yes, he replied. It was amazing to him that London had been to see her mother twice this week. After ten years of estrangement. But it seemed to be going well, and he wanted to do whatever he could to facilitate the relationship.

London: Thank you. I'll see you there at seven.

Derek checked his watch and realized that he'd better hurry if he was going to make it. Grabbing his briefcase and jacket he looked around his empty office and shook his head. Tomorrow was another day, and at least he knew he'd be getting laid by a beautiful woman tonight. He grinned to himself. Life wasn't all bad.

**

Derek nodded to Owen who was on duty at London's door when he arrived. He thought they could dispense with the security in the next couple of weeks, but there were still the occasional paparazzi hanging around and he didn't want to risk London being harassed. She'd been going out to restaurants and stores some in the last few days. So far she'd only had to endure a few whispers and stares, this was D.C. after all, a scandal a week, and Derek and London were last week's news.

"Ms. Sharpe's not home yet," Owen said.

"Okay. I'm sure she'll be here soon, and if her mother arrives, please let her in. Farrah Amid."

"Yes, sir, Mr. Ambrose."

Derek went inside and set his belongings down in the foyer then headed to the kitchen where he'd stashed a bottle of scotch the last time he'd been over. He poured himself a couple of fingers in a tumbler and was about to sit on the living room sofa when he heard a commotion outside.

He opened the door to the flash of a camera, and raised his arm in front of his eyes to ward off the blinding light.

"Mr. Ambrose!" a man called out.

"You're trespassing on private property," Owen called out.

Derek lowered his arm, and looked around. There was a reporter with a photographer standing on the sidewalk in front of London's small front yard. On the walk leading to her front door were Owen and a dark-haired middle-aged woman who he knew in a moment was London's mother.

"We're on the public sidewalk, asshole," the reporter said in response to Owen.

As the shock wore off and his vision cleared, Derek's temper flared. "Listen, I don't care if you're in the middle of the damn street, if you don't back off I'm going to have the cops out here and charge you with harassment. You need to find someone else to bother." He stepped off the small front porch and walked down the sidewalk to Owen and Farrah.

"Please come on inside," he told her smiling.

She nodded at him quickly. "Thank you."

He could smell the sweat coming off of the reporter a couple of feet away. The guy had greasy hair and an untucked plaid shirt that looked like it had been worn for a few days straight. The photographer snapped another photo and the flash lit up the faces of everyone around like ghosts in the night.

"Get her inside," Derek instructed Owen. Owen took Farrah's elbow and moved to take her up to the house.

"Is this the first time you've met your girlfriend's family?" the reporter said, sneering at Derek.

"You need to go," Derek responded, arms crossed, feet spread in a wide stance.

"Farrah!" the guy shouted as she moved away. "Do you keep in touch with London's father?"

Derek heard a gasp and turned to see Farrah with a look of shock on her face. He pivoted back to the reporter just as another question shot out through the dusky night.

"Does he write letters to your daughter? Maybe call her?"

The insensitive ass. Derek fought the urge to punch the fucker and be done with it. "What the hell are you talking about?" Derek scowled at the guy. "Her father's dead."

"That's not right though is it, Farrah?" the reporter shouted. "Your daughter's father isn't dead, is he? In fact, he was just indicted last month in an international court for war crimes for the tenth time, wasn't he?"

Derek's stomach lurched. He turned to look at Farrah. Her hands were over her mouth, her eyes wide with horror as she shook her head. His thoughts spun in confusion and he rotated back to the reporter, but instead his eyes fell on London standing a few feet away on the sidewalk, her face was pale, but her mouth was set in a grim line. She stared at him without blinking. His heart beat once, twice, then stopped for a long breath before it started up again, and in one burst of the camera's flash he knew that it was true. It was all true.

**

"Please, Derek," London cried as she followed him out of the house. He kept his steady but highly determined pace and proceeded down the sidewalk toward his car.

"Derek, let me explain." She jogged to keep up with him, thankful that she had worn flats and jeans today instead of a business ensemble.

Her heart raced and her skin itched, as if it were going to split and things would start spilling out of her. He reached his car and placed his hand on the driver's door just as she caught up to him.

"Derek!" She grabbed the lapel of his jacket, hanging on for dear life as she looked up into his icy stare. Yes, those ice chip eyes were back, and she realized with stunning clarity that it was only her Derek who had warm eyes. This was the other man, and she was terrified her Derek had left for good. "Let me tell you how this happened, about what I know and why I didn't tell you sooner."

He stood stock still, as if he were made of stone, and in that moment she would have believed his heart too was stone, like the rest of him. His gaze held nothing—no affection, no regret, no yearning. It was as if his love for her had drained away while he stood in her front yard and listened to the last secret she had to guard.

"Do you have any idea what you've done to me?" he asked quietly.

She nodded rapidly, several times in a row. "We'll make sure to tell them you didn't know, that it's all my fault and that I've never even met the man."

"Is that true?" he asked, his head tilted slightly to one side as if he were assessing her answers. "Is it true you've never met him? Because I'm having a hard time understanding what's true here and what isn't."

"I've virtually never met him," London corrected. "I was only two at the time."

"So you have met him then." Derek shook his head in disgust. "How could you not tell me? How could you let me stake my entire life on you, and not mention that you're the daughter of a man who's been called the Hitler of the twenty-first century?"

She cringed.

"I'm in politics, for God's sake. In a nation under siege by Islamic terrorists. My entire adult life has been dedicated to institutions that enact democracy, and protect freedom. I've been in the inner circle of some of the greatest leaders the Western world has ever known."

His arm lay across the roof of the car and he hung his head, the pose weary and defeated. "In my world, my patriotism, my allegiance to this country, is everything. No one has ever doubted my love for this country."

He took a breath, and London watched him, warily, fear throbbing through her veins.

"If and when the day ever came that my love for this country did come into question?" He shook his head. "I can't even imagine it. I can't fathom what it would feel like to have my entire life's work laid to waste like that. To have the very core of everything I do, the very core of *me*, in doubt—by an entire nation. *My* nation."

"Derek," she whispered, tears rolling down her cheeks.

"I gave you everything." His voice was rough now, as broken as his posture. "And I did it willingly, happily. I did it because I love you. But when three hundred and twenty-million Americans wake up tomorrow and read the news that I've been fucking Mohammad Rouhani's daughter?" London jerked back at the vehemence in his voice and the bitterness of his words. "You will have destroyed the only things I had left. My love of this country, and my love of you."

He swung open the door of the car then, and she sobbed. "No, please no. I'm sorry. I'm so sorry. I should have told you. I should have. And I'll tell everyone you didn't know. I'll hold a press conference or give an interview—whatever will work the best."

He looked at her sadly, and she knew it was because he pitied her desperation. How could he not? She was a prostitute, and a liar. She was a woman who destroyed—reputations, trust, love. She was pathetic, and they both knew it.

He reached out, stroking one finger along her jaw. Then he shook his head slightly, because he was out of words, and so was she.

He got into the car and shut the door, never looking at her again as she sobbed alone in the street and he drove away, out of her life, but not out of her heart.

CHAPTER XVI

Derek looked out the window of his office, watching the rain fall on the cars and concrete below. He sighed and turned back to the computer screen on his desk, rereading the email, although he had it memorized at this point.

Dear Mr. Ambrose: This correspondence serves as my thirty day notice of termination of your consulting contract with my campaign for the Sixth District Congressional seat in the Great State of Florida. While I consider myself an open-minded man, and I was prepared to stand behind you when you made it known that you were personally involved with a paid sex worker, I'm afraid that her relationship to a known international criminal has crossed a line that I cannot. Dating a former prostitute is a far cry from dating the daughter of an enemy of the United States. I cannot, in good conscience continue my working relationship with you under these circumstances.

Derek had seen exactly eight versions of the same email over the last week. His eight remaining clients, all gone. Every contract cancelled, every account closed, every back turned. Even before that, the Department of Homeland Security was at his front door, and while they'd seemed satisfied with his very truthful answers to their questions, he still noticed a plain dark car parked near both his office and his home each day. He had to assume his phones were tapped and his Internet monitored as well.

It had taken forty-eight hours for the national party to send their email, detailing that he was being pulled from the exclusive list of preferred consultants. They'd also been just petty enough to revoke his VIP pass to the national convention the next year. He was now persona non grata. Congressmen wouldn't take his calls, donors wouldn't sign checks they'd promised to his candidates months ago, and the President had respectfully withdrawn his standing invitation to monthly White House policy luncheons. She'd contacted him personally, explained that she supported him privately, but that she couldn't court the ire of the opposition and the Congressional leadership by hosting him at the White House. He assured her he understood, then hung up the call and threw his thirty-pound desk chair across the room.

But no matter how much his guts twisted at the loss of his business, his reputation, and his influence, they twisted more when he thought of the loss of her. At night he woke, dreaming of her hair, her skin, her eyes. He could almost feel her silky touch on his cock, almost taste her tart sex on his tongue. Her voice haunted him in his head, and her face haunted him in his mirror. Try hard as he did, he couldn't hate her, he could only miss her.

Every morning he woke, exhausted from sleeplessness, wracked with doubt, and bruised both inside and out. He ran his body and his mind ragged, working out at Spar for hours at a time, staying at the office late into the night, looking for new clients, composing emails to old contacts, searching for new and better ways to spin the story of him. It was the only way he knew to deal with the pain, the aching pit that had lodged inside his chest when she stood on that sidewalk in Dupont Circle and told him with her eyes that she'd lied about the only thing that really mattered, her loyalty to him.

**

"Are you ever going to talk about it?" Kamal asked as they bounced around the sparring ring one afternoon a few weeks after he'd learned the identity of London's father. The two men had been gradually making their way back to one another. Kamal made the first overture, asking for Derek's advice on an Embassy matter. Derek reciprocated by inviting Kamal to their favorite sports bar to watch the U.S. Men's soccer team play a World Cup qualifying match. The soccer had helped, the alcohol had helped more, and now they were on their third 'date' as Teague had teasingly called it. It was, however, the first time they'd broached the subject that had come between them.

"What is there to say? You were right, she lied to me. You win."

Kamal's fists dropped and he ripped off his head gear. "Dammit!" he snarled. "Do you think I'm getting some sort of enjoyment out of this?"

Derek shrugged.

"Well, I'm not. Not even close. The last thing I would ever want was for you to get your heart sliced out. Not to mention the crucifixion in the press. You can't really think I'd ever want you to endure being called a traitor and a national security risk, do you?"

Derek pointed to Kamal's head gear, motioning for him to put it back on, then began bouncing around, looking for an opening to take a shot.

"It doesn't matter now anyway," Derek said. "What's done is done, and I'm ready to go back to my life and forget all of it ever happened."

"And how does that work?" Kamal asked.

"I don't know, but I'm sure as hell going to try."

"I think you're making a mistake."

"You always do." Derek made a face as Kamal got him with a left jab to the shoulder.

"It may be true that she deceived you, but it was an entirely different kind of deceit than what I thought was going on." He feinted right and dodged one of Derek's famous uppercuts.

"She didn't lie to you because she was trying to take advantage of you. She lied because she was afraid of losing you."

"Well, she was right. She's lost me. But I think you're exaggerating how much she cares about that."

Kamal shook his head. "No, I'm not."

Derek fought off a stabbing pain in his midsection. Kamal hadn't touched him there, so he knew it wasn't from the sparring.

"There's too much water under the bridge. Whether she loves me or ever did, I don't know, but I do know that she ruined the campaign we'd been designing for eighteen months. She ruined my spotless reputation, she ruined Melville's chances of ever moving past the Senate. Hell, he won't even get reelected to his Senate seat now." And silently he thought that she'd ruined him for any other woman as well.

Kamal stopped bobbing and weaving for a moment. "I think Melville and his father-in-law had a little to do with that." He took up the dance again, catching Derek by surprise with a jab to the biceps that truly hurt. "Doesn't she deserve a second chance?"

"No." Derek's tone was final. "I just want to act like none of it ever happened. Can we do that? At least for right now?"

Kamal sighed, shook it off, and soon the two men were sparring like they had every other week for years.

Kamal had only one more question: "Do you still love her?"

Derek gritted his teeth and answered, "Unfortunately, I'll always love her."

**

After Derek left her standing alone on a sidewalk, London did what she knew, she hid. She hid in her own house, too exhausted and heartbroken to brave the big world outside her front door. But after weeks and weeks of hiding, she was sick of it. Joanna had been to her house every day bringing food and little trinkets, hiring masseuses and nail techs to visit. Her mother, readmitted to her life, hadn't been able to stay away for more than twelve or fourteen hours at a time. London's kitchen was stocked in true Persian fashion, feta cheeses, olives of all varieties, the many spices of her childhood.

So, while she was enjoying the renewed connection to her past, the fussing of the two women was enough to make her want to hide in bed all day. That's what she was telling herself anyway. It wasn't because Derek was gone for good. Of course it wasn't.

"Oh my God," Joanna moaned around a mouthful of lamb stew. "This is heaven. What does your mother put in this stuff?"

London sat at the bartop in her kitchen and shook her head at her friend's newfound love of Middle Eastern cuisine. "I should have cooked more Persian all these years," she said. "It seems to agree with you."

"You can do whatever you want. But leave me your mother, please."

"She's something, isn't she?" London said, unable to keep from smiling a little at the thought of the woman she'd hated—no, not actually hated, just blamed—for so long.

"I know she should have told you the truth about your dad, but she's amazing, London. Beautiful, brilliant, strong, and she cooks like an angel. She must have to beat the men off with sticks."

London paused, eyes squinting as she thought over what Joanna had said. "You know…I've never seen her date anyone. Maybe she has in the last ten years, but while I was growing up she never did, and she hasn't mentioned anyone in the last few weeks. I guess I should ask her about that." She shrugged. This was her mother after all. She really didn't tend to think of the woman in those terms.

"Speaking of dating…" Joanna gave London a sideglance as she pulled out a container of yogurt and figs from the refrigerator.

"Don't," London warned, her muscles tensing at the very thought. It had taken her six full hours to stop crying, two full days to be able to eat again, one full week before she could manage a shower, and now an entire month had gone by, and she still couldn't bear to leave the house.

She was a prisoner in her own gilded cage, a cage that she wasn't going to be able to afford much longer if she didn't do something to earn a living.

Joanna's voice grew soft, her eyes pinned to London's, empathy oozing from them.

"I know you hurt each other, but you love him, don't you?"

London sighed. "It doesn't matter."

"Yes it does." Joanne ate a spoonful of the yogurt then opened another container of flakey pastry layered with honey and walnuts.

"He doesn't love me back. How could he after what I did? Knowing who I am?"

"I think you're selling him short. A man like Derek Ambrose isn't going to be scared away by some bad in-laws. That man is notorious for his single-minded pursuit of what he wants, and for his humane agenda. Did you know that he got into politics because he wanted to press for things like environmental reforms? He's donated millions of dollars to programs for women's education and wildlife protection. Last year he held a fundraiser for a tiny organization in Ghana that builds schools for local children and doesn't require them to wear uniforms. That's the number one reason kids don't go to school in countries in Africa. They can't afford the uniforms."

"You're like a walking encyclopedia of Derek Ambrose facts, aren't you?" London snapped, feeling envious that Joanna knew things about him that she didn't.

"You could be too, if you'd go after him," Joanna answered coolly.

"Sorry," London muttered.

Joanna finally released her clutch on the food and came around the countertop to face her.

"I don't know Derek like you do." She picked up one of London's hands and held it in both of hers. "But I do know a man who's in love, and every single thing I've seen tells me he's in love with you. That doesn't go away because you find out the person kept a secret from you.

Derek hasn't fallen out of love with you because you kept something from him out of fear."

London felt the anguish bubbling up in her center. She worked so hard to keep it buried, but Joanna would not let it be. Didn't she realize how much it hurt?

"He's sad," Joanna continued. "And hurt, but he can get over that. You can get over that. But only if you talk to each other."

London shook her head, biting her lip so she wouldn't dissolve in front of her friend.

Joanna patted her hand before releasing it. "Think about it? For me?"

Taking a deep breath, she nodded. "Okay. I'll think about it."

"Good. Now, is your mother coming back anytime soon? Because I just ate the last of that baghlava and we're going to need more."

**

Derek looked up from his laptop as his brother walked into the office. "I can't take the time to go out to dinner, but if you want to order a pizza I'll take a break to have it with you."

Marcus threw himself into one of the armchairs across from Derek's desk.

"What's keeping you here so late?"

"First district Tennessee congressional campaign."

"Ah Standish." Marcus nodded thoughtfully. "That's a good new client to have. How'd you get her anyway?"

"You'd never believe me if I told you."

"Try me."

"First of all, she's half Pakistani." Derek leaned back in his chair and swiveled from side to side as he talked.

"Second of all she's transgendered. The first transgendered State Senator in Tennessee to be exact. She contacted me and said that her entire life was predicated on people putting away their prejudices, so she wanted to lead by example—put away the prejudice that's been shown toward me, and hire me to manage her groundbreaking campaign."

Marcus nodded in agreement. "That's fantastic thinking."

"Six months ago she wouldn't have been able to afford my fees, but now, I need the client, she gets my know-how, and we give the State of Tennessee a candidate who is brilliant, and dedicated, and savvy as hell."

"Is she going to be able to pull it off?"

"Early polling numbers are decent, but not great yet. We're working on developing her signature issue. I think that will help move her numbers up and give us a foundation for solid fundraising." Derek raked a hand through his hair. He was exhausted and frustrated, the lack of sleep and a diet of carryout food taking a toll on his demeanor.

"I'm happy for you but you look like hell," Marcus observed.

Derek leaned back in his chair. "I'm tired," he answered.

"Why don't you take a night off?"

"Can't," he said.

"Or won't?"

Derek eyed his brother. "What's that supposed to mean?"

Marcus leaned forward, putting his elbows on his knees. "You've been running yourself more ragged than usual." Marcus raised an eyebrow at him. "I think you're avoiding something."

Derek shifted, uncomfortable and irritable. "Thanks for the amateur psychology lesson. I'll keep it in mind." He rolled his eyes.

"Seriously." Marcus stared at him until Derek gazed back. "There's not enough work or time at Spar or plotting or polling to forget about her. You're in love with her. I think you're going to have to do something about it."

Derek snorted. "Yeah? You've got a girlfriend now so you're going to lecture me about my love life? You've just started seeing Renee. I hardly think you're an expert."

A slow smile spilled across Marcus's face. "I've got the world's best girlfriend and I'm in love with her, so yeah, I think I've got a little more experience than you do. I've sure as hell had more success at it."

Derek growled and shoved a stack of papers across the desk.

"What would you suggest then, Mr. Expert?"

"I'd suggest you quit trying to ignore your obvious misery and talk to her."

"You do remember the whole story, right? She didn't tell me who her father was, she lied to me, after I'd given up everything to stand by her. Every single thing in my life."

"And I agree she fucked up, but like I've never fucked up?"

"Hardly comparable."

"Why? You love me and that means when I screw up you tell me so, then you forgive me. I do the same for you. Seems to me that if you really love someone you do that—forgive them." He shrugged as if it were a foregone conclusion.

Derek stood from his chair. "We going to order a pizza or not?" he asked.

Marcus shrugged. "Fine. But I'm going to keep asking about her until you get off your ass and do something about it."

Derek shook his head. "Is that a promise?"

"Definitely."

Derek smiled for what felt like the first time in weeks. "Okay. You do that and maybe one of these times I'll listen."

"You will," Marcus answered. "And when you do you'll thank me."

**

It was after eight p.m. when London's doorbell rang. She assumed it was her mother or Joanna and didn't worry too much before she looked through the peephole. However, it wasn't either of them. Standing on her front steps was Kamal Masri, the Egyptian Ambassador himself. She shivered, wondering what he could possibly want since she was no longer involved with Derek.

She opened the door with a flourish. He'd scared her in the past, but with everything in the open, and her affair with Derek at an end she didn't think there was anything he could do to her. She was tired of being scared, and tired of being tired.

"Yes?" she asked as she stood in the doorway, arms crossed.

"May I come in?"

She considered it. She would have loved to tell him to go to hell, but he might have something to say about Derek, so she couldn't stand the possibility of missing whatever tidbit of information she could glean about the man she still hadn't stopped dreaming about.

She gestured for Kamal to come inside, then led him to her living room. "I would ask you to sit, but somehow I don't think you'll be here that long," she told him.

His lips pulled back in a grimace. "I deserve that," he said. "I was cruel to you, and I apologize wholeheartedly."

She crossed her arms and gave a short, sharp nod, indicating he should continue.

He sighed. "I've spent the better part of fifteen years being Derek's right-hand man. I backed him up on the soccer field, in college classrooms, through bar fights, and political campaigns, and yes, a few sketchy women as well."

London glared, and Kamal had the decency to look sheepish.

"It's second nature to me to defend him, to protect him. I've spent many years in this country, away from my people and my culture. My family in Egypt is large, and I'm the second son. There are heavy expectations of me, but those don't include staying close to home because my older brother fulfills that role. My job is to take the family's reputation and interests out into the world, spread the Masri name throughout the world however I can. My father is an empire builder and my place in the empire isn't at home, it's here, in the U.S. It's a good role, but sometimes a lonely one."

He paced around her living room slowly, and even though he wasn't obvious, she could tell he was taking it all in—the knick-knacks, the photos, even the Persian vase that sat in the place of honor on her fireplace mantel.

"Derek and our small group of friends, who you met, have become my family, and in my culture you kill for your family, you die for your family, your family is everything. I realize that when he got involved with you I took that too far.

"I owe you both an apology and I've given one to him. I behaved poorly. I didn't understand—" He paused as if searching for the appropriate word. "I didn't understand how strong his feelings for you were."

She blinked at him, not sure what his point was.

"Do you feel the same way about him?" he asked.

She dropped her chin to her chest before looking up at his dark eyes. He was an exceedingly handsome man, but she couldn't feel anything other than resentment toward him.

"Why do you even care?" she asked. "I thought you'd be thrilled that he's away from me."

Kamal smiled weakly. "That's the thing—he isn't away from you, far from it. You're haunting him, and I think if he can't resolve this with you he won't be happy again for a very long time."

London's heart ached with regret. She'd done that to him. Caused Derek pain, embarrassment and doubt, when all he'd ever done to her was be kind, accepting, and considerate.

"I certainly don't hate him," she said. "I couldn't hate him even if I wanted to."

He looked at her, but she didn't flinch or turn away.

"I hope you'll consider speaking with him," Kamal said. "He needs you. One of you has to take the first step and I'm not sure he's able."

She shook her head, confused and sad.

"Think about it. Think about him. Please." With that he turned and left her house.

**

The weeks went by and still London didn't hear from Derek. Her savings weren't going to last forever so she needed to decide what to do next. Returning to prostitution was out of the question for many reasons, the biggest of which was that she couldn't bear the idea of having another man touch her after Derek had. He was branded onto her very soul. She couldn't imagine letting anyone else near her ever again.

Joanna and her mother wanted her to go to college. Farrah said she would pay London's tuition just as she would have when London was eighteen. London was considering it, but somehow it didn't feel right. She had been through so much in her life, learned in an entirely different way than formal education, college seemed like a step back, an attempt at being someone she could never be again. So she delayed any decisions, and she sat, and she thought, and she ached.

Even though she had her mother back, and Jo's undying devotion, she was lonely, feeling Derek's absence more acutely each day that passed. She realized that she was paralyzed, unable to move on because her heart and her mind were caught in that one moment in time when he drove away from her. The lack of resolution was poisonous, and until she fixed it, she wasn't sure she could have a new life, or any life at all.

Then Joanna showed up at her house with a tiny white ball of fur—a Maltese puppy.

"You got a dog?" London asked, kissing the tiny thing on the nose as it squirmed in Joanna's arms.

"No, you did." Joanna plopped the little bundle into London's hands.

"What?"

"It's for you." Joanna grinned. "You're rebooting your life, you need a friend to keep you company."

London held it up in front of her face and looked into its tiny black eyes. "Really? You think I can take care of a puppy?"

"Of course you can." Joanna sailed past London into the kitchen. She set down her Chanel shopping bag and began removing everything a new puppy could use—food and water bowls, a collar, leash, small cans of food, and a book on housebreaking.

"You really thought about this," London said, tucking the puppy under her arm as she inspected the loot.

"I really thought about all of your possible objections." She grabbed a plastic packet from her purse and unwrapped it. When she was done it popped open into a small, soft-sided dog kennel.

"Oh my God. What is that?" London peered at the little box with the mesh sides.

"It's his kennel of course. When you go somewhere and don't want him to be loose in the house you put him in this."

London held the dog up to her ear. "He says he doesn't like it," she told her friend. "He says that when I go places he should go with me."

Joanna tried to hide a smile as she filled the food and water dishes. "I'm glad you two understand each other."

London snuggled the puppy to her face. "I guess you're staying," she said. "And I think I'll name you Kingmaker."

"What kind of a name is that?" Joanna asked, scowling.

"It's between he and I, we already have secrets don't we, King?"

Joanna rolled her eyes. "I've created a monster."

London looked at her across the kitchen counter, eyes shining. "Thank you, Jo. You're amazing. You're an amazing friend, and I'm so lucky to have you."

Joanna sniffed and turned to the sink. "Stop. Just be good to the dog. And do something really great with your new life, okay?"

"Okay," London whispered.

**

Kingmaker served his purpose, he forced London to give life another chance. A tiny life was dependent on her now. She had to go outside to walk him, had to go to the store to get him food. She had to go outside her own thoughts to pay attention to him, and go outside the broken limits of her heart to give him love. And as each day passed and she devoted herself to caring for the tiny dog with giant needs, she kept hearing Kamal's voice inside her head—one of you has to take the first step, and I'm not sure he's able.

If Derek felt even half of the destruction that she did, but he didn't have his own Kingmaker, he might not be able to move forward, he might not be able to move at all. If Derek was caught in that state of paralysis that she was only barely moving on from, then he was suffering, and while she could bear her own pain, the idea of his was too much.

Ten days after Joanna gave London the most important gift of her life, London sat down at the desk in her kitchen, opened up the Internet browser on her chic Apple desktop, and finally made a plan.

CHAPTER XVII

Derek was surprised that a Powerplay meeting had been called. Usually he or Kamal called the meetings, but it was Teague who had sent him the text that afternoon, instructing him to be at the club condo by eight p.m. sharp. Derek picked up a large pizza on his way and arrived five minutes early.

"There he is, the man of the hour," Teague joked as Derek walked in.

"I know I'm special, but why tonight in particular?"

Teague and Kamal exchanged glances and Derek's eyes narrowed.

"What's going on?" he said, suspicions raised.

"Nothing except you've got the pizza," Scott interjected, walking over and offering Derek a beer while he snatched the pizza box away at the same time.

As everyone tore into the pie and found seats in front of the big screen TV, Derek asked, "So what's the occasion really?"

"There's a show we're going to watch," Kamal answered, around a mouthful of sausage and peppers.

"Is there a fight on that I didn't know about?" Derek squinted at the TV as the picture focused.

"Not exactly," Jeff mumbled.

Teague turned up the volume as the WNN logo flashed and the announcer's baritone vibrated through the stereo speakers. "Tonight, live from Washington, D.C., a WNN special edition of Politics in America."

Derek looked at Kamal who merely shrugged in return.

A perky blonde who normally anchored the morning news, came on the screen.

"Good evening, and welcome to this special edition of Politics in America," she said. "Tonight's guest and the topic of discussion rocked the nation and the bid for the White House." She turned in her chair to face a different camera, and there, sitting to her left was London.

Derek's heart flew into his throat and he struggled to swallow it back down. "What the hell..." he whispered.

As the blonde went on to introduce London and give the background of Melville's failed campaign, Derek's eyes were glued to the screen, his ears tuned only to her voice. His entire body swayed toward the television. His instinct to go to her was that strong.

"Ms. Sharpe," the reporter began. "Tell us why, months after this story first broke, you've agreed to do an interview?"

London's cheeks were pink, but she faced the camera and spoke clearly, her voice and her eyes strong and confident. God, she was the most beautiful thing he'd ever seen.

"Because I made a terrible mistake, and I have to try to correct it," she answered.

"Working as a prostitute?" the blonde asked. Derek felt nauseous. He might never get used to hearing people describe her that way. It conjured images of Melville and men who didn't realize how amazing she was, men who didn't respect her inside, and only used her outside.

London gave the reporter a sad smile. "Prostitution was a mistake, but not the mistake I'm referring to. You see..." She looked at the camera, and Derek knew that she was looking at him. Across the airwaves, across the miles, across town, she was looking at him, this was all for him.

"One day, several months ago, I met a man, and he was unlike any man I'd ever known. Derek Ambrose was...is...one of the hardest-working, brightest, most committed men that I've ever met. He also has more heart than anyone I've ever known. Derek gave me the benefit of the doubt. He was willing to have his name and his reputation tied to mine even knowing how I'd been supporting myself for the last eight years. He was willing to defend me, to protect me, and to help me find myself again, after a very long time of being lost."

Derek swallowed around his dry throat, and onscreen London reached for her glass of water, as if they could feel each other's need.

"I'm ashamed to say that I repaid Derek for his devotion by keeping the identity of my father from him."

"I see," said the blonde somberly. "And what do you want to say about that now?"

"I want the American people to know that Derek Ambrose loves this country. He loves its government and its people, and he's devoted his entire career to electing the kinds of leaders who can facilitate all of its promise. Derek had no idea who my father was. I didn't even know who my father was until I was seventeen years old. To the best of my knowledge my father has only seen me one time, and that was for a very brief few minutes. My mother had hidden my existence from him because of who he was. When he discovered me two years later, he tried to take me from her, which in Iran, he could do legally. That's when my mother escaped the country and immigrated here."

London paused, and the camera stayed on her beautiful face as she struggled to maintain her composure.

"My mother was a rebel in Iran," she continued. "And her involvement with my father was conducted to get information about the fundamentalist regime that took over the country in the 1980s. So you see, everyone has focused on my father, who I've only seen once in my life, but they've ignored my mother, who raised me. She fought for a democratic government in Iran, for laws free of the subjugating influence of religion. She gave up everything for a cause that aligns with and has been supported by the United States for decades."

The reporter nodded, shifting subtly in her seat. Derek realized that he'd stopped breathing and inhaled deeply, a twinge wriggling its way through his heart.

"And when she had me, she had to give up her cause. She had to hide, and live a secret life in order to protect me. When she was discovered she had to rely on underground connections to flee the country and gain asylum here. Everyone focuses on the man whose DNA I share, but no one focuses on the woman whose convictions I share."

"Ms. Sharpe," the reporter said, her face serious and if Derek wasn't mistaken, on the verge of tears as well, "the public wants to know, with a mother who was seemingly so devoted, how did you end up as a prostitute servicing prominent D.C. politicians like Senator Melville?"

London smiled sadly. "My mother loved me too much I guess. She tried to protect me from the knowledge of who my father was, just as I tried to protect Derek Ambrose from that same knowledge. When I found out the truth about my father, I was seventeen, and stubborn, and dramatic. I was horrified, I felt like I didn't know who I was anymore, as though my entire existence had been a lie. So I ran away from home, and I ended up doing what so many desperate young women do, I entered the sex industry."

"And what are you hoping to accomplish here today?"

"Derek found out about my father the same time that the rest of the country did. I just want people to understand that he would have never kept something like that hidden. He probably would have never dated me in the first place. It was entirely my fault, and I accept full responsibility for any deception that occurred."

The reporter smiled encouragingly at London. "Why are you coming forth now, Ms. Sharpe?"

London took a deep breath and looked deep into the camera again, so deep that Derek felt her gaze touch his soul.

"Because I love him, and I never got the chance to say it."

**

It was a chilly night, but Derek could feel spring coming. In another month the cherry trees would blossom and D.C. would be overrun with tourists snapping pictures and visiting monuments. It used to be his least favorite time of year, but he thought that maybe this year he would take some time off of work and see the Smithsonian with everyone else. Take a ride out to Mt. Vernon, maybe get a tour of Monticello. It had been a long time since he'd visited the places that reminded him what it meant to be an American, how the nation started, what the vision of those first prescient men had been.

He leaned forward and put his elbows on his knees, breathing in the crisp night air as he waited. When he saw her coming up the walk his heart stopped, and so did she.

"You came," she said softly.

"I did." He stood, stepping off her porch. She walked closer, and when they were within touching distance they both stood and stared, almost too in awe to speak or move.

"God, I've missed you," he breathed, reaching up to brush a finger across her cheek.

"You saw the interview," she stated, her breath quickening at his touch.

"Yes."

"What did you think?"

He gazed at her, his eyes hungry to see her silken skin, her glossy hair, the way her bones curved beneath her cheeks, and the tiny notch in the center of her upper lip. He was a man starved, and he knew that if he looked at this woman every day for the rest of his life it wouldn't satisfy his appetite. If he listened to her voice, touched her skin, knew her thoughts—for decades—it would only touch the tip of his need for her. He was going to have to spend the rest of his life drinking her up in order to survive.

"Will you marry me?" he asked suddenly.

She stared.

"What?"

"Marry me," he said, wrapping his hand around the back of her neck and drawing her closer. "It's just come to me, I'm not sure why I thought it could be any different. I can't live without you. I can survive, but I can't truly live. I'm so in love with you that all I can think about, dream about, wish for, is you. To see you, hear you, touch you, feel you. You. Are. Essential."

She made a small choking sound, and she blinked rapidly before her lips curved up and her face glowed.

"You mean it? Even after everything? After I betrayed you, and you lost so much?"

He tilted his head and leaned his forehead against hers. "I know you. I know you didn't do it to hurt me. I needed some time, and I needed your words tonight. You had the perfect words."

"Which words?" she asked. "I said a lot of them." He chuckled as he gave her a gentle kiss on the lips. "I love you."

"Oh. Those words."

"Yeah, those words."

She stepped closer and wrapped her arms around his waist beneath his jacket. "I do. Love you. Beyond reason, beyond measure, beyond this life. I love you."

He swept her up then, relishing the weight of her in his arms, the flesh and muscle and the sweet curves that made her real and made her his. He knew every inch of that body, and he was going to remind every inch of how much he worshipped it.

"You never answered me," he told her as they fumbled with the key in the front door.

But before she could respond, a yapping ball of white fluff landed on his foot. He stopped, midway through the foyer, and looked down as Kingmaker yipped and jumped in a futile effort to reach his mistress.

"What...is that?" Derek laughed as he looked at London, one eyebrow raised.

"Kingmaker," she said, grinning.

The little dog yipped again and pawed at Derek's leg.

"You named it Kingmaker?"

London shrugged, her cheeks turning pink. "I missed you too."

Derek felt his heart thump against the cage of his ribs, and he kissed her softly on her full lips before he continued up the stairs to her bedroom, Kingmaker scrambling to follow them. "That's good to know. Now will you please answer my question?"

"What was the question?" She giggled when he used her ass to press the lever that opened the bedroom door.

"Will you marry me, dammit," he growled before nipping her in the curve that joined her neck to her shoulder.

"On one condition."

"What's that?" He slammed the door shut, closing Kingmaker in with them, and went straight to the bed where he tossed her down and began yanking off his tie.

"You get more of the whipped cream. I really liked it."

"Gorgeous, you'll be my dessert every night for the rest of our lives."

EPILOGUE

The scent from the White House rose garden carried across the small lawn on the humid late summer air. London had on the lightest dress she could find and still be decent, but even then the humidity and heat threatened to melt her like an ice sculpture.

"Do you think if I stuck my head in that fountain over there anyone would notice?" Derek whispered in her ear.

"I don't know, but if you get to I do as well."

"Not a chance," he reprimanded. "After you've given your speech you can do whatever you want, but until then you have to look camera ready."

She smirked as she glanced at him over the rim of her champagne flute. "You sound like you're coaching one of your candidates."

"Well, in all fairness, my candidates need a little more coaching these days. Being the consultant to the underdogs has changed the way I do business. When you're in the business of helping women, minorities, immigrants, and any other assortment of non-traditional candidates you modify how you train them up."

"But it's worth it, isn't it?" she asked, pressing her palm against his cheek and staring at him with pure love in her eyes.

"Absolutely. I'd have never known how good it can feel to put someone in office who is there for purely altruistic reasons, someone who wants to be the standard-bearer for an entire constituency, and can use their own experiences being doubted and challenged to make them better leaders, more compassionate, more cautious."

She stretched up and kissed him on the cheek. "I'm so proud of the direction you've taken your firm. You have the best candidates in the country."

"Hey, as popular as you've become with your foundation for victims of sex trafficking, you might be a great choice for a congressional seat."

She pinched his elbow, one of the few places she could get any loose skin on him. Spar kept the man so taut that he was one big slab of muscle.

"Bite your tongue, Derek Ambrose. I can't imagine a worse idea than me as a congresswoman."

"Why is that?" He snaked an arm around her waist and drew her closer, his voice gravelly.

She melted into him. "Because I have needs, and I have to have time for my husband to take care of them. If I'm always on the Hill fighting battles over legislation, I might not be able to visit him at lunch for a quickie." She winked at him, remembering their rendezvous on Derek's desk the week before.

"That was very nice," he whispered, nibbling behind her ear.

"Stop," she giggled. "We're at the White House."

"Yes, and we're not the only ones who are breaking protocol. Look at that pair in the window."

London turned to where Derek gestured, and saw a set of French doors leading into the Oval Office. The sheer curtains that covered the glass doors had slipped to one side, and she could see the legs of a man and woman.

He had her pressed against the smooth glass, his suit clad knee wedged between her legs, hitching up her pale blue silk skirt. Pale. Blue. Silk.

"Oh my God."

"What?" Derek asked.

"That's the President," London gasped.

Derek squinted and swore.

"And Kamal," he gritted out. "That's the president and Kamal."

London stared at him for a moment, until the crease in his brow relaxed, and before they knew it they were both laughing so hard they could barely breathe.

When she'd regained control, she pulled on his hand. "Come on," she said. "It's time for my speech. We need to distract everyone so they don't see the President of the United States making out with the Ambassador from Egypt."

"The fact that you can say that with a straight face, much less devise a way to facilitate it proves that you're the perfect woman for me." Derek grinned.

"Oh I am, the absolute perfect woman for you."

And they were perfect together.

THE END

ACKNOWLEDGMENTS

I sort of hate writing acknowledgements, not because I'm not thankful, and not because I don't realize all the help that I get for each book, but because it all seems so rote after a dozen or so books. So, sometimes I don't write them. But it's time to do one again, so here we go:

Thank you so much to my critique partner, Jamie Raintree, and content editor, Bev Katz Rosenbaum. Your careful reading and observations of where I fell down rabbit holes (of the plot variety) were amazingly helpful. Also to my copy editor who keeps all the little details straight, Nicole Bailey.

Thank you to some wonderful groups that keep me sane on a professional level: ASN, RAU, and MM. And to the lovely reader groups who are so supportive of my work: BU, Divas Inc., and iBooks Readers and Authors.

And last but not least, thanks to all of you—the romance readers who take a chance on me, and on my books. I love giving you stories, thank you for reading them.

ABOUT THE AUTHOR

Selena Laurence is a USA Today Bestselling Author who loves Putting the Heat in Happily Ever After. In 2014 she was awarded the Reader's Crown Award for Contemporary Romance of the Year.

Selena lives in the foothills of the Rocky Mountains with her kids, Mr. L, "Goldendoodle" and "Demon Cat." When she's not writing she can be found at soccer games and tennis matches, or one of her favorite coffee shops.

You can find Selena online at these places:
Facebook: SelenaLaurenceRomanceAuthor
Twitter: @selenalaurence
Instagram: @selenalaurence
Pinterest: @selenalaurence
Web: www.selenalaurence.com

CPSIA information can be obtained
at www.ICGtesting.com
Printed in the USA
BVOW06s0843010217
475053BV00010B/67/P